The Airplane

The Airplane

The Story of the Next Big Thing

A Thriller

Karl Milde

Author of *The Commuter Train*

iUniverse, Inc.
Bloomington

The Airplane
The Story of the Next Big Thing

This is a work of fiction. All of the characters, names, incidents, organizations, and dialogue in this novel are either the products of the author's imagination or are used fictitiously.

iUniverse books may be ordered through booksellers or by contacting:

iUniverse
1663 Liberty Drive
Bloomington, IN 47403
www.iuniverse.com
1-800-Authors (1-800-288-4677)

Because of the dynamic nature of the Internet, any web addresses or links contained in this book may have changed since publication and may no longer be valid. The views expressed in this work are solely those of the author and do not necessarily reflect the views of the publisher, and the publisher hereby disclaims any responsibility for them.

Any people depicted in stock imagery provided by Thinkstock are models, and such images are being used for illustrative purposes only.
Certain stock imagery © Thinkstock.

ISBN: 978-1-4620-4942-4 (sc)
ISBN: 978-1-4620-4941-7 (hc)
ISBN: 978-1-4620-4940-0 (ebk)

Library of Congress Control Number: 2011915961

Printed in the United States of America

iUniverse rev. date: 09/21/2011

Acknowledgment And Dedication

This book is dedicated to my loving wife, Cheryl, without whom I would not have had the belief that I could write at all, never mind write a best-selling novel like this one!

BOOKS BY KARL MILDE

CHILDREN'S BOOKS

Jason and the Detectives Series:

The Case of the Missing Trophies

The Case of the Haunted Summer Camp

The Case of the Burning Schoolhouse

Grandmother's Farm Mystery

The Mystery on Governors Island

ADULT NOVELS

The Commuter Train

The Airplane

Prologue

Carl Collingwood sat alone in his office, studying the plans for his new airplane design. It was close to midnight, and all of Carl's employees, including his son, Bruce, had left after another long day of constructing the prototype. They would all be back tomorrow by six in the morning to go at it again as they had done day after day for nearly a year, but the end was in sight. They would finally finish and test the aircraft in only a few days' time.

Carl stared at the CAD drawing of the new, barrel-type engine they had just installed to power the wing fans. It was extremely small for the power it could develop and was perfectly suited for lifting the aircraft vertically off the ground and hovering in the air. The rest of the airplane was really quite conventional with a second, front-mounted engine and a propeller to power the aircraft forward.

The only problem, Carl foresaw, was the cost of the special new engine. To fulfill his vision and his plans for the future, his aircraft had to be within the financial reach of an American family. It could be no more expensive to purchase than a luxury automobile. Carl wanted to fill the skies with his airplanes, transporting people quietly and fuel-efficiently from point to point, wherever they wished to go, without the constraint of having to land at an airport.

Carl knew that if the test went well and if he could mass-produce the aircraft to keep the costs down, there was scarcely a limit to how many he could sell. It was conceivable he could start a new industry and put thousands of people to work, manufacturing and selling this new vertical takeoff and landing aircraft with its wings like an airplane. His vision would no longer be just a dream. It would be *real*.

As he scanned the CAD drawing, his initial feelings of admiration for the details of the design gave way to a sense of concern for the unknown. What was it about this engine that was somehow off-kilter and gave him pause? He examined the assembly diagram and looked carefully at each part in turn, but everything seemed to be in order. Still, there was this feeling of foreboding.

Finally he stood up, switched off the light in his office, and walked out into the darkness to head home for the night. In just a few days, he would test his airplane and, he hoped against hope, fly it into the future.

Chapter 1

Hello! My name is Julianne Gables, "Juli" for short. If you've read about the hijacking of the commuter train to New York City, you know all about my husband, George White, and me. Shortly after the trial of Carl Collingwood and his son, Bruce, George and I got married and honeymooned in Bermuda. Yes, Bermuda! The very same place where we got shot at and narrowly escaped by helicopter.

When we came back home to New York, we set to work again investigating and reporting the news on our website, www.GablesReport.com, which, by the way, just kind of *took off*. We've been getting thousands of hits a day now, and every day there are more.

We post up-to-the-minute news on the site before it's reported on TV or in the newspapers. We leave the murders and break-ins to the local media and focus on political and corporate corruption. We also do sex scandals when they apply to a presumably responsible public figure such as Eliot Spitzer, Arnold Schwarzenegger, or even John Edwards, but I'm getting ahead of myself. Let me start from the beginning and tell you what happened to Carl and his aircraft. Tighten your seatbelt, dear reader, and hear me out—

George and I left early in the morning and drove way out to the Suffolk County Airport in Westhampton, Long Island, a trip of more than an hour. When we arrived at the airport gate, we stopped and asked directions to our final destination, the Hummingbird Aircraft Company. The security guard handed us a sheet with a map of the airport and noted the route. We finally pulled up in front of a huge metal hangar, and there, on the tarmac, in front of the open hangar door, stood the thing we had come to see: It was what Carl Collingwood, the inventor, once dubbed his "personal aircraft."

The craft looked like any other airplane one might have seen, but it was supposed to take off and land vertically. Carl and Bruce had been working with their team of engineers for nearly two years to build this first prototype. Carl had asked us to come today to watch the very first test flight.

George and I got out of our car and walked toward the open entrance of the cavernous building. Carl and Bruce were over in the far corner on the right, holding coffee cups and chatting with their engineers. There were nine of them in all—members of his team, I mean—each with a different skill set that was needed to build such an aircraft. No one was dispensable.

As we joined them, we saw Carl and Bruce locked in a heated exchange about who would pilot the plane. His handy cam always at the ready, George held back and started quietly to record the scene.

"You've got to be kidding, Dad. You're twice my age for God's sake! Pardon my saying so, but your reflexes are a bit *slow*." Bruce dragged out the last word for effect. "It's going to act more like a bucking bronco than an aircraft."

"I can handle it. Don't worry. It's my baby, and I want to be the first to take it up."

"Why don't we let our people decide?" Bruce turned to the Hummingbird team for support.

"Yeah, right," Carl said dubiously. "If they choose you, I'll be annoyed at you, and if they choose me, you'll be annoyed at everyone, including me."

"Okay, here's Juli! Maybe she can settle it." Bruce turned in my direction expectantly as I walked up.

We had asked for, and Carl and Bruce had granted us, an exclusive on this story. We were the only reporters allowed anywhere near the hangar today. Whether the test was a soaring success or a fatal flop, we were entitled to the first broadcast. After that, ours would be the only video footage available, so we could license it to the media. Considering the publicity we got at the Collingwood trial, I figured there'd be a heavy demand for our pictures.

"This is the big moment," Carl explained. "It'll be the first time a fixed-wing aircraft could do this, rising straight up from the ground. The military brass will be here in a minute to watch this test flight, and if it goes well, the army has agreed to give us an order for five thousand units."

"I still don't get it," I said. "What's makes it so special?"

"The fixed-wing aircraft, as we know it, has been developed and refined for over a hundred years. It is incredibly fuel-efficient at producing lift, once you get it moving through the air, but this is the first time an aircraft of this type is going to go straight up and hover. No downward pointed jets. No spinning chopper blades, which are the helicopter's wings, by the way. No complex mechanism to control those spinning blades. Much less noisy, too!"

"Like flying a *magic carpet?*"

"Exactly! Someday we'll all be able to take off from our own backyards. This is going to be big, really big!"

I heard a sound behind me, and all heads turned to see a black SUV pull up and stop just outside the hangar. Three men in uniform got out. I could tell by the stripes on his sleeve that the driver was a sergeant. The other two wore those military hats with gold graffiti on their visors proclaiming their elevated status. They all headed our way.

Carl just stood there, staring at them blankly, without moving. The arrival of the military had triggered something, and he froze. Maybe it was the enormity of this moment—to have arrived at this final test, which, if successful, would result in fulfilling his lifelong dream—or maybe it was fear: fear of authority, fear of the military, fear of the future, whatever. I didn't have a clue.

As he sensed his father's difficulty, Bruce quickly stepped forward to greet the visitors. "Hi, I'm Bruce Collingwood." He held out his hand. "Thanks for coming."

"I'm General Bellamy, and this is Major Hendricks and Master Sergeant David Schulz."

They shook hands all around, and Bruce introduced his father, who was still standing silently for some reason, and the other members of his team. Finally, they got around to greeting George and me.

"We still haven't decided who will fly it, Dad or me," Bruce continued, while Carl still seemed to be tongue-tied. I just couldn't believe it! "We'll have to flip a coin or something."

"Is that a problem?" the general demanded. "It's *your* invention," he said and turned to Carl. "*You* decide who flies it," and that was that.

Without a word, Carl reached for his flight jacket and carefully put it on. George kept the camera rolling as Carl walked out to the aircraft on the tarmac. Bruce followed and helped him climb into the cockpit and close the door.

At Bruce's signal, Carl opened the side window and shouted, "Clear prop!" I figure he had finally found his voice. The front propeller cranked a couple of turns and awakened the engine, which sputtered briefly before it settled into a smooth, comfortably quiet hum. Then, strangely, a *second* engine buried somewhere in the middle of the fuselage started up, turning fans partly buried in the wings with a muffled bustle. The combined sound was not unpleasant, something like the sounds one hears in a Laundromat.

The wheels of the craft were blocked, which kept it from moving forward or back. Bruce moved in and grabbed little ropes that were attached to each chock and then pulled the chocks away, at first from the front wheel and next from the main landing gear under each wing. He backed off a safe distance, carrying the chocks, and watched the aircraft vibrate as the rotating blades in its wings churned the air with a flutter.

The aircraft shuddered slightly as its engine sound increased in pitch and then moved forward a bit as it slowly lifted itself, seemingly by its own bootstraps, off the ground. The landing gear extended downward at first, leaving the wheels on the tarmac beneath, and then it picked the wheels up off the surface. The craft was airborne!

The tiny group of people, who stood by with their eyes glued to the levitating aircraft, spontaneously broke into wild applause. "Hurray!"

The aircraft continued to rise, first by a foot and then five feet, and eventually held steady at about ten feet off the ground, rotating horizontally a little as it hovered. We all stood there in awe, especially because it was impossible to see how the aircraft could fly at all. Except for a tiny shroud above each wing, the aircraft looked like a conventional airplane, but it was not flying forward. It was just sort of . . . defying gravity.

The aircraft remained motionless for a few seconds. Then, without warning, there was a huge explosion, and it ignited into flames right before our eyes. The fire burst forth and quickly engulfed the aircraft just like what had happened to the dirigible Hindenburg.

Chapter 2

The flames were horrible! I could feel the heat from one hundred feet away. The aircraft wobbled like an out-of-round Frisbee and then suddenly fell as a dead weight and crashed against the tarmac. By the time it hit, it had practically burned itself out and had turned everything within itself to black ashes.

George—God bless him—had the presence of mind to keep the camera rolling the whole time.

I stood transfixed, unable to move. The explosion, the fire, the crash had happened in no more than an instant, but it seemed to occur in slow motion. I heard silent screams in the background. Eventually, my own screaming voice pierced my consciousness.

Even before I came to my senses, I realized that sirens were approaching, and within a minute or two, public safety vehicles with airport insignia converged on our location—an ambulance and two fire trucks. Soon after, several police cars, their overhead lights flashing, arrived, too. An odd feeling of relief and gratitude came over me because I knew I was helpless to assist in any way. I learned later that the general had instantly called 911 on his GPS phone and demanded help, so help did descend on us—big time.

As fast as the feeling of utter helplessness had come and turned me into a statue of stone, the feeling evaporated, and my body switched into hyperdrive. My first concern was for the safety of Carl's son, Bruce, and his team of engineers. They had witnessed Carl's death in the explosion firsthand and must have suffered more shock and trauma than any normal person could possibly bear. I ran over to Bruce, who stood there trembling, and put my arms around him to give him whatever comfort and solace I could. The rest of the team stood by in a nearly catatonic state, not even understanding their own reactions to the crisis, much less coping with their distress at this moment.

When they were finally able to control their emotions and function somewhat, Bruce and his men went back to their office in the hangar and waited for the public safety people to quench the remaining fire and start their investigation. This left me free to do what a reporter is supposed to be doing under the circumstances of a breaking story, and boy was I *energized*. I quickly ran back to the car to grab my notebook and then moved about the scene like a maniac, taking names and transcribing comments and quotes from the numerous public safety personnel who had arrived. George, who had been zeroing in on one heartrending face after another, now had his camera focused on the police chief in charge, who was interviewing General Bellamy.

"Your name is?" The police chief had probably picked him out to speak to first because the general's uniform gave him away as somebody important.

"General Bellamy. David Bellamy."

"You saw this happen?"

"Yes, I was standing right there." The general pointed to a spot near the hangar.

"Why? Why are you here?"

"I came to see the flight test. The military is interested in this aircraft. *Was* interested." The general emphasized the past tense.

"Well, what did it look like?"

"I'd say it was a bust. It went up. It went *boom* and then came back down and crashed."

"The pilot didn't have a chance," the chief said.

"No, I guess not. Too bad."

"Any idea what might have caused this . . . this *boom*, as you say?"

"I'll leave that one to you professionals. Must have been a faulty design."

"Or maybe a bomb of some kind?"

"I wouldn't think so," the general said.

"Why not?"

"Who would want to do such a thing? It was just a flight test."

"I see your point. The pilot was the inventor, wasn't he? A Mr. Collingwood?"

"Collingwood, right. Carl Collingwood."

"Not much left of him, is there?"

"No," the general said.

"Did he have any enemies that you know of?"

"Doesn't everybody?"

"Spoken like a true military man," the chief said.

"Why don't you talk to his son, Bruce? I'll bet he knows where the bodies are buried."

"Believe me, General Bellamy, we intend to. But right now I'm talking to you. When was the last time you spoke with Mr. Collingwood?"

"Before today, you mean?"

"At any time."

"I talked to him today, of course. Just before the flight."

"What did you talk about?"

"We shook hands. I said hello. That was about it," the general admitted.

"Did everything seem normal?"

"Now that you mention it, well . . . *no*. Mr. Collingwood was acting a bit strange. He didn't say much."

"How do you mean 'strange?'" the chief questioned.

"It was like he was under some kind of strain or something. I assumed it was because the test was critical."

"Was anyone with you when you spoke with him?"

"Yeah, his son, Bruce. Like I said, you should talk to him. I've got to go now and get back to my base."

"And like I said, we'll talk to Bruce. I have just a couple of more questions if you don't mind—"

"All right," the general said. "If you insist."

"Did the military have some kind of contract with this company? Collingwood's company?"

"No, but like I said, we were interested. If the aircraft had flown according to specs, it would have solved a big problem we were having, and we would have placed a rather large order."

"And what problem was that?"

"Noise. You can hear a helicopter coming a mile away. This airplane is designed—correct that, *was* designed—to hover quietly. The concept was to have a low-flying, slow-flying aircraft for emergency rescue, surprise attack, that sort of thing."

"Kind of like a stealth aircraft, only for ground operations?"

"That was the idea anyway."

"Thank you, general," the chief said. "That'll be it for now. I'll need your contact information in case I want to follow up."

General Bellamy took out a business card and handed it to the chief. Not to miss an opportunity, I stepped in and asked for a card, too. One can't be too pushy in this business, and you never know when the information might come in handy. Without thinking, the general gave me one. I took the card and jammed it in my pocket. Later when George and I got back to the car and headed home, I looked at what it said:

Major General David Bellamy
Director of Procurement

US Army Ordnance Command
Aberdeen Proving Ground, MD
david.bellamy@usarmy.mil

Chapter 3

The mental image of that plane blowing up kept playing itself out in my mind over and over as George drove us home. I really didn't want to see the video George had taken that morning—it would be too horrible—but I had to see the explosion in slow motion. I was hoping against hope this recording would reveal some clues.

And the reporter that I am, I couldn't help thinking we had to get the story out . . . fast. We had some valuable footage here, but I wasn't about to release anything that was grisly or otherwise disrespectful of the Collingwoods. Carl Collingwood had burned to death, and that was big news; however, a tight shot of his final agony didn't have to float around the Internet like so much flotsam and jetsam.

Also, I wanted to make sure that nothing went out before Bruce had time to tell his mother about the tragedy.

An hour later, back in our apartment in New York, George and I sat in front of the computer and watched the terrible scene unfold again before our eyes. We saw it through once at regular speed and then again in slow motion. Finally, we reexamined the video record once more, frame by frame. What we saw was absolutely shocking.

The video began with a long orientation shot, starting with the hangar and panning around a full 360 degrees. Carl, Bruce, and their entire team were there, and so was I, all of us talking and joking, completely oblivious to the terrible tragedy that was about to take place. Out on the tarmac stood the aircraft like the huge bird that it was, both sleek and, perhaps with hindsight, menacing.

Then the military arrived. To his credit, George kept the camera rolling the whole time as the three men walked up and introduced themselves.

And finally, the test flight itself. It was all there on permanent record. The aircraft lifted off, hovered a few seconds, and then exploded and burst into flames from within.

George and I stopped the video at this point and ran it in reverse to a frame just prior to the explosion. This was easy to do with George's video equipment. We then ran it forward again until we saw the very first glint of the explosion. When we examined that frame, we were able to see where the explosion had started—somewhere within the center of the fuselage where that high-pitched whine had come from.

The explosion blew apart some of the metal skin of the aircraft, so we could see inside. On the fourth frame following the commencement of the explosion, we had pretty much an open view, so we took a closer look. George zoomed in on the innards of the aircraft, and we both looked at the picture.

"Look at that!" George pointed to a round metal object at the center of the fire. "What do you think it is?"

I looked carefully at the image, but the closer I looked, the more blurry it seemed to become. George tried zooming in and zooming out to get a clearer view, but that didn't help. We just couldn't decipher what it was.

"Maybe we can have the picture digitally enhanced," George said hopefully.

"That works only if you know what you're looking at. We don't."

"There *are* some clues we can use to enhance the image. We can also speak to Bruce to find out what was *supposed* to be in there."

Just then, my cell phone rang. I looked at the caller's number. It was the Collingwoods.

"Hello, this is Juli," I said with some trepidation. I instantly recognized the caller's voice. It was Sylvia Collingwood, Carl's wife and Bruce's mother.

"Juli—" Sylvia could barely speak through her tears. "Bruce tells me you were there—"

"Yes, Mrs. Collingwood. I am *so* sorry. I—"

"After all that Carl's been through . . . and now this. I can't stop crying—" Sylvia stopped for a second to compose herself. "The, uh . . . the reason I'm calling is to ask you . . . to implore you to find out what happened. I know you have that ability . . . the ability to get at the truth."

"I will do my very best, Mrs. Collingwood. I promise."

"Thank you, Juli. You and George have been a comfort to us. We can't tell you how much we appreciate all you have done."

"Thank you, but that's our job as investigative reporters. Oh, but Mrs. Collingwood, may I ask you something?"

"Yes, of course," Sylvia said.

"Would you let us know about the funeral? When you make the arrangements, I mean. I will post it on our website. And George and I would like to attend."

"Bruce is here. We will talk about it and let you know as soon as we can."

"Thank you, Mrs. Collingwood. Call any time, day or night. My cell phone is always on."

"I will. Good-bye, Juli." I heard a soft sniffle just before the phone went dead.

Who would do such a dastardly deed? The world of business may be rough-and-tumble, but killing one's opponent is just not an option in a civilized world. Whoever did it—and *someone* must have done it—had descended down to a lower level of the animal kingdom. With an animal, though, it's about survival. In business, it's only a game they play. If you win, you get to live in a bigger house and buy expensive toys like a fancy car, a boat, or a vacation home. If you lose, you still have food and shelter. What evil mind would want to snuff out someone else's precious life?

I got to work on the story. I wrote it, rewrote it, and still wasn't satisfied. In view of the time constraints, I posted it anyway. So here it is—the story that appeared on my website, "The Gables Report" that afternoon, *dateline October 24*:

INVENTOR DIES IN AIRCRAFT TEST FLIGHT

<u>Westhampton, NY.</u> A huge explosion killed Carl Collingwood during the first ever test flight of his vertical takeoff and landing (VTOL) aircraft, an invention he had been working on for many years. Well known for hijacking a commuter train headed for New York City to deliver one of its passengers to Washington, DC, Collingwood and his son, Bruce Collingwood, were acquitted of wrongdoing, allowing them to continue development of the aircraft. The prototype was undergoing its first flight when the tragedy occurred.

Authorities have been unable to determine the cause of the explosion. Foul play is suspected, and the police are investigating. The intense fire that followed the explosion reduced the aircraft to black ash, leaving virtually no human remains.

One theory is that someone planted a bomb aboard the aircraft prior to the test flight. The bomb could either have been triggered by a timer after the start of the aircraft engine or triggered manually by someone watching from a distance.

I figured this last statement was just logical, so I threw it in. It was really just speculation at this point.

I went on like this for a few more paragraphs, giving some details about the effects of the explosion but not too much. I mentioned that the event was witnessed by representatives of the US Army, including General Bellamy, and then closed the article by saying, "Carl Collingwood is survived by his wife, Sylvia, and their son, Bruce, who helped his father construct the prototype. Bruce had tried to persuade his father to let him conduct the test flight, but Carl Collingwood had insisted on flying the aircraft himself."

It seemed important to me to tell the world that Bruce was not a suspect. There are a lot of cranks out there who have all kinds of theories. Some of them are still debating who killed JFK.

George and I posted the article on the website along with some still images we extracted from the video footage. In a microsecond, the wire services picked up the story and rebroadcasted their version. It has always startled me how fast the bad news gets around.

In comparison, good news doesn't go very fast or very far.

Chapter 4

George knew what he had to do. If there were any clues hidden in those video frames, it was his job to decipher them. As he said to me, he would stay at this task "as long as it takes."

"Okay, you work on that," I said. "I'll start by pounding the pavement and speaking to anyone who might have an interest in killing Carl . . . or maybe Carl's aircraft."

"I'll bet I know who you're going to start with."

"Yeah?" Juli said. "Who's that?"

"Somebody who runs a big company that supplies aircraft to the military."

"You know what they say: 'Great minds think alike.'"

Just then my cell phone rang, so I glanced down at the screen. It said, "Michael Snead, Chm. & CEO. Transport International, Inc."

I answered, "Hello, Mr. Snead."

"Juli Gables, is that you?"

"Yes, Mr. Snead. It's me."

"I just heard that Collingwood's aircraft exploded. Do you know about this?"

"As a matter of fact, I was there."

"You were?"

"Yes, it was horrible. I saw the whole thing."

"How is . . . Sylvia?" Mr. Snead hesitated over the name. My guess was he didn't know whether to call her "Sylvia" or "Mrs. Collingwood."

"She's devastated, as you might imagine."

For a moment, there was silence. Then he said, "I'm so sorry."

"I posted the news on my website."

"Well, I'd like to offer my assistance in any way I can."

"I'm sure the family would welcome it. You should call Mrs. Collingwood. Perhaps some time after the funeral—"

"Yes, yes," he said. "I'll call her, but first, I need to ask you for a favor."

"Oh? What's that, Mr. Snead?"

"I need you. I would like to hire you and your husband, George."

"Hire us?"

"Yes. Naturally, the police are going to suspect that I had something to do with this, Carl's company and mine being direct competitors for the military business."

"So?"

"Well, I'd like to hire you to find out who did this . . . *thing*. I don't trust the police *or* the DA to give me a fair shake. Knowing you, you're going to do whatever it takes. My company will pay whatever you wish."

"So you didn't do it?"

"I may have had my differences with Carl, but murder is not my style. Juli . . . may I call you Juli? You know me better than that."

"I'm not sure I do, Mr. Snead. You're offering me money to influence our reporting."

"It's not like that, Juli."

"It's not? What's the money for then?"

"I just want to make sure you're well-funded. I want you to spare no expense to get to the bottom of this," Mr. Snead said.

"It's still a bribe. We're news reporters. We don't shade the truth."

"Knowing you, you'll tell it like it is, no matter what."

"You're not worried?"

"Worried? Should I be?"

"Worried that we'll find someone in your closet with a smoking gun?" Juli asked.

"No, not at all. I'm not worried because neither I nor my people had anything to do with it."

"Then why don't you just hire a detective agency, Mr. Snead?"

"It's not so simple."

"Oh?"

"Detectives work to confirm a fact that's presumed. Here we have no idea what is going on."

"So if you didn't do it, you have nothing to worry about."

"Well, yes, I have to say I'm . . . uh . . . *concerned.* Concerned about what others *think* of me and my company. And that's where you come in."

"Very sorry, Mr. Snead," Juli said, "but we're not for sale."

"You have it all wrong! I'm not trying to influence you. I'm just trying to do what I can to—"

"You can keep your money," I cut him off. "We're going to conduct our own investigation *independently*, and we'll report whatever we find."

"You do that. But Juli, please remember I'm counting on you. The sooner you get to the bottom of this, the sooner they'll take the heat off. There's going to be a media frenzy, and I'm a sitting duck here."

I hung up the phone and stared for a moment at George. He stared back with a big question mark on his face.

"Mike Snead didn't do it," I said. As a reporter, I'm a truth machine.

"So what was that stuff about money?" George's eyes were wide.

"Snead wanted to fund us to do our job."

"And you . . . *turned him down?*" I think I detected a crack in George's voice.

"Yeah, I did. Is that okay?"

"Yeah, I guess." That's all George said, and he let it drop.

George and I spent the next minute or two posting a postscript to our story on the website: "Mike Snead, the Chairman and CEO of Transport International, called the bombing a 'horrible tragedy' and pledged support to help Mr. Collingwood's family through this ordeal."

I knew this was not the first time that Mr. Snead had come to that family's aid, and I privately predicted it would not be the last.

Chapter 5

It was time for me to start digging for evidence, so I returned to the scene of the crime.

The police were still there sifting through the ashes that remained of the burned-out aircraft and—do I dare say it?—Carl as well.

The chief of police was gone, leaving investigators in charge of mopping up the evidence.

The chief investigator, it turned out, was a fairly good-looking white guy in his midthirties with a really bad attitude.

"Hi, inspector," I began cheerfully and upbeat. "I'm a reporter, Juli Gables. Do you have a moment to speak with me?" I smiled my most beaming smile, trying my best to ingratiate. The technique does work for me sometimes.

The guy didn't even look me in the eye. "Okay, get this woman outta here!" he shouted to no one in particular.

Two officers instantly appeared, one on each side of me. They grabbed hold of my arms and were about to use unnecessary force to drag me away.

"What's your friggin' problem, inspector? We were here watching the test flight when the plane blew up. You need to talk to me, you *butt head*."

The guy finally looked at me. I guess he didn't like what he saw because he didn't soften one bit.

"You have evidence? Okay, what is it?" he growled.

"Not so fast. I thought we could make a . . . uh . . . *trade*."

"Trade?" he asked. "What kind of a trade?"

"I give you information, and you give *me* . . . uh . . . information."

"No deal, Miss . . . whatever your name is. We don't leak to the media, *period*. Okay?"

"You don't leak. We don't leak. We're both plumbed tight."

"The difference is your information belongs to the *state*. If you're hiding anything, I'll run you in for obstruction of justice. Got it? Okay?"

"All right, you can see the video, but you won't learn anything from it."

"You have a *video* of this?" The guy suddenly seemed interested.

"Yeah, like I said, we were here. I'm a reporter. Connect the dots, dumb ass."

"Okay, okay! I'm Inspector Gavin. Dan Gavin. Your name is?" He actually extended his hand, and I accepted the handshake.

"Juli Gables. Call me Juli."

"Okay." If this guy said "okay" just once more, I was going to scream. "So where's the video?"

"We can e-mail you a copy if you like. In the meantime, how about at least telling me who's running this investigation."

"I am," the inspector said.

"How many people you got on it?"

"Three, full time. It's top priority."

"Was a bomb on the plane?"

"Yeah, we—" the Inspector stopped himself. He had already said too much.

"Found traces of explosive?"

"I didn't say that."

"You mentioned a bomb."

"You print that, and I'll run you in."

"I already did before you said it. It's the only way it could have happened."

"Clever, aren't you?"

"You'll get to know me better," Juli said.

"I don't think so."

"So we're looking for a bomber, is that it?"

"You figure it out."

"Got any suspects?"

"Okay, lady, you just crossed the line. You're choice: Leave now, or I call over the officers."

"You don't want to know my list of candidates?"

"What the fuck do *you* know?" the inspector said. "You're just a goddamn reporter. And an annoying one at that."

"I know more about the Hummingbird aircraft development than anyone. I've been following this story for two years now. The airplane was supposed to be the next big thing."

"Your knew this guy Collingwood?"

"Carl Collingwood and his son, Bruce—both. Me and my husband, George, covered their trial when they hijacked that commuter train."

"That was *you*? Why didn't you *say* so? Damn, we should be working *together*."

"You never asked, and yes, we should."

"Okay, you've got my attention." That "O" word again!

"Do we have a deal?" Juli asked.

"Deal. But everything stays in confidence unless and until I say so."

"Fair enough. So tell me what you found out so far." Finally, I was getting somewhere.

"I will, but first, there's something I want you to do for me."

"Oh yeah? What's that?" I was looking at Inspector Gavin but became suddenly aware of a noise of increasing loudness coming from somewhere behind my back.

"Get rid of those damn reporters!"

I turned around and saw what looked like a convoy of cars and vans of all assorted types traveling straight toward us along the airport road. Normally, I would have been in that boisterous crowd myself, but in a moment, I was going to see what it was like to be on the receiving end of a media frenzy.

Chapter 6

"String that police tape across the tarmac. Quick!" I pleaded and then stepped forward to greet the phalanx of TV and newspaper reporters that had just parked their vans and cars and were advancing on foot toward me like an army. There were about fifteen of them followed by their entourage of support people—photographers with telephoto lenses, audio and video technicians with handheld microphones and mics mounted on poles, video cameras supported on dollies and handy cams of various types. The newspaper reporters just carried clipboards or notepads or handheld computers they used for taking notes, composing their stories and transmitting them to the home office.

As I scanned the advancing group, I could make out only a few familiar faces—field reporters I had seen on the TV news and a columnist from the *New York Post*. I stood my ground as the cops strung up the yellow "Police Line—Do Not Cross" tape behind me.

"Hold it right there!" I commanded, and believe it or not, the army stopped advancing. In my next life, I'd like to be a drill sergeant!

Assembled in front of me, waiting to record every single word I uttered, were a dozen microphones held up by as many reporters, all urgently pressing forward to ask me questions. It was unnerving, but to tell the truth, it made me feel a bit like a rock star. Lil' ol' *me* in front of all these microphones!

A particularly pushy reporter I recognized as Aleksa Williams from Channel 2 News fired the first question at me. I had seen her many times on television but had never had the displeasure of meeting her face-to-face.

"Who's in charge here? Why are we even talking to *you*?" Aleksa was drop-dead gorgeous, but I didn't hold that against her. It was just that she was too overconfident for my taste and, well, a tad too capable. Good looks, self-confidence, and smarts were a potentially hazardous combination—too much competition for my comfort.

"Because the chief inspector wants me to get rid of you guys. He has a job to do."

"Not going to happen. *Sorry!* We want the chief inspector, not you, lady."

"My name's Juli Gables. If you have any questions, I'll try to answer them. I was on the scene when the tragedy happened." The reporters, most of whom had never met me in person or had even seen a photograph of me, quieted down somewhat at the mention of my name. They stood there, staring at me, perhaps because they'd heard I had solved so many crimes. The word gets around in this media business.

"All right, Juli Gables," Aleksa began. "What were *you* doing here when the airplane blew up?"

"I was here covering the story. I have—correction, *had*—an exclusive on this test flight."

"You saw the whole thing?"

"Yes, and we videotaped it."

The reporters, a rowdy bunch who were jockeying for position in front of me, were stunned for a moment.

"You have it on *videotape*?" Aleksa was incredulous.

"Yes, but we don't plan to release it. Carl Collingwood died in that explosion."

"So? That videotape belongs to the *people*. It's news. We want a copy . . . *now!*"

"I don't *think* so, Aleksa." I stood my ground. "It's not for publication."

"You greedy little *bitch*, holding out for more money. So how much do you want for it?"

Something inside me snapped. At that moment, Aleksa became the enemy.

"It's not for sale. Not to you. Not to anyone else."

"We'll see about that. When our legal department gets through with you, you'll wish you gave everyone here a free copy." I could hear chuckles in the crowd.

I was floundering, and Gavin must have noticed because he came to the rescue. He ducked under the yellow police tape, stood by my side, and glowered. The reporters stepped back a bit, maybe out of respect, I don't know. Anyway, he delivered the very speech that I should have be able to give, but couldn't.

"All right, calm down," he said. "A man has died here. Carl Collingwood died during the maiden flight of an aircraft, his aircraft. He spent half his lifetime developing this aircraft, and now he has died for it. It was his dream. When you report on this tragedy, I want you to get that message out. I want you to eulogize him. He was an American hero."

The press reporters were copying every word. "What caused the aircraft to crash?" one of them asked, still scribbling on his pad. It was the question on everyone's lips.

"I'm told it was an explosion of some kind. We're investigating that."

And then everyone started with their questions.

"Do you suspect foul play?"

"How high was the aircraft when it blew up?"

"Did an ambulance come?"

"Did the fire department come?"

"Who saw the test flight?"

"Has Carl's family been notified?"

"Who notified *you*?"

"What police are here?"

"Who's your supervisor?"

"Who gave Juli Gables permission to be here?"

"Will you have a press conference?"

"When and where?"

The questions were coming in from all directions now. I just stood there and let Inspector Gavin field the answers. I could see a storm brewing, and I was right smack dab in the center of it.

Chapter 7

Home alone in the apartment he shared with Juli, George viewed his video of the exploding aircraft over and over again until his brain was nearly numb. Then he viewed the scene again, frame by frame, until he came to the precise moment of the explosion. He drilled down on the area of the engine inside the fuselage until the picture became an assemblage of individual pixels. But the closer he looked, the more the image disappeared. It was a futile exercise.

Sitting in front of his computer, dejected, wondering what to do, George had an idea. He lifted the phone, selected a number, and pressed speed dial.

"Jim, it's me, George. I need your help," he said.

George first met Jim in Metropark, New Jersey, when Jim drove a TV van for channel WTNJ. Jim had broken all the rules to transmit George's video footage to a competing TV station, Channel 8 in New York, and George never forgot the favor. Sometime later, after he and Juli had founded their investigative reporting business, George used their investigative tools of the trade to find Jim and thank him for what had turned out to be a significant turning point in George's career. One thing had led to another, and Jim became best man at George and Juli's wedding. Now George needed another favor from his loyal friend.

"What's up, man? Is everything okay?" Jim said.

"You know me. I'm always in over my head."

"Not so! You're the smartest dude I know. What you need, bro?"

"I have this videotape—" George explained that maybe, just maybe, secrets were locked in the frames of the video. If only he could decipher them.

"Have you tried to blow it up?"

"Sure, but that just made the pictures worse. You don't see anything, just a bunch of colored pixels when you look at them up close."

"I know the problem. There's a well-known cure for that—kind of like "smoothing," only not so simple. I have some very expensive software that'll work."

"Really? It can make the pictures better?"

"There's all kinds of things you can do to enhance the images. I'll come over and bring the software."

"Thanks, Jim. That would be *great!*"

"That's what friends are for, bro."

An hour later, Jim sat at George's computer and loaded some advanced applications software he had brought with him from his photo business at home. "Okay, I'm ready," he said when the computer finally flashed on the screen that the installation had been successful.

George, who was sitting next to Jim and watching his computer's brain get smarter by the second, pointed to a video file in the "My Docs" menu. Jim used the new software to retrieve the video from memory and then clicked an icon to play it.

"Fast forward to the flight test," George suggested.

Jim operated the keyboard controls to move quickly through the video until he could see the aircraft propeller begin to turn. He made note of this video frame and then let the video play at normal speed until it came to the moment in time when the aircraft exploded. He stopped at the frame that most clearly showed the beginning of the explosion and enlarged this image until he could see the individual pixels. After he briefly examined the colors and hues of these pixels, he selected a number of parameters from a drop-down menu and pressed "Enter." The hard disk made clicking sounds, and the computer started crunching numbers.

Within minutes, the pixels on the screen blended together to form a clear, finely pixelated image. The result was like giving reading glasses to a farsighted person for the first time.

George stared at the screen in amazement. The image processing had turned a mosaic of disparate, individual pixels into a clear picture of the aircraft with a fire in its belly, a fire that had incinerated the craft in a matter of minutes.

"*Now* I can see what happened!" George said excitedly. "Look at *that!*" He pointed to a place inside the fuselage. "The flames shoot out right there . . . from inside that engine!"

"You're right!" Jim agreed, looking closely at the screen. "That's definitely a bomb. But how was it detonated?"

"It couldn't have been set for a specific time," George reasoned. "No one knew exactly when the test flight would take place. Someone had to have been there, watching the airplane, in order to press a button at precisely the right time."

"How about a timer connected to the engine ignition? It could have been set to go off at a certain time *after* the engine started. Here, let's see how long that was—"

Jim subtracted the frame number at the start of the test from the current frame number shown on the screen. "That's 21,127 frames at thirty frames a second. That's 704 seconds or about twelve minutes. They could have set the timer for twelve minutes."

"I don't think they'd do it that way. It would be much too risky. What if the pilot started the engine and, for some reason, decided right away to abort the test flight?"

"The explosion would still have destroyed the aircraft," Jim reasoned.

"But that wasn't the point, was it? They could have blown up the aircraft at any time, but they didn't."

"They waited for the test flight."

"They must have wanted to blow up the airplane *and* its pilot, Carl Collingwood!"

"That's horrible! *Why*, do you think?" wondered Jim.

"Must be they wanted to kill the project. To do that, they had to kill the inventor."

"The bomb must have been detonated by someone there at the test flight. They had to be sure that the pilot was still on board."

"*And* that Carl Collingwood was actually the test pilot," George added. "It could just as well have been someone else like his son, Bruce."

"So who was there?" Jim inquired. "Any competitors from the aircraft industry?"

"No, only the people who built the plane, three people from the US Army, and Juli and me."

"Assuming you and Juli didn't do it and assuming the people who built the plane didn't do it, that just leaves—"

"The army," George said, shaking his head. "But that doesn't make sense. They wanted to buy the aircraft if the test was successful."

"You're assuming they wanted it to be successful."

"Well, *yeah*. We can assume that. Why wouldn't they?"

"You can't assume anything. Just for argument's sake, let's suppose the aircraft posed some kind of a threat."

"A threat to who, what?"

"Oh, I don't know. Maybe some corrupt inside deal with an army supplier."

"Okay, then why would they even show up at a test? They could just refuse to buy the aircraft."

"And let Carl Collingwood sell the thing to the US Navy or Air Force? Or worse yet, offer it to some foreign country? I don't think so."

"So you're saying—"

"They'd have to kill the inventor and destroy the prototype."

"So they planted a bomb in the engine compartment." George was finally catching the train of thought.

"Maybe someone snuck into the building at night," Jim offered.

"Or maybe the engine manufacturer installed it right in the engine."

"Sure! It could have been the same corrupt military supplier that wanted to kill the project."

"All that was left to do was to press a button of some kind."

"Right! So how could a person press a button without being seen?" Jim raised his eyebrows as he posed his rhetorical question.

George paused and then looked squarely at his friend. "He'd have to press the button with a hand in his pocket."

Quickly, Jim tapped a few keys on the keyboard and replayed the video, starting from a time prior to when the aircraft took off from the tarmac. Before he zoomed in on the aircraft, George had purposely taken a wide-angle shot of the entire scene. There stood the three military men, and one of them was watching the test flight with his left hand in his pants pocket.

Chapter 8

Aleksa Williams knew an opportunity when she saw one, and this story, she recognized, was an opportunity of a lifetime. Investigative reporting 101!

Not only was there a murder mystery to solve, but there were some *great* visuals to showcase, if only she could get her hands on them. And getting what she wanted was her specialty.

Aleksa was one of those lucky women who were blessed with great physical beauty. She knew it, and she *used* it. It was an advantage she had over not only other women but also men, most of whom could never know what it was like to be stared at and admired for their good looks. In her view, it was her birthright.

Ever since Aleksa could remember, going back to age two or three, people told her how *cute* she looked and later, as a teenager, how *stunningly beautiful*. Of late, Aleksa was used to hearing the terms *sexy* and *hot*. Not that she minded. Not at all. It gave her leverage over others, and anyway, she knew it was true.

Whereas some young women would have been content to learn the tricks of the beauty trade, spending their time and money on cosmetics, hair lotions, and body crèmes to flaunt their beauty, Aleksa was driven to do more. She was driven to *succeed* in what she believed to be "the serious game of life."

As a young girl growing up, she watched and admired her father as he struggled to build a business—an African-American in a white man's world. Not many avenues were open to black businessmen in those days. The music industry, sports, and also religion were among the few fields in which black leaders were permitted to excel. Jack Williams, undaunted by the odds against him, purchased old buildings in New York, refurbished them with a team of loyal and dedicated construction workers, mostly African-Americans, and sold them at a good profit.

Jack had started before Aleksa had been born with a ten-thousand-dollar "minority" SBA loan to buy and renovate his first building. When he returned less than a year later with a check to prepay the money and cancel the loan, the loan officer was so impressed that he insisted on lending Jack even more money, this time fifty thousand dollars. Jack, in turn, was so taken with the appreciative smile on the loan officer's face that he promised himself he would never default on a loan or even be tempted to take an unnecessary business risk that would jeopardize his reputation as a responsible and reliable businessman. Thereafter, little by little, Jack patiently and quietly acquired assets, both in real property and liquid securities, until his untimely death at the age of forty-eight.

Aleksa was twelve at the time when the events of that day permanently seared the neurons of her memory. Recalling the events, as she did many times since, was like projecting a motion picture in an IMAX theater.

She accompanied her father that Saturday as he went to a job site to talk with his men. They were working overtime, as they usually did, to complete a complicated reconstruction of an office building in Harlem. These were heady times, because President Bill Clinton had located his office and library nearby, and Harlem was undergoing a long-anticipated resurgence of activity. His men had completely gutted the building down to its frame. Even the front wall had been removed to make way for a new façade.

Aleksa remembered riding up in the open elevator cage on the outside of the building and stepping out with her father onto the empty twenty-fourth floor. From there, one could see toward the south, over the buildings in front of them, all the way to Central Park and the buildings beyond. Jack talked with his men for a while, gave her time to enjoy the view, and then turned to go. He grasped her hand, and they entered the elevator together again. The cage door closed behind them, and they headed down to the relative safety of the street level.

As they descended, Aleksa noticed that her father seemed agitated, as if something were not quite right. He was deep in thought, and she knew better than to interrupt by making small talk.

When they landed and exited the elevator, he looked down at her apologetically and said, "I'm sorry, honey. I have to go back for a minute. Just wait here for me." Those were the last words she ever heard him say.

Ten minutes later, Jack's body came down in free fall and landed with a loud but muffled "thud" right next to where Aleksa was standing.

No one ever came forward to explain what had happened that day. Aleksa and her mother cried continuously for two days, but this crying gave way to stoic determination during her father's wake and eventually to a semblance of relief when she and her mother met with their family lawyer. Jack Williams had died a multimillionaire.

Over time, Aleksa took on a self-determined, self-centered, and decidedly selfish attitude. The experience of losing her father that day coupled with the way people reacted obsequiously to her wealth and beauty had an unfortunate, negative effect on the development of her character. By the time she entered college, Aleksa had acquired all of the attributes of a *bitch*.

Not content to run with the pack of cub reporters, Aleksa was constantly on the lookout for some news story that would afford her the opportunity to break out of the pack and make her a star. With the murder of Carl Collingwood, she knew she had found a vehicle that would carry her career to an entirely new level. And she was going to drive that vehicle as fast and as far as it would go.

Chapter 9

Aleksa stood in front of the camera at Suffolk County Airport, police tape visible in the background, and spoke into the Channel 2 News microphone. Her luscious mouth, glossy with freshly applied lipstick, and her soft hair exquisitely coifed, her face generated a powerfully attractive force for human eyes, male and female alike. And as a bonus for male eyes, the slightly open neckline of her jacket hinted at the possibilities of two spectacular breasts.

Aleksa responded to the voice of the news anchor, Cynthia Brooke, in her earpiece when the red light came on: "Thank you, Cynthia."

"Right behind me is the scene of a terrible tragedy that happened about eight o'clock this morning. A new type of aircraft undergoing its maiden test flight exploded, killing the test pilot and its inventor, Carl Collingwood.

"If the name Carl Collingwood sounds familiar, it's because he made national news just two years ago by hijacking a commuter train. Acquitted by a jury in a sensational trial, Carl and his son, Bruce, immediately founded a company to develop this new type of aircraft that was supposed to take off and land vertically.

"The police are trying to piece together what happened. They have cordoned off the area, and right now, they are interviewing everyone who was present during the test flight. They are not releasing any names of the witnesses, but a black sedan belonging to the US Army command was seen leaving the airport a half hour ago. We are checking on this lead and will follow this breaking story throughout the day.

"Back to you, Cynthia."

Aleksa stripped off her earphones and her lapel mic and stared disapprovingly at her cameraman, Brian, who couldn't stop shooting footage of the beautiful woman in front of him. "So what do you think *you're* doing? How *dare* you! If you release so much as *one frame* of that video, I'll have you *fired* for infringing my right of persona. Shut that thing off and take all of your equipment back to New York . . . *now!*"

The man complied instantly, switching off the camera and retreating to the satellite communications van with it and all the other electronic paraphernalia.

Aleksa pulled her mobile phone out of her pocket and called into the station. "John, send a car. I'm going to stay here a while and snoop around. And tell Cynthia to call me the instant she takes a break. It's very *urgent!*"

"Yeah, yeah. With you, it's always urgent." John's voice could be heard in reply as Aleksa snapped the phone shut.

Aleksa ducked under the yellow police tape and headed straight for the airport buildings.

"Hey, you!" a uniformed police officer interrupted her determined advance. "Where do you think you're going? Stop right there!"

"Hello, officer. I'm Aleksa Williams. I'm working with Juli Gables," she lied. "She's here somewhere, right?"

Aleksa gave the officer the radiant, full-face treatment, with her smile wide and her eyes innocent.

Smitten, it was all the officer could do to point toward the hangar and say, "Yes, she's in there." Aleksa continued on in that direction and almost made it to the hangar door before another officer who was standing guard accosted her. "Just a minute, lady!" Just then Aleksa's cell phone rang, and she held up her hand for the officer to wait while she took the call.

"Oh, hello, Cynthia," her voice was saccharine smooth. "Thanks for returning my call. I just have a hunch this story is going to be big, *really* big. I want your permission to drop everything *and* go deep. Cynthia, you're a doll. I'll come back with the goods. I always do, you know. Don't forget to tell John. Be well."

"The bitch," Aleksa muttered to herself as she popped the phone back in her trouser pocket. When she looked up, she realized the officer was still standing there, blocking her way to the hangar. "Oh, *hello.* Now where were we?" Aleksa composed herself quickly and fluttered her eyes at the officer. He melted visibly and stood there, not knowing what to say or do.

"I have to see Juli Gables. It's very important," Aleksa said as she opened the door on the side of the hangar and pressed past the officer. She stepped into the cavernous space and walked purposefully toward the group of people standing near the internal hangar office.

"Hi, fellas," she said cheerfully as she walked up and beamed her ingratiating smile. "I'm Aleksa Williams from CBS News. Mind if I ask a few questions?"

The group of men didn't know what to say. They just stared at her, and there being no spokesman for the group, no one replied so Aleksa continued.

"Who was here when it happened?"

Several of the men took a step forward and instinctively raised their hands. Again, there was an awkward silence, and Aleksa pressed on.

"I'd like to take names, if I may, and talk with each of you, uh . . . *privately.*" She emphasized the word "privately" in a conspiratorial sort of way, just as though an audience with her were something to be coveted. However, the men again did not respond. *This is like pulling teeth*, Aleksa thought to herself. She tried another tactic.

"Is Bruce Collingwood here?"

"He's inside the office," one of the men who had raised his hand said with a nod toward the inner office door.

Finally, someone said something! Aleksa took the opportunity to address this man, summoning all the feminine attractiveness in her arsenal. "What is your name?" she asked sweetly.

"I'm Bill Paley, one of the employees of Hummingbird Aircraft."

"You worked on the prototype that exploded this morning?"

"Me and the rest of the guys here."

"Any idea how it could have happened—the, uh . . . explosion?"

"We figure it had to be a bomb," he said.

"A bomb?" Aleksa feigned surprise. "What kind of a bomb?"

"We have no idea, and no idea how it got there."

Just then the office door opened, and the detective, Dan Gavin, stormed out.

Chapter 10

I was inside the office, talking with Inspector Gavin and Bruce Collingwood, when I heard a commotion and glanced out the bay window that overlooked the inside of the hangar. There she was again, this time at the center of attention among the police officers and the employees of the Collingwood Aircraft Company. My God, was she annoying or *what*?

I nodded to Gavin with a silent query: Did he want me to deal with her? He rolled his eyes, took a deep breath, and stepped outside himself to read her the riot act. Bruce and I stood in the open doorway to watch the fireworks.

"How did that woman get in here?" Gavin shouted rhetorically to no one in particular. "What the hell's the matter with you and those guards outside?"

Aleksa excused herself from the group surrounding her and walked over toward Gavin.

"Hello, inspector, pardon my intrusion, but I *would* like to render my assistance. Channel 2 News is at your service." She gave Gavin the full blast of her radiant sex appeal.

"Oh, brother," I said under my breath. "Gag me with a spoon!"

"I heard that," Bruce mumbled. I didn't know if he approved or disapproved. He was in a horrible place emotionally. I felt another pang of sorrow for him at that moment. It was so sad and upsetting, what had happened.

Thank goodness Gavin wasn't buying. "We have all the help we need from Ms. Gables, thank you. Now, if you don't leave voluntarily, we'll use whatever force we find is necessary. Trust me."

"Ms. Gables? You're getting help from *her*?" Aleksa pronounced the word "her" as if the thought were so disgusting she had to hold her nose. "What can *she* do that the whole CBS News team can't do a lot better?"

"For one thing, she can keep our investigation confidential. For another, she was here by invitation of the Collingwoods, and she has a video recording of the entire test flight."

"I know. I know. Don't rub it in. And we're entitled to see that video, inspector," Aleksa said, batting her eyelashes, looking up at him, and widening her pupils. *How the devil does she do that?* I wondered. "Ever heard of freedom of the press?" Her voice trailed off, sweet and smooth as honey. She was coming on to Gavin with all her female powers of persuasion. "Maybe you and I could have coffee sometime, and—"

"Out!" Gavin roared angrily, pointing to the side door of the hangar.

"All right, I'm going. But I'm always available . . . to you especially. Just call me." She tossed her head seductively. "Until we meet again, my dear inspector." Oh, *brother!* Aleksa made a pretense of bowing deferentially to Gavin, shot a brief but telling look my way, and then walked off, wagging her tail from side to side. Everyone stared after her in amazement. Men!

When she finally disappeared by way of the hangar door and let it swing closed with a bang, the spell was broken. I gave a sigh of relief and turned back to the business of investigating and hopefully solving the biggest, most hideous crime I had ever encountered. Had I known that Aleksa was heading straight for our home in an attempt to pry the video away from my husband, George, I would not have been so quick to let her image drop from my consciousness.

For the next two hours, Gavin and I worked together, going over the video on my laptop and interviewing all of the people on the Hummingbird team who had worked on the aircraft. Bruce made every effort to be helpful, but I could see that this investigation was extremely trying on him. I persuaded Gavin to complete his interview of Bruce and allow him to return home to be with his mother, who was now a widow, and give whatever comfort he could.

After Bruce left, Gavin and I bore down on the central issue: We knew there had been a bomb. We just didn't know where and when it had been installed on the aircraft. Hummingbird Aircraft had no video surveillance, but the team had been working around the clock and someone had always been in the hangar with the prototype.

After Bruce left, we interviewed each of the employees, and they all agreed it would have been impossible for anyone to have entered the hangar and plant a bomb on the aircraft. We, therefore, focused our attention on the engine mounted in the middle of the fuselage, which rotated the vanes in the aircraft wings. The bomb *must* have been in the engine when it had been installed.

None of the employees knew where the engine had come from, and Bruce had gone home, so we decided to go through the files in the office. A file on the engine should be easy to find, we figured, and this file would tell us who the manufacturer was.

Gavin started on one file cabinet and I on another, but after an hour of searching, we were no closer to the answer than we had been when we had started. After we looked through all the cabinets along the wall, we gave up in frustration.

"Nothing on the engine!" Gavin called out as he finished checking the last file drawer on the last file cabinet. "I can't believe it!"

I sat there at Carl Collingwood's desk, frustrated and exhausted from searching, and tried to imagine where he would have filed the papers: the correspondence with the manufacturer, the purchase order, the warranty certificate, the delivery bill of lading, *everything* relating to that engine. The documents had to be somewhere. How could we be missing them, and where could they be? What file would they be in?

It *finally* dawned on me! Instead of looking at a file for the object being manufactured, we should look at a file for the *manufacturer* itself. But what company could that be? None of the files I saw during my search through the cabinets were labeled with the name of any company. I assumed that Gavin's search was equally devoid of company names, but I had to check anyway just to be sure.

"Dan, did you see the names of any companies on the files you looked at?"

"Yeah, I saw just one. Why?"

"That could be the manufacturer."

Dan stared at me for a moment and then dashed back to a file cabinet. His fingers flew through the folders until he found the one he was looking for. He picked it up and glanced through it. "Bingo!" he said.

"The engine?"

"Yeah!"

"What file is that?"

"Transport International. Mike Snead's company."

Chapter 11

Aleksa walked out of the Hummingbird Aircraft hangar to the waiting car, slipped into the backseat and gave Juli and George's address to the driver. The driver entered the address into his navigator, and they were on their way. An hour and a half later, they pulled up in front of a modern apartment building with a doorman standing at attention. The driver got out, walked around to the opposite side, and opened the car door for Aleksa.

Aleksa had taken good advantage of the trip to refresh her lipstick and adjust her accessories to maximum advantage. She added a brilliant silk scarf to her outfit and put on deep drop earrings to complement her gorgeous face. As a final touch, she applied a dab of her favorite perfume to each side of her throat.

As she stepped onto the curb, the few pedestrians who happened to be walking by literally stopped in their tracks to steal a glance at her. She stood there on the street for a moment and looked up at the tall building to prepare herself mentally. She tried to imagine what Juli and George's apartment would look like but was unable to draw any images in her mind. The two reporters were an enigma—so far from her own life's experience. She knew, however, that George would be there alone, and that was what counted on right now.

"Wait nearby, and I'll call you when I'm ready to leave," Aleksa ordered the driver and took his business card. After she entered the building, the doorman holding the door, she walked straight to the front desk and asked the concierge for "Juli Gables."

"Is she expecting you?"

"Not exactly. But either she or her husband, George, should be here. This is my card." Aleksa handed her own business card to the concierge, and he placed the call.

"Hello, George. There is a—" he said and looked down at the card. "An *Aleksa Williams* here to see you. From Channel 2 News. Should I send her up?" The concierge glanced at the card again and then at Aleksa.

"He says he doesn't know you." The concierge looked at her expectantly.

"Tell him I have some important information about the Collingwood tragedy."

The concierge spoke into the phone again and exchanged a few words.

"All right. Go on up. It's on the forty-seventh floor. Apartment B."

The concierge followed her with his eyes as Aleksa proceeded to the elevator bank.

When the elevator reached forty-seven, George was already standing in front of his open apartment door and waiting to see who would emerge. When Aleksa stepped out onto the landing like a vision, George blinked and blinked again.

"Is Juli Gables here?" Aleksa knew full well she was still back at the airport.

"No. I'm her husband, George. Can I help you?"

"George? Why, as a matter of fact, you can. May I come in?"

"Sure. I guess."

Aleksa swept past George and entered the apartment. "Why, this is nice!"

"Thank you. We like it."

Aleksa took a look around and eventually went to a window. "The view is nice, too!"

"Yeah, it's pretty high up."

"You must be very comfortable here." Aleksa turned to face George, and for the first time, he received the full effect of her good looks. "Can you offer a girl a drink? It's late enough in the day, don't you think?"

"Uh, sure." George went over to a cabinet on the side of the room. "What would you like?"

"Some white wine would be nice."

"Your name is?"

"Oh, I'm sorry. I'm Aleksa Williams from Channel 2 News."

"That's what I thought. I've seen you on TV a couple of times."

"Just a couple? I'm on almost every night these days."

"We don't watch TV much anymore," George said. "We're on the Internet."

"I know. *Big* competition for broadcast news."

George poured two glasses of cool Chardonnay and handed one to Aleksa. They clinked glasses, and each took a sip.

Aleksa squeezed her eyes closed for a moment to savor the flavor. "Oh, yes, that soothes the soul."

"So what's it like being a TV celebrity?"

"I just love being on camera. That's why I took this job, you know."

"I'd rather be behind the camera than in front of it. I'm much too shy."

"A good-looking guy like you? If you were on TV, the girls would be falling all over themselves to get to know you."

"I never thought of myself that way."

"Take it from me," she said. "I know an attractive guy when I see one."

"Flattery will get you everywhere," George said graciously. "But I'm married, you know."

"I know . . . what a waste." Aleksa raised her glass again and downed a couple of more swigs. George followed her lead and did the same.

Aleksa smiled at George, and the whole room lit up, or so it seemed to him.

"I, uh . . . think you'd better go," George suggested. The visit appeared to be spinning out of control.

"But we haven't even talked about our business yet."

"Our business?"

"You know, the Collingwood thing," Aleksa said.

"What about it?"

"You shot a video?"

"Yeah?" George wondered now where the conversation was going.

"Does it show anything about what happened?"

"Yeah, it shows everything, but—"

"*Everything?*"

"I can't let you see it. It's confidential."

"Confidential from whom? Me included?"

"Well, yeah, you and everyone else."

"Can't it be just between us . . . and your wife, of course?"

"No, I'm sorry." George countered shyly.

"I won't show it to anyone. I *promise*." Aleksa moved closer to George with an inviting smile and looked deeply into his eyes and put her arms on his broad shoulders.

"Well, I'll have to ask Juli about—"

"Does she have to know?"

Just then the phone rang, breaking the spell of the moment. George disengaged himself and walked over to the desk phone to pick it up "It's Juli calling," he said innocently, glancing at the caller ID. "Maybe she's learned something."

Aleksa frowned.

"Hi, Juli. Yeah, I got Jim to help analyze the video. We have clear images of the explosion, frame by frame. But more than that. Remember General Bellamy standing there? The video shows he may have set off the bomb!"

Chapter 12

When I heard George tell me that over the phone, I could hardly keep myself from screaming out loud, "Shit!"

"I'm on my way to pick you up," I told him, "We've got to drive down to Aberdeen Proving Grounds *now*."

"I'll be ready."

"And George—"

"Yeah?"

"Be sure to wear your special belt."

On the way to New York City, all I could help thinking about was how and why would General Bellamy blow up the aircraft . . . with *Carl in it*. It was Bellamy who told Carl to fly the plane. He wanted to kill him?

George was waiting for me when I pulled up in front of our apartment house. He stood there on the sidewalk, looking a bit sad and forlorn for some reason. Me, I was so excited I could burst!

George had his camera equipment with him as he always did when we took to the road, and on the way, we talked together about our strategy for interviewing General Bellamy. As was our routine, George was to stay in the background and try to blend in, camera quietly rolling, while I engaged the interviewee in conversation. It would seem natural that we would want to interview Bellamy about the aircraft explosion—after all, it was top news of the day—but the general didn't know we knew what we knew, namely that he apparently had a hand in triggering the explosion. Armed with this information, we felt we could ambush Bellamy on the record and surprise him into revealing more than he would ever care to reveal about his role in the tragedy.

It took about four hours to get to the military base. Between spurts of conversation, there were long stretches where we didn't say much. This was not unusual with George and me, and we were nervous about the forthcoming interview. But we should have been talking about our strategy so we could take full advantage of our surprise attack.

When we finally arrived at the base, we were stopped by the guards at the main gate. A sergeant stepped out of the gatehouse, came up to my window, and peered into the car. "What can I do you for?" he inquired, not unpleasantly.

"We're reporters. We're here to interview General Bellamy."

"Does he expect you?"

"No, I don't think so."

"What's going on? You're the second reporter today that's asked for him."

"Someone else was here already?"

"That's their chopper." The guard pointed to a helipad within walking distance from the gatehouse. On it rested a dark blue helicopter with "Channel 2 News" on the side. "We just gave them a ride in to the main office."

"*Aleksa!*" I growled under my breath.

"You'll have to get out of the car. We need to look it over." George and I got out and watched as a couple of soldiers examined the vehicle, inside and out. They looked under the hood in the engine compartment, not to mention the trunk, the glove compartment, under the dash, and everywhere else.

"You can never be too safe!" I commented as cheerfully as I could. The soldiers didn't say a word but went on about their business.

"Okay, you can go," the sergeant said finally. "Follow this access road about a mile and a half till you see some buildings. There'll be some signs there for the headquarters building. I told the general that you're coming."

I thanked the guards, and we were on our way.

I don't know what I expected—maybe some big guns or tanks or something—but the base was pretty low key for being the headquarters of the US Army's Ordnance Corps. This was where they tested and procured almost all of the army's new stuff, ranging from night-vision goggles to the most advanced antitank weapons. All kinds of aircraft, too, for transporting troops, aerial photography, weapons delivery, whatever. But the base looked so ordinary. Just a bunch of nondescript, low-rise buildings all painted white. I guess it was a good thing. Our military was expensive enough without adding luxurious accommodations and offices for its personnel.

We followed the signs to the headquarters building, which turned out to be a two-story, white clapboard structure that was no fancier than the rest. When we pulled in to the parking lot adjacent the building, we found a space in the marked-off area with a sign for "visitors," got out of our car, and walked over toward the main entrance. Near the entrance were a number of parking spaces reserved for the top brass. The sign closest the entrance read, "Post Commander." Others read "Adjutant General," "Arms Control Officer," stuff like that. We also saw a sign for "Procurement Officer," which we assumed marked General Bellamy's spot. There was a car in that spot, a dark blue Ford Taurus that we assumed was General Bellamy's POV. That was a good thing because it showed the man was there working.

When we entered the lobby, we found a sign listing all the different offices and looked for "Procurement," the department listed on General Bellamy's business card. It was upstairs.

The procurement office took up pretty much the whole floor, or so it seemed. It was more an "area" than an office, with computer desks everywhere. Maybe about a hundred people, mostly in civilian clothes, were working away, presumably buying stuff at taxpayer expense.

"Can I help you?" One of the many office workers stopped her work and came up to us.

"We'd like to see General Bellamy. Is this his office?"

"Yes, but he has a visitor right now." The receptionist nodded toward an interior office with the door closed. "Would you care to wait? She's been in there quite a while, so I don't think it should take much longer."

My mind immediately conjured up an image of Aleksa. And sure enough, the door opened, and out she came! General Bellamy emerged right behind her with a wide smile on his face, and he was followed by two young guys carrying cases of camera equipment with the CBS logo. At first, none of them noticed George and me standing there on the side.

"Thanks for stopping by, Ms. Williams. I wish I could have been more helpful."

"Please call me *Aleksa*, general. Everybody does."

"Well, Aleksa. It was a pleasure to meet you. I'm at your service if you have any further questions."

"I just might take you up on that, general. Bye." As Aleksa turned to go, both she and Bellamy noticed our presence at the same time. Aleksa shot me a superior glance as if to say, "You're too late, you big losers," and walked briskly past us on her way out, followed by her camera crew. Bellamy just stood there, staring at us with a slightly serious look on his face.

"Do you have a moment, general?" I seized the opportunity to talk with him, preventing him from retreating to his office, while George proceeded to do his camera thing.

"I'm afraid I'm late for a meeting. So if you'll excuse me—" The general started to head back to his office, but I intervened.

"You had better speak with us. We have evidence of a homicide."

He froze. "Homicide?"

"Yes, we need to talk. Privately."

"All right. Come in then." The general waved us into his private office and shut the door. "Evidence of homicide?" His face turned suddenly dark, and he stared at me sternly, as if *I* were the one guilty of some heinous crime. George kept the camera rolling. "You mean Carl Collingwood?"

"Yes, Collingwood. We know who triggered the bomb on the aircraft."

The look on the general's face, a blend of fear and sudden anger, told it all. He must have realized it though, because he walked stiffly to his desk, pressed a button on the intercom, and gave a sharp command, "Security!"

In an instant, two MPs appeared at the door.

"Take away this man's camera," he ordered, "and escort these people off the post."

"Just a minute!" George protested. "This camera is *mine*."

"You'll get it back *after* we remove your recording. This base is off limits to reporters. Now I must ask you to leave . . . *immediately*."

The two MPs did as they were told and ushered us out of the office. As they did so, I noticed George did his best to continue to face toward Bellamy and at one point toward the guards who were straining to force him out the door. Good for you, George!

We didn't resist, so the MPs simply walked us to the front entrance of the building and let us go. Out in the parking lot, we passed General Bellamy's car. I looked at George, and he looked at me. The same idea must have clicked in our heads at precisely the same time.

"Do you have the tracer with you?" I asked George, hoping against hope that he did.

"Sure do. I carry a couple of them in the trunk just in case."

George unlocked the trunk, reached in to a small compartment on the side, and pulled out a small black disk. He moved a tiny switch on the side of the disk to the "on" position and carried it over to Bellamy's car. After he first looked around to make sure no one was watching, he reached down and affixed the device to the inside of the left rear fender in one quick motion. It was magnetized and held itself tight just like a magnet to the side of a refrigerator.

Chapter 13

By the time we returned to the front gate, the Channel 2 chopper was gone. George was driving, so I sat back and took a deep breath. We had gotten *something*, but I wasn't sure just what. In addition, Aleksa's quick trip to see General Bellamy was eating at me. Why was she there? What did she know? There were other issues, too, like what he had told her. And ultimately, what did he know?

Over time, George and I had developed quite a rapport. Together, we could usually figure things out.

"I don't like that Aleksa. She's getting on my nerves."

"She's just doing her job." George apparently didn't have the same problem with her that I had.

"Well, she had better stay out of my way. That's all I can say."

"Maybe we should invest in a helicopter." George was joking, right? Helicopters *cost*.

"Maybe we should keep a couple of steps ahead of her. That shouldn't be too hard, with her . . . *attitude*."

"She outsmarted us on this one," I said.

"Yeah, why was that? How come she was there, anyway?"

"She must have found out General Bellamy was at the airport, watching the flight test. Routine interview for background information."

"She got to him awfully fast."

"Bellamy didn't seem to mind the interview."

"She's got something up her sleeve," I said. "I just know it."

"She gave him softball pitches, which he slugged to the outfield."

"Well, whatever she got from him, we'll see it on Channel 2 News tonight."

"So what do we put on our website?" George queried.

"I wonder. The world is waiting for us to break some news."

"Do we expose Bellamy?"

"I'm not sure it's time yet. Maybe hold back and follow the trail. What do you think?" I always ask George for his opinion on important decisions like this.

"We have the goods. We should use them. It'll make a great story."

"Let's review then," I said. "What goods have we got?"

"We have footage of the test flight that no one has seen yet."

"I'm not sure we want to show it, but go on." I sure as *heck* didn't want to show it.

"We can show who was there. And show that Bellamy watched with his hand in his pocket."

"I'm not sure that's convincing. There might have been another way to trigger the bomb."

"We can also show our interview with Bellamy. You scared the shit out of him."

"I thought so too. Give me the memory stick, and let's take a look."

While he was steering with one hand, George reached down with the other and pressed a button on his belt buckle. He slipped out the memory and handed it to me. I grabbed a laptop from the backseat and fired it up. Within a minute, I had the video of the interview playing on the screen.

"Not bad for a belt buckle. Focus is good. The sound's a bit fuzzy though."

I ran through the entire scene from the time General Bellamy emerged from his office to when he ordered the MPs to take away our camera. Then I replayed the video and freeze-framed it at the point when I told him we knew who had triggered the bomb. Was that a guilty look or what?

"I'm tempted to put this on, just this frame." I said. George glanced over and quickly looked at it while he was attending to his driving.

"What a great picture!" George agreed. "As long as we don't accuse him, we should go with it."

With that decided, we drove home in silence and then went to work uploading our video onto the website. By the time we were through, it was 6:30, so we turned on the CBS Evening News. The Collingwood aircraft was the lead story, and sure enough, there was Aleksa on screen, telling the world about the explosion: "In an interview today, General Bellamy explained how much the army wanted the flight test to be successful. The army desperately needed an aircraft of this type because the leading supplier of military aircraft, Transport International, does not have anything comparable."

The CBS News cut to footage of Aleksa interviewing General Bellamy. After he had confirmed that he had witnessed the test flight, there was this exchange:

Aleksa: "Did the tragedy that happened today appear to you to be a homicide?"

Bellamy: "Yes, I would say so. There was definitely a bomb on that plane. The explosion was so intense."

Aleksa: "Do you have any idea who might have triggered such a bomb?"

Bellamy: "I can't imagine who would do such a horrible thing."

Aleksa: "Could it possibly have been a competitor of Collingwood?"

Bellamy: "Possibly. I can't really say."

Aleksa: "Who are the competitors?"

Bellamy: "There's only one for this type of aircraft."

Aleksa: "Who is that?"

Bellamy: "Transport International. It's one of our military suppliers."

Aleksa: "Transport International? As head of procurement for the US Army, could you tell us how much business they would stand to lose to the Collingwood aircraft?"

Bellamy: "We have budgeted close to two billion dollars for this type of aircraft. We have a mandate to provide our troops with this capability."

> *Aleksa:* "Thank you for taking your valuable time to speak with us, General Bellamy. I have just one more question: Who is the chief executive officer of Transport International?"
>
> *Bellamy:* "A man named Mike Snead."

Aleksa concluded her report with one of those veiled challenges that news people use to cast doubt on someone's innocence: "After the interview with General Bellamy, we attempted to contact Michael Snead, CEO of Transport International, but he did not return our phone calls."

The news program cut back to Cynthia Brooke, who closed the story before she moved on to the next segment: "Thank you, Aleksa. We'll follow this important story and give you updates, so stay with us."

There was, of course, no mention of the fact that the *real* inside story could be found on *The Gables Report.*

THE GABLES REPORT

WELCOME TO OUR WEBSITE

YOU ARE THE

002,597,328th

VISITOR

OUR MISSION IS SIMPLE:

To shine a bright light on criminals and their criminal activity.

Our mission is to proactively investigate criminal activity and to pass the information we uncover along to the police and to the public as rapidly as possible. After all, the police could use a little help!

By the way, if you have information about possible criminal wrongdoing, contact us.

Breaking story . . .

ARMY GENERAL SUSPECT IN SETTING OFF BOMB ON COLLINGWOOD AIRCRAFT

<u>Westhampton, NY.</u> *A huge explosion killed Carl Collingwood during the first ever test flight of his vertical takeoff and landing (VTOL) aircraft, an invention he had been working on for many years. Well known for hijacking a commuter train to New York City and bringing it and one of its passengers to Washington, DC, Collingwood and his son, Bruce Collingwood, were acquitted of wrongdoing, allowing them to continue development of the aircraft. The prototype was airborne and hovering about fifteen feet off the ground when the tragedy occurred.*

Authorities have been investigating the cause of the explosion, which left traces of C-4 on the blown-apart fuselage. Attention has focused on representatives of the US Army who were present at the airport to watch the flight. The army was intensely interested in the aircraft as a much less expensive and a much quieter alternative to the helicopter.

The army representatives who witnessed the test flight were led by General David Bellamy, US Army. Gen. Bellamy serves as director of procurement for the US Army Ordnance Corps. Others present at the flight test were Major Oliver Hendricks and Master Sergeant Samuel Schulz.

*A video taken at the scene of the tragedy revealed that **the explosion was triggered manually by Gen. Bellamy**. We attempted to interview Bellamy about his role in this tragic bombing of the aircraft. He not only refused the interview, but he unlawfully confiscated our camera equipment.*

*We recorded our attempted interview with Gen. Bellamy by means of a **hidden camera**. Click HERE to view Gen. Bellamy's reaction when he found out we knew who triggered the bomb.*

Collingwood's VTOL aircraft flew successfully for less than one minute before it exploded. Had the flight test been completed as planned, it was Collingwood's intention to initially sell this type of aircraft to the

US Army as an airborne "Jeep" and then to offer them to industry as a quick and efficient means of personal transportation.

The aircraft was designed to carry four adults for up to 500 miles at a cruising speed of 100 miles per hour. Collingwood called it a "personal aircraft" or "PAC" for short.

Visit our Web Site EVERY HOUR, EVERY DAY to follow this breaking story. www.gablesreport.com/articles/collingwood

Other Stories to Watch!

Justice is waiting, department:

Corporate top exec cashed in big time just prior to company bankruptcy
$400M payday while his company goes under. Click HERE.

Another congressman in another sex scandal
Can't these guys use their time more wisely? Click HERE.

Presidential pardons for sale
Ever wonder why certain people get pardoned? Click HERE.

And now, enter the PLATINUM parachute
Why do stockholders keep putting up with this legal theft? Click HERE.

Justice is served, department:

Gambino Mob headed for trial
Murder, extortion, money laundering, drug trafficking, and prostitution. You just want to lock each of these wise guys up in the trunk of a car or maybe administer some electric shocks to his sensitive body parts. They'd quickly learn why the rest of us choose to live by the rule of law. Click HERE.

BLOGs

Comments welcome! To comment on any post, please click on the title of the post.

The world desperately needs a "personal aircraft" like the one Carl Collingwood invented. Every year, they make ten million more cars, but they don't make any more roads. Little by little, our roads are becoming so clogged that eventually we won't be able to *move*. With Carl's aircraft, we could land in our own backyards and travel on "highways in the sky" that keep us from bumping in to each other. There is a *lot* of room up there. Let's use it! *Steve B.*

That Gen. Bellamy sure is arrogant. Like a lot of military men, he thinks he's hot shit. I'll bet he pressed the "death button," and he enjoyed watching Carl die. *Just a thought.*

Good going, Juli and George! You're definitely on to something. As a next step, figure out how the bomb was planted. *Your secret admirer.*

Juli, you'd better keep tabs on your husband, George. Aleksa is out to get him, and she comes fully equipped. *Anonymous.*

Go get 'em, you guys. The whole country is watching this one. There aren't enough crusaders like you. The regular news media are a bunch of ass lickers. They're just in it for the money, not to seek justice or to keep us informed. *Someone who cares.*

You bastards! Don't you see what you're doing? You are trying to undermine the military industrial complex. They are what make this country *great*. We need them to *kick butt* all over the world. Do you want us to end up a "has-beens" like France or England and get no respect? *Charlton, a/k/a "Moses".*

Did it ever occur to you that everyone is destined to die someday anyway? Why are we so quick to blame the killer? He's just doing his part to fulfill their destiny. Who are we to pass judgment? *Just a thought.*

www.gablesreport.com/weblog

Chapter 14

Inspector Dan Gavin was beside himself. Was Juli Gables making him irrelevant? How dare she publish a story like that without checking with him? Should he cite her for obstructing justice? If he did so, would there be a public outcry against him for picking on her? If he didn't call her on this fiasco, would she continue to upstage him and possibly interfere with his homicide investigation? Should he bring General Bellamy in for questioning?

That would surely be a waste of time. Surrounded by military lawyers, Bellamy would avoid saying anything incriminating.

Absolutely livid, he dialed Juli's number and left a voice mail. "Juli, it's me, Dan Gavin. I read your recent news report on your website. Please call me *immediately!* You know the number."

Gavin called his two assistants in for a status meeting on the crime. Peter and Jack appeared at his office door within seconds, and he motioned for them to sit. They both wore nondescript sweatshirts and dirty jeans, the department uniform for non-uniformed police officers.

"What have we got so far?" Dan was not at all hopeful there was anything they might call progress.

"Not a whole lot," Peter acknowledged. "Transport International yielded *bupkis*. We interviewed everyone at that company who had anything to do with the aircraft engine and came up with nothing, so we don't have a single good lead."

"Yeah," Jack agreed. "And our interviews with those aircraft engineers at the airport were a total waste."

"Somebody's lying. How else could a bomb have been installed on the plane?" Gavin was incredulous.

"They all say the same thing, boss. At least two people were working on that aircraft night and day, sometimes four or five. Nobody had exclusive access. Not even Carl or Bruce."

"Well, from what we heard, Bruce wanted to fly it. That tells us he didn't know what was coming."

"We can rule him out," Jack said firmly. "He was still crying like a baby when we left the airport. He'd have to be one hell of an actor to put on a show like that."

"So, bottom line is—" Gavin pressed.

"We don't have shit," Peter said and threw up his hands for emphasis. "So far anyway. Maybe we should be interviewing those military guys again."

"Or the CEO of TI, Mike Snead?" Jack offered.

"It's way too late for that. Snead would be surrounded by layers of lawyers, and Juli Gable's put the military on their guard."

"Yeah, we saw her website. Damn smart going in like that. Bellamy was like a deer in the headlights. Looked guilty as hell," Peter volunteered.

"So how do you suggest we follow up?" An edge in Gavin's voice revealed his annoyance and frustration.

"Why don't you talk to Juli?" Jack asked. "She's way ahead of us anyway."

"Yeah, it can't hurt," Peter agreed.

"I have a call in to her already, but I'm *really* pissed."

"Yeah? You jealous?" joked Jack.

"Damn straight! Who's running this investigation? Me or her?"

"So far, looks like she is!" Jack grinned.

Just then Gavin's cell phone beeped, and he looked at the caller ID. "It's *her!*" he said with disgust and pressed the green button to take the call.

"Inspector Gavin," he answered

"Hello, inspector. It's me, Juli. You called?"

"Yeah, I called. Who do you think you are, going down there and ambushing General Bellamy? You didn't get squat from him, and now he'll never talk to us without an attorney present, which means he won't talk."

"You don't think we got anything? Did you see his picture, inspector?"

"Of course I did. He looks guilty as hell, but that's not evidence we can use to nail him. We need physical evidence. Stuff we can take to the bank."

"I know, inspector. I know. We're working on it, believe me."

"That's just what I'm afraid of."

"Oh? And you have a problem with that?"

"You'll screw everything up for us, you and your cockamamie cameraman-husband. You're just a couple of amateurs."

"Your ego is showing, inspector. I had hopes that we could work together."

"We can solve this case without you, thank you very much."

"Then I wish you the best of luck, inspector. We'll go our separate ways and see who brings the bad guys to justice."

"Just wait one minute!" Gavin quickly interjected before Juli hung up. "You said you had a video of the test flight. I want to see it."

"Sure, inspector. I thought you'd never ask. George will send it right over. Check your e-mail."

"Does it show anything?"

"That's for us to know and you to find out now, isn't it?"

"Juli, I'm warning you! Stay out of my way on this case."

"No problem. But inspector, I just want you to know—"

"What's that?"

"If you need any help, feel free to call."

Chapter 15

Carl Collingwood's farewell was the biggest I'd ever seen. As a reporter, I had been to quite a number of funerals for popular local officials and for even a congressman who had had a heart attack, but this event was bigger. Over five thousand people showed up to pay their respects to a man whom most of them had never known or even met. Carl was a symbol for all of us who tried our best but just couldn't seem to get recognition.

Like all the kids who went out for sports and tried their best but weren't picked for the team.

Or like all the actors who worked as waiters while they waited for breaks that never came.

Or like all the writers who couldn't get published.

Or like you and me, who tried and failed to get a job.

Or those of us who did have jobs and worked hard every day to just scrape by.

Carl was every man. There was a little bit of him in all of us. We know we're basically losers—most of us were anyway—but you don't have to rub it in.

The difference was that Carl tried to strike back. *That* was what he became famous for. He just couldn't take the injustice of it all. And deep down in our hearts, neither can we.

The media was there in full force to experience the mood of the crowd and to report every minute detail. It was definitely the news event of the day.

Poughkeepsie is a city of churches. In fact, one of its main thoroughfares is called "Church Street." The service was held in the largest church on Church Street, a cathedral really, one made of red brick and stone at the turn of the nineteenth century. The place was packed to the point where many were left outside to listen to the ceremonies from loudspeakers set up on the front steps on either side of the huge front doors.

The Rev. John Horton officiated, but his role was more like that of an emcee than the pastor of his congregation. One at a time, he called upon Carl's relatives and friends to present their last farewell addresses and eulogies to the assembled audience. There was no casket, not even an urn with ashes of Carl's remains. This was a memorial service, pure and simple.

I sat in the third row and recorded everything, hoping to catch some clue that might help solve the mystery of Carl's death. George roamed with his camera.

Bruce's eulogy came first. It wasn't what he said but *how* he said it that made an impression. He cried his way through it, and we cried with him.

Next came Carl's employees—all nine of them—who told little stories about how much Carl cared about them and also their families. Yes, he worked them late into the night many times, but they did so willingly, because he unfailingly showed them his appreciation and respect. No one had a critical word to say.

A few parishioners took their turn. By the time they were through, there wasn't a dry eye at the church, inside or out.

Finally, Rev. Horton called upon the man all the media had come to hear, Michael Snead, chairman and CEO of Transport International or "TI," as it was called. He didn't have to give a eulogy; however, he did, and what he said moved us all.

Snead came forward from the back of the church someplace, and as he came abreast of the first pew, he stopped to say a few words of comfort to Carl's widow, Sylvia. She sat front and center, dressed in the traditional black, doing her very best to keep her composure, but not at all able to say anything to anybody, much less a church filled with well-wishers. I couldn't hear what Snead said, but I could see that it was heartfelt and that Sylvia saw that as well. The comforting words had their intended effect.

As he stepped up to the podium, Snead began with a short quote from a Shakespeare sonnet:

Farewell! Thou art too dear for my possessing,
And like enough thou know'st thy estimate:
The charter of thy worth gives thee releasing;
My bonds in thee are all determinate.

He then started, "Carl Collingwood and I had a business
relationship. It was nothing more than that at first. He had made
a remarkable invention. My company had invested in it. We make
investments like that from time to time.

"One of my jobs as CEO of our company is to put out fires.
I don't pay much attention to details when things are running
smoothly, but when they are not, I get involved. That is how I got
to know Carl.

"It's not easy to develop a new aircraft during the best of
circumstances. But Carl had invented a radically new design for an
aircraft, and it was taking all too much time to develop the prototype.
I ordered my company to pull the plug on the investment.

"What I didn't know then but what I eventually learned was
that Carl's invention was his *dream* for a better world. He knew it
would work, and all he wanted was the chance to prove it. He was
not about to give up just because I said so. He filed suit against our
company for breach of contract, but he lost.

"Carl must have died a little bit inside when the jury came
back with that decision. He would never forgive me, I knew, for
stopping the project, but I did what I had to do. After all, business
is business.

"What Carl did then was the most remarkable thing of all. He
hijacked a train I was on to take me to Washington to testify about
my company to the people who make the laws for our country.
He assumed they would find something wrong with the way the
company did business that needed legislative correction. As it turned
out, no new laws were needed or made.

"What I admired most through all of this was Carl's passion,
his drive to succeed against all odds. Carl was undeterred by his
setbacks. He kept on fighting, even though his chances of success

were next to nothing. He believed in his aircraft, and he held fast to his dream to make it fly.

"We are assembled here now because Carl died for his dream. He built the aircraft, and it flew! It rose up and hovered for ever so short a time before it exploded, but its flight was enough to show that the aircraft could do what Carl had always said it could do.

"I will make a prediction here and now: Someday you will look up in the sky and see many of Carl's aircraft flying overhead. They will become as commonplace as the jet aircraft of today, filling the airways with people traveling from here to there, wanting to get where they're going as fast and efficiently as possible. People will eventually take them for granted and will never know the effort and passion that went into the development of this automobile in the sky.

"But you and I will know. We will never forget the man who brought us the personal aircraft. It is men like Carl who change our lives and, in doing so, make this country great."

As Mike Snead stepped away from the podium and walked down the aisle toward the doors in the back of the church, you could have heard a pin drop. But at that moment, I remembered that Snead was an accomplished actor.

Chapter 16

Aleksa stood facing the camera outside the church and gave her report. She was energized by the little red light in front of the camera that showed the camera was rolling:

"This afternoon in this church behind me, an overflow crowd came to pay their last respects to Carl Collingwood, a man with an impossible dream, a dream to build and fly what he called a 'personal aircraft' that could take off and land vertically from your own backyard. Unlike most of us, Collingwood almost achieved his dream. But on its maiden test flight, the aircraft exploded violently, killing Collingwood and bringing a final end to this project.

"Tons of tears were shed today as person after person came forward and related how Collingwood had made a positive difference in their lives. To hear them tell it, there is no one on earth who could have had any possible reason to harm this man. But someone did, and the police are conducting a broad investigation.

"One of the witnesses to the tragedy was Juli Gables, a one-time Channel 8 television news reporter. Gables has now accused US Army General David Bellamy of triggering a bomb on the aircraft, an allegation that General Bellamy vigorously denies. Gables has produced no evidence to support her accusation other than a photo of General Bellamy allegedly showing his reaction when informed of her accusation.

"Ms. Gables achieved some notoriety for her inept reporting when Carl and his son, Bruce, hijacked a commuter train to New York City. At that time, Gables also made a wild accusation that a passenger on the train, Michael Snead, bribed a jury in a lawsuit Collingwood brought against Snead and his company, Transport International. The accusations were never substantiated, but Gables was never sued or called to account.

"Mike Snead, who is president and CEO of Transport International, delivered a remarkable eulogy at this memorial service. He reminded us all that it is dreamers like Collingwood who make this country great, and he predicted that Collingwood's dream, his personal aircraft, would someday become a reality.

"This is Aleksa Williams for CBS News."

When Cynthia Brooke watched this report in preparation for the CBS Evening News, she was absolutely furious—so furious, in fact, she did something she only rarely needed to do. She ordered her staff to delete part of the report.

She also ordered her administrative assistant to call Aleksa on the carpet straightaway.

However, Cynthia was not so furious with Aleksa that she ignored the report altogether. Because it was clearly the most important story of the day, she ran it as the top story on the evening news. As she stared directly into the camera as if to gaze into the TV viewer's eyes, Cynthia introduced Aleksa with a lead-in that set the solemn mood: "Carl Collingwood, inventor and entrepreneur who died last week in a fiery explosion while testing his new aircraft, was remembered today at a memorial service in Poughkeepsie, New York. Aleksa Williams was there and has the story."

The story ran without any mention of the involvement of Juli Gables.

At 7:00 p.m., immediately after the news broadcast, Cynthia walked to her dressing room and confronted the waiting Aleksa. "How *dare* you, Aleksa! Who do you think you *are*?"

Uncharacteristically subdued for the *prima donna* that she was, Aleksa was at a loss for words at first, but then she quickly found her voice. "I'm just trying to find the *real* story, Cynthia. It's not, you know, the *Death of a Salesman*."

"What the hell does that mean?"

"It means that the death of one old guy is not the news. It's who's involved and why."

"You can't just go throwing rumors out there and calling it news. Our reputation is at stake! And did I mention *libel and slander*?"

"I was just reporting the facts about Gables. She's *accusing* Bellamy of triggering the explosion. Look on her website if you don't believe me."

"Who cares? Why do you give credence to that rag? What is it, Aleksa? Are you *jealous* of *her*?"

"Of course not! Why should I be jealous? I'm just trying to find the killer like she says *she* is."

"You have a shitty way of going about it, I must say. So far, all you've done is try to seduce Juli's snooty, cameraman-husband. What's his name? George?"

"You know about that?"

"I guessed it. It's what *I* would have done. Anything to get that video."

"We're two of a kind, aren't we?"

"Remember, I was in your shoes once. You just watch it, young lady. You're *not* going to get my job."

"Don't be too sure, Cynthia. I'm a bigger bitch than you are."

"You don't know me. I'll cut your balls off."

"You don't have the balls to do that, and besides, I'm better looking than you."

"You say one more word like that, you bitch, and you're *history*. You'll never work in TV news again."

"You're in the anchor seat right now, so be my mentor. Groom me. Make me perform. You know I've got what it takes to be the top bitch someday."

"Why should I put up with your insolence?"

"One reason, Cynthia. You do it, and I'll make you look good. *Really* good. You'll get the ratings. You'll knock 'em dead over at ABC and NBC. You'll be unstoppable."

"Okay, I'll give you a shot. But in return, I want some *major* suck-up. I want you to kiss my fat ass . . . *big time*."

"You just watch me."

Aleksa genuflected to the media queen and walked briskly out the door.

Chapter 17

With his grieving mother sitting beside him, Bruce rode home in the back of the limousine after the memorial service at the church. He stared blankly out the window, little snippets of his life flickering in the background on the small screen in his mind. It was a strange feeling. True, he now felt sadness and sorrow for his mother, who had endured so much during her marriage to Carl, and just when Carl seemed to be able to achieve some measure of success, she had lost him entirely. Yet, oddly, he himself felt neither depressed nor even saddened by his father's death. The sudden fiery explosion that consumed his father had been a shock to his system, but what seemed to have been a diffuse weight between his shoulder blades was now fading away. He had never noticed it before, this "weight," but now that he could feel it disappearing, he sensed it must have been real.

So real, in fact, that he nearly accepted the guilt that accompanied it. Was his father the weight? How could he be so uncaring?

By the time the limousine arrived at their driveway, Bruce knew exactly what he wanted to do. He assisted his mother out of the car, signaled to the driver he was free to go, and walked his mother up to the door of the house. After he unlocked the door, he stood there on the threshold and kissed her tenderly on the cheek.

"Mom, I'm going back out to the airport. We've got some unfinished business there."

"Whatever it is, it can wait until tomorrow. Come on in and let's have a nice supper."

"No, Mom, I really have to go."

"What's the emergency?"

"It's nothing, Mom," he said. "I'll handle it. Don't you worry."

"You *know* I'll worry. Now that Carl is gone, you're all I have left."

"Well, don't wait up for me. I'll be home late."

"What is it then? What's going on? Can't I help?"

"No, Mom, I don't need help. I just need to spend time—"

"Well *tell* me!" she interrupted.

"You don't want to know. Just let me go."

"Yes, I do. I *insist!*"

"I'm going to finish what Dad started. I'm going to build and fly the aircraft."

"Oh my *God*, no! The *aircraft?*" Sylvia Collingwood suddenly burst into tears. "That aircraft has *ruined* our family. Please *no!*"

"That's why I didn't want to tell you! I don't want to hurt you, Mom."

"Then don't go! Find something else to do—go back to school, get another job, *anything*. I can't *bear* to hear more about that aircraft. It's as if it was . . . *cursed.*"

"I know, Mom. I know. But Dad started this, and it's such a good idea that I can't let it go. And I want to . . . I need to do it for *his* sake."

Sylvia looked up at Bruce, saw the desperate pleading in his face, and softened. Involuntarily, she reached up and softly held her son's head between her two hands to better see deeply into his tear-filled eyes. "You are my only son. I am so afraid of losing you. As sure as the sun comes up in the morning and goes down at night, that cursed airplane will take you away from me if you go back to it. But I will do what every mother must do. I will let you go."

Bruce felt his mother's body shake with emotion and couldn't bring himself to go. Not just yet.

"Can I at least have supper, Mom, before I get started?"

Sylvia grabbed her son in her arms and held him tightly while she buried her face in his shoulder. She didn't want him to see her cry.

When she was able to compose herself, she released him and stepped back and stood erect. "Bruce," she said with a slightly wavering voice, "I would be delighted if you would join me for dinner."

Making dinner for Bruce was part therapy and part expression of love. She made Bruce's favorite meal, lasagna with layers and layers of ricotta and mozzarella cheese interspersed with her own special recipe of Italian meat sauce. She baked it at 350 degrees for fifty minutes and then took it out and topped it with a layer of parmesan cheese. After she returned it to the warm oven to bake over, she prepared a green salad with slices of avocado and onion and added a dollop of blue cheese dressing in sour cream. Finally, she set the table with her finest china and tableware, poured Bruce a tall glass of Ballantine ale, and announced that dinner was ready.

Bruce fully understood the significance of this meal to his mother. Over time, she would have to transfer her allegiance and loyalty from her deceased husband to the next generation in her tiny, close-knit family. Her expression of love was palpable. In spite of her grief, she had taken a small step forward. She was trying as best she could to adjust to her new life without Carl.

"Thank you, Mom. This is great!" Bruce kissed her on the cheek, helped her with her chair as she sat down, and then took his own seat and tried his best to act normal.

Chapter 18

Finally, on the way home from the funeral, George and I had a chance to put our heads together and work out what we were going to do about finding and proving who had planned and carried out this horrible crime. I say "finally" because ever since that day, it seemed that neither George nor I had a chance to *breathe*.

I had promised Sylvia Collingwood that we would bring those people to justice. I had also told Mike Snead that I would do the same, although I didn't feel at all obligated to him as I did to Mrs. Collingwood.

And finally, George and I considered it our *job* to solve the crime. That was our calling, and that was what we *did*. We felt like the whole community depended on us. The community had more faith in *us* than they did in the local police.

"I got some great footage," George told me as he finally found the main road and we headed out of Poughkeepsie. "I can't wait to show you." George was driving as usual, and I was in the passenger seat, staring out the window as the city quickly turned into suburbs, which less quickly turned into the rolling countryside of Dutchess County. Once pure farmland, the county was now more or less just a nice, relaxed place to live.

"So, George, what do we do now?"

"Ever see a movie called *Marty* with Ernest Borgnine?"

"Didn't that come out about hundred years ago?"

"There's a scene where the guys are standing around, trying to decide what to do for the evening, and Marty says, 'What do you want to do?' And his friend says, 'I don't know, Marty. What do *you* want to do?' It goes back and forth like that, and they never decide."

"Sounds hilarious."

"Well, you have to see the movie."

"So, what do we do?"

"I don't know, Juli. What do you want to do?"

"I don't know, George. What do *you* want to do?"

"Very funny," he said. "Like I said, you have to see the movie."

"I'm serious. I'm really kind of stumped."

"Want to talk to Aleksa? See what she's got?"

"Aleksa? No, I don't *think* so."

"Mind if I talk to her?"

"Suit yourself," I said. "But I'll stay miles away if you don't mind."

"Shall we talk to Inspector Gavin?"

"What for? He can't sleuth his way out of a paper bag." I was adamant.

"Bellamy?"

"Been there, done that."

"Mike Snead?"

"If he knew anything that would prove his innocence, he would have told us, and he's not about to reveal any bad stuff."

"Who's left?"

"We need Deep Voice," I said, remembering back to the time when Shelley Bernstein led us through the maze of that corporate conglomerate when we investigated the hijacking of the commuter train. Just then my cell phone rang. Without looking at the caller ID, I took the call. "Hello? This is Juli."

"Hello, Juli. How are you holding up?" I instantly recognized that deep gravelly voice. "It's been a long time."

"My God, it's you! I'm here with George. We were just thinking about you!" I put my hand over the microphone and clued George in, "It's Shelley!"

"Positive thoughts, I hope." I put the phone back to my ear and just caught the end of that remark.

"What are you saying? You're our hero!"

"I'm glad you think so, because I really need your help. I have a problem here."

"If there is anything we can do—"

"It's our famous CEO, Mike Snead. I'm afraid he's unwittingly putting our company in jeopardy."

"Again?" I asked. "Can't he keep out of trouble?"

"I'm afraid not. It's a long story, and I'd like to meet with you privately to paint the picture—and believe me, it's not pretty. Have you got a couple of hours for an old friend?"

"Of course, Shelley. You just say when and where. Does it have anything to do with Carl Collingwood's death?"

"It has everything to do with it. When I saw your story about General Bellamy on your website, I started putting the pieces together. I've got a lot to tell."

"So when and where?"

"How about this evening? Here in the city. I leave work every day at seven. I don't want to change my routine, or Snead will get suspicious."

"No problem. Let's make it 7:30. Next question's where?"

"I know a little place on Restaurant Row called Orso's. It's down below street level. Quiet. No one will know we're there."

"Can I bring George?"

"I'd rather you came alone. Nothing personal, but I think it will attract less attention. And I don't want any cameras."

"That's okay. George will understand. I can trust him to stay home alone one evening. Come to think of it, it'll be the first time since our marriage."

"He just might like the privacy. See you tonight." Shelley clicked off.

I put down the phone and explained the situation to George. He didn't seem to mind at all that he couldn't join in this meeting to end all meetings, but I felt bad nonetheless for leaving him at home, all alone by himself.

Chapter 19

Although protocol indicated that he should go, General David Bellamy had decided not to attend the Collingwood funeral. *It is too risky,* he thought, *with the press presence there. People who would ask pesky, probing questions.* He knew his temper was not always under his control and didn't trust himself to answer such questions without his anger level rising.

Juli and George's visit to the base had been truly unnerving. What had prompted them to come? What did they know? Bellamy felt like a mouse in the same room as a cat. He needed to retreat to his hole in the wall and stay there.

Bellamy left the headquarters building and walked briskly along the sidewalk to another building some significant distance away. Although painted white like all the other structures on the APG campus, this building was not at all attractive. Made entirely of cinder blocks and walls with no windows, it looked like a huge toy or building block.

Bellamy inserted his security card in a slot for the front door and entered the building. Immediately inside was a small anteroom, no bigger than a medium-sized closet, with a locked door facing straight ahead. To the right was an ATM-like console built into the cement wall. To the left, the wall was partly formed by a thick glass pane with a silvered surface. "Good morning, sir," came a voice from an overhead speaker. "Just press your thumb on the sensor and pose for the photo."

Bellamy knew the drill, having done it many times, and quickly completed his biometrics security test. A green light came on in the console after his thumbprint, face image, and retina image had been processed. "Now just punch in your code, sir, and the door will unlock automatically."

Bellamy did so and gained entry to one of the most secure buildings in the US Armed Forces.

Once inside, a Sergeant Major greeted him warmly. "Glad to see you again, general," he said with obvious respect for the senior officer. "It's been a long time since we've seen you in here. What can we do you for?"

"I'd like—" Bellamy hesitated. "I'd like a secure phone to call the VP."

The sergeant was visibly startled. "You mean you haven't heard?"

"Heard what?"

"About the vice president. He had a heart attack this morning, and he's at the Georgetown University Hospital, undergoing surgery right now. It doesn't look good."

Bellamy's face suddenly lost color, and he was speechless for a moment. Then he managed to say, "How did you find this out?"

"It's on all the news channels. The POTUS is going to hold a press conference at four o'clock. I'm surprised you didn't know. You of all people."

"Why do you say that?"

"I know you and the VP have been close."

"Well, maybe not close, but it's good to have *acquaintances* in high places." Bellamy emphasized the word "acquaintances."

"Well, we'll know more at four."

Bellamy excused himself and quickly withdrew through the door from which he had come. Once outside, he hurried back toward his office, but without entering the building, he jumped in his own POV, a late model Ford sedan. Starting the engine and backing out of his parking spot in one swift motion, he turned the wheel, gunned it forward, and shot out of the parking lot.

"Shit, shit, shit," Bellamy kept saying to himself as he sped out the APG main access road to the highway south to Baltimore. "I've been fucked. What am I going to do now?"

All the way to Washington, DC, on the Baltimore-Washington Parkway, Bellamy listened to the news on the radio. Indeed, it wasn't good. Eventually entering the city traffic on New York Avenue,

Bellamy continued to press ahead, timing his way through the traffic lights to speed his way toward the Georgetown University Hospital. He had to get to the vice president and speak with him privately before the patient became overwhelmed by the many others who would crowd around to debrief him, taking advantage of his weakened condition—or God forbid, he died.

Bellamy made a quick right on L Street, left on 10th Street, and then right again on K Street, following it to the Whitehurst Freeway. From there, he turned left onto Canal Road, bore right onto Foxhall Road, and eventually turned right at Reservoir Road to reach the hospital. All of this took less than twenty minutes, but each minute drew a band tighter around Bellamy's chest. When he finally entered the hospital parking facility, his head was pounding, and it was all he could do to slip his car into one of the few tight spaces he found. He shut off the ignition and sat motionless for a moment, his eyes closed, holding the car keys in his sweaty palm. "Get a grip, get a grip," he kept telling himself.

When the panicky feeling had subsided somewhat, he exited the car and walked quickly to the nearby hospital entrance. As he went, he tried to formulate a plan.

He swept through the lobby and headed purposefully toward the elevator bank. His officer's uniform allowed him to pass right through the security screen at the lobby level, but Bellamy knew that security would be much tighter at the floor with the vice president. He headed up the elevator and got off on the top floor landing. Sure enough, the doors leading to the corridors were shut, and several military police with holstered weapons stood guard in front of them.

"I'm General Bellamy, US Army Ordnance, and I've come to see the vice president," Bellamy explained to the guard who appeared to have the senior rank.

"Our orders are to let no one in," was the reply. Standard procedure, Bellamy knew.

"Use your phone and call his aide, Charles Brodsky. Tell him it's me, and he'll make an exception."

"Your identification?"

Bellamy handed the guard his military pass with his picture and other biometric information. The guard glanced at it, inserted it in a slot in a tag reader, and gave it back. After the officer grabbed a telecom from his belt, he pressed several buttons and brought it up to his ear. "We have a General David Bellamy here. Says he wants to see the vice president." After a few seconds, the guard nodded and terminated the call. "Mr. Brodsky says he'll come out and speak with you."

A moment later, Brodsky stepped out through one of the doors and greeted Bellamy with a handshake. His face was grim. "He's just come out of surgery," Brodsky reported. "He's not doing at all well, but there's still hope. We'll know more when he wakes up from anesthesia."

"I can't talk with him?"

"Definitely not."

"He's the only person who can deal with this," Bellamy said.

"What's it about?"

General Bellamy whispered in Brodsky's ear. He really didn't think Brodsky knew about the matter, but to his great surprise, Brodsky whispered back, "I'll get you in."

A short time later, Bellamy left the hospital via the elevator by which he had come. His coming in and going out were not only logged by the guards, but they were also recorded by closed-circuit surveillance video.

Chapter 20

Orso's is an Italian restaurant on the south side of 48th Street just off Eighth Avenue. It's kind of hard to find because it's in the basement of a brownstone, but that location makes it all the more interesting as a secluded, intimate place to meet. If you like Italian food, take a tip from me and give it a try. Get yourself a reservation far in advance, though, or you won't get in. Shelley Bernstein must have known the owner of Orso's, or he could not have gotten us in on such short notice.

When I walked in, I saw Shelley sitting at a cozy table for two in the far left corner of the room. He rose when he saw me and smiled the broadest smile. It had been a long time since we had last met, and during our encounter over Collingwood's hijacking the commuter train, we had developed a relationship of mutual trust and respect. We also genuinely liked each other. It was an honor and a pleasure to meet with him.

"How have you been?" Shelley asked warmly as he pulled out a chair and helped to get me comfortably seated.

"Can't complain," I replied. "Our new website is going like gangbusters, and we're posting new stories every day. How about you?"

"Not so good. That's the reason I called you, Juli," Shelley began. "There's something strange going on, and we haven't been able to sell to the military like we used to."

"Something? What something?"

"I'm not sure. It's like a cold front has moved in, cooling down our relationships with all our usual customers. They're holding us off for some reason. I don't understand it, and neither does Mike Snead. He's tearing his hair out, and I can't blame him."

"Do you think it has anything to do with Carl Collingwood's death?"

"No and yes. This freeze started several months ago, before Carl's plane blew up, but I can't help thinking there's a link."

"Really? How's that?"

"I read your website. I know you think General Bellamy had something to do with the tragedy. He's the director of procurement for the US Army for God's sake."

"He's in charge of buying your stuff?"

"Partly. He and his people. For the army anyway, but the US Air Force and Navy are involved, too. They all work together, and they're not returning our calls."

"What do you want me to do?"

"I know that Mike reached out to you and wanted to hire you and George to investigate for us. You rightly turned him down, and he respects you for that. So do I. But I want to be sure you get all the clues we have to work with. This is important to us, Juli. We could go out of business if this keeps up."

"You're *that* dependent on military sales? Don't you have other business?"

"That's the weird thing. Our commercial business is drying up, too. Nobody's buying."

"What do your customers say?" I asked. "Any idea why?"

"It's a jumble. They all have a different excuse. It's like a conspiracy, and they've been told not to reveal anything. I don't mind telling you we're running scared."

"Any suggestions where we should look?"

"Not a whole lot, but here's one thing we learned: There's a mega-company in Russia called InterMil that seems to be doing really well on the international market. They've been selling arms to small African nations for many years, and quite recently, they have gotten into nuclear power. Nuclear arms too, we think. A man named Nikki Borisnikoff is the majority owner of this company and is chairman of the board. He's the kind of guy who'd stop at nothing to gain some advantage."

"You really think a Russian company could affect your sales like that? In this country?"

"Doesn't seem likely or even plausible, but we don't know who else would stand to gain."

I sat there, dumfounded, and stared at Shelley. If what he was implying were true, this would be the first worldwide attempt to corner the market on military arms by an international corporation. The prospect was just too scary to imagine.

"Mike's running scared, Juli. Really scared. I've never seen him like this. A homicide detective, a guy named Dan Gavin, is circling around with his men like a bunch of vultures. They think Mike had someone plant a bomb in the engine, and there's no way to prove the negative."

"Have they found any evidence at all?"

"That's the worst part! They found some guy in the plant who claims he saw something. They won't say what that's about, but this other shoe is about to drop. I just know it!"

With the foreign competition, the falling sales and now the possibility of an indictment, I would also say that Mike and his company were in some deep trouble.

Chapter 21

The very next morning, as George and I sat in our kitchen having breakfast, the phone rang. It turned out to be one of the saddest and most difficult calls I have ever received in my life.

At first, all I heard in the receiver was a woman's voice attempting to say something but making no sense. I recognized her voice though. It was Mrs. Collingwood.

Through the crying and whimpering sounds, I was able to make out, "I saw it. It's on the TV right now. My husband—" Her voice dissolved into a sound of heartrending pain.

I cupped the microphone for a split second and whispered to George, "Turn on the TV news. *Quick*."

What I saw was inconceivable to me. Our video, the one that George had taken of the horrible, fiery tragedy of Carl Collingwood's death, was playing on our own kitchen television set.

"Oh, God!" I said out loud. Mrs. Collingwood heard me and started sobbing uncontrollably. "I'm so sorry!" was all I could offer. Mrs. Collingwood had seen her husband burn to death on broadcast television news.

Somehow, I stumbled through that call without making matters worse for Mrs. Collingwood. I didn't know what to say, and to this day, I can't remember what I said; however, whatever it was, it seemed to help the situation. Mrs. Collingwood eventually apologized to *me* for calling and revealing her pain in such a personal way. Good God, what a gracious lady she was and *is*.

But when I got off the phone, I glared at George. Truth detector that I am, I saw guilt written all over his face.

A reporter's mantra is "who, what, why, when, and where." There's a "how" thrown in there sometimes, too. I knew "who" the person must have been that gave the video away, so I asked George, "*Who* did you give it to?"

"Aleksa," came the sheepish, hardly audible reply. "But she promised to keep it confidential."

"She *promised*? Just *what* did you give to her?"

"I gave her a disc with the video."

"You *gave* her a—*Why*?"

"She asked me for it. She said she wanted to see the proof that General Bellamy blew up the airplane."

"*When* did you do this?"

"Last night while you were having dinner at the restaurant with Shelley."

"Just *where* were you when you gave her the disc?"

"I was at home. In our apartment." George looked really pathetic at this point. He was *so* wrong.

"Let me get this straight. Correct me if I don't get it right. Aleksa came over to *our* apartment, and you gave her a disc with *our* Collingwood video on it?"

"That's right," acknowledged George in a very small voice.

"*How* could you think of doing such a thing? She's out to kill us. Take our jobs away. Why would you do her any favors? She of all people?"

"She seemed so nice—"

"So *nice*? You gave her the video because she was *nice*?"

"No, not exactly."

"Then *what* exactly?"

"I don't know. I guess I thought she was pretty."

My head was starting to pound about this time. I was about to lose it, so I took a different tactic. "How long was she in the apartment with you?"

"Maybe an hour, I guess."

The answer to each question I asked seemed worse than the previous one. I almost hesitated to ask this one last question: "Then *what* were you *doing* with her in the apartment all this time?"

"Nothing. We just . . . talked."

"You talked, and she ended up getting the video?" I asked incredulously.

"Yeah, that's all we did. She said she wouldn't show the video to anyone else."

I felt awful. My head was aching something fierce. I had to get out of there *fast*, or I'd do something I was sure to regret. How could George betray me like that after all we'd been through? I thought for sure I had found my soul mate, but now it was all ending so suddenly. I couldn't deal with the thought of this betrayal. I pushed back from the table, grabbed my purse, and ran out of the apartment without looking at George.

Down in the lobby, I dashed past Nigel, the concierge, and was about to leave through the front door of the building when it dawned on me. I turned around and walked back to Nigel. I could trust him to tell me what he knew, and I was determined to find out anything I could about Aleksa's coming and going.

"Last evening," I began, "did you let a good-looking black woman go up to our apartment?"

"You mean Aleksa Williams from Channel 2 News? Yes, I called, and your husband, George, said I should send her up."

After I got all of this information in such a short time, I was nearly struck dumb. I must have showed it because Nigel continued, "I thought you knew about her visits."

"Her *visits*? More than one?"

"She was here a couple of times. Yesterday and also a couple of days ago."

My heart sank. There was not even a glimmer of hope any more that George had been true to me. I walked out of the lobby in a daze and roamed the streets for hours until I eventually calmed down enough to think reasonably straight. When I was good and ready, I marched right back to the apartment and stormed in the front door to confront George. To my dismay, George was nowhere to be found.

George had had the good sense to stay away for a couple of days. I found out later that he went back to live with his mother in her apartment. To this day, I wonder what he told her had happened between us.

Chapter 22

My life was falling apart, but I had to soldier on. *Someone* had to keep our news business alive and, more importantly, had to solve the crime of the year, if not the decade.

I began by looking up InterMil on the Internet. A big company like that would have a website, you would think, but not this one. There was precious little information out there, not even a list of the board of directors. Not even a mention of the company's products and the services that it sold and offered to various governments throughout the world. It was all hush-hush.

The only lead I had was from my encounter with General Bellamy, and he was not talking. I was reaching a dead end, so I turned on the TV news again.

There, for the first time, I saw the breaking news story about the vice president's heart attack. It was of interest to me as a reporter, but I had no inkling of its huge significance to the country and particularly to me in the coming months.

What I saw on CNN was an up-to-the-minute report of the VP's condition and a replay of some of President Bradley's four o'clock press conference the day before. The VP was still in intensive care at that moment and might conceivably have irreversible brain damage. "Only time will tell," said the chief of surgery at the Georgetown University Hospital, but he was "very hopeful" that the vice president would fully recover all of his faculties. If he didn't, well, there would be a vacancy in government that the president would have to fill. Another press conference was scheduled for later today, again at four o'clock.

The VP's name was Richard Chernoff, a first-generation American whose parents were well-known dissidents in the Soviet Union. His parents had succeeded in leaving their country and coming to America during the rule of Nikita Kruschev. It was reported that "Rick," as he was known, had close ties to a lucky few who were in the right place at the right time to benefit from the upheaval in the late 1980s, when the Soviet Union dissolved into the separate but closely connected "CIS" countries. Many Americans thought that President Bradley chose Rick Chernoff to serve as the vice president precisely because of his supposed influence in Russia.

"We all pray that vice president Chernoff comes through this ordeal and will be able to assume his duties again soon," the president had said yesterday. There appeared to be no change in his condition since then, so I wondered why the president felt the need to hold another press conference today.

I was at a dead end. I was tempted to call Inspector Gavin and ask if he had any leads I could follow. Not that he'd tell me if he had any. There was only one more thing I thought I could do. I'd check to see where Bellamy's car was parked.

With the computer, I pulled up the software for that application and typed "GPSLink29," our code for that tracking device we put on Bellamy's car, in the login box, and I added my password in the box just below it. I mouse-clicked on the word "login" and waited while the computer found the information on the Internet. Within a few seconds, a roadmap appeared with a little red icon showing the location of Bellamy's car. It took me a few seconds to realize I was staring at a map of Washington, DC, and that the car was parked somewhere in Georgetown. I zoomed in closer and saw the legend, "GU Hospital." Pondering this, it took me almost a full minute to connect the dots: Bellamy was at the same hospital where they had taken Vice-President Chernoff. Could this have been just a coincidence? Now *this* was a lead I could follow!

Too bad George wasn't with me. I could have used his expertise right now, not to mention his moral support and his companionship. I was beginning to miss him, darn it—betrayal or no betrayal. He was still my George. If I got my hands on that bitch Aleksa, though, I'd wring her neck!

Where *was* George anyway? He'd been away since yesterday. It was time for him to come *home*, damn it.

I called downstairs to the lobby and asked Nigel to call me a cab. I packed a few things in my valise and was soon on my way to LaGuardia Airport to catch the next Delta Shuttle flight to Washington. Within two hours, I was on the DC Metro blue line headed for Foggy Bottom. While I was passing through Reagan National Airport, I took a moment to call home and leave a voice-mail message so George would know where I was just in case he *ever* came back to our nest to roost.

I got out at the Foggy Bottom station and took a cab to the GU Hospital. I didn't know what I'd find there, but I was not deterred. There *had* to be some reason why Bellamy was at the hospital, and my intuition told me he was up to no good. But how could I find this stuff out? Just ask him? Yeah, right.

The cab dropped me off at the hospital, and I walked into the lobby. I tried to use my press pass to get upstairs, but security was really tight, so I got nowhere. If only George were here, he'd know what to do!

I looked around, but nothing occurred to me. I could just sit there and wait to see if Bellamy happened to walk by, but that was too much of a long shot. Even if he did, he'd refuse to talk to me. Then what? I was stumped. I'd come all this way for nothing.

I turned to leave with nothing to show for this boondoggle of mine when whom do I see coming in the front door? None other than Aleksa with her cameraman and George!

Chapter 23

I didn't know whether to hide from them or scream bloody murder. In the end, I did neither. I just stood there until they practically bumped right into me on their way to the security station. It was not like me to have such a snotty attitude, but I was not in the mood to be nice to either Aleksa or George. Aleksa's cameraman, whose name turned out to be Brian, seemed nice enough, but I lumped him together with the other two.

"Watch where you're going, you . . . you—" I was so tongue-tied, I couldn't even think of what to call them.

George, God bless him, kept his counsel in this incredibly awkward turn of events. I'm sure he was dumbfounded at seeing me there, but he didn't show it. It was all I could do to keep myself from slugging him.

Aleksa, on the other hand, was saccharine sweet. I'll bet she could handle any weird social situation, ranging from a football locker room brawl to a romp in a gay bathhouse. "Ms. Juli Gables, I presume?" as if she were Stanley meeting Mr. Livingston in the heart of Africa. "It's truly an honor to finally meet you."

Yeah, right! She had stolen my man and now she was saying it was an honor to see me here, standing in the lobby of some hospital in Washington, DC, like an absolute *jerk*.

"Well, I'm not sure I'm glad to see *you*, especially together here with my husband, George."

George finally piped up. "Honest, Juli, it's not like it seems." All the guys who are caught red-handed say that, don't they?

"Oh? How does it *seem* to you?"

"I . . . uh . . . guess it looks pretty bad. But that's not the case. Aleksa and I just came down here to check on Bellamy."

"You came to check on Bellamy with *her*?"

"You kinda . . . uh . . . *disappeared* on me. I found out that Bellamy was here—using our bugging device, remember?—and I figured I had to come down here *quick*. That's when I contacted Aleksa and explained everything, and she agreed to come."

"So why do you need *her*? Why didn't you come by *yourself*?"

"I'm just a *photographer*," George said meekly. "I couldn't do this alone."

"Can I get a word in here?" Aleksa started to butt in.

"No! You stay *out* of this," I literally screamed. I was really pissed at this point. "You are *not* just a photographer," I admonished George. "You're an investigative reporter just like me."

"I'll agree with you on that one. George has real talent for scoping out the news," Aleksa said anyway.

"So what do *you* know? He's *my* husband." I was about to strangle her.

"At first, I couldn't believe that Bellamy could possibly have been involved. He was so nice to me during that interview at Aberdeen. That guy really had my number. But George explained to me how he was the only one who could have set off that bomb. And your video proved it."

"The video he gave to you after you said you wouldn't show it to anyone?"

"Yeah, well, I didn't have a choice. Cynthia, my boss, found out I had it and made me put it on."

"Like you expect me to believe that bull—"

"Believe it or not, it's true. But the point is that George has a nose for this stuff, and I began to take notice. So when he called me about Bellamy taking this trip to Washington, well, wouldn't you have wanted to come along?"

I couldn't help but want to agree with her. "Okay, so Bellamy is here, but the security is so tight no one can get to him. What do we do? Turn around and go home?"

"I have an idea," George spoke up with his meek voice.

"Yeah, *what*?" I didn't really want to hear it.

"There's always a back room in these places where they watch the video surveillance cameras. A couple of guys who just sit there and stare at the screens. That's all they do. Maybe we can get to *them*."

"That's a *great* idea," Aleksa said brightly. "See, Juli? George really knows his stuff."

"And why do you think they would give us the time of day?"

"They're men, aren't they? Just watch me," Aleksa said.

We found out from the hospital information desk where the security room was—or I should say, Aleksa found out from the guy at the desk who didn't hesitate to tell her whatever she wanted to know. And we headed directly to room SB29 down in the subbasement. There was no indication on the door who or what might be behind it. At first, we carefully tried turning the doorknob, but it was locked, so we knocked. Nothing happened, so we knocked again, louder this time. We must have wakened someone up because we first heard a muffled noise. Then the door opened a crack, and a good-looking African-American man peered out at us. Because she was the pretty one, I let Aleksa take the lead.

All she said was, "Hi, honey," and I could see the guy start to melt already.

"What can I do you for?"

"Could you let a girl in for a moment? I need to ask a question."

The man hesitated—would you believe it?—notwithstanding a winning smile by Aleksa that even I thought was a sure door-opener. The man's eyes scanned George and me up and down.

"I'll leave my friends out here. Just let me come in a minute."

"All right, but just for a minute." The man opened the door just enough to let Aleksa in and then closed it again, leaving George, Brian, and me standing alone together out in the hall.

A minute passed and then two and then five, and George and I could only wonder what was going on in there. After what seemed like half an hour but turned out to be only ten minutes, the door opened again, and Aleksa reappeared, all smiles, holding a DVD. She gave the man who had let her in a kiss on the cheek and stepped out into the hallway. The door snapped shut behind her, and she told us, "I've got Bellamy going in to Chernoff's room! Not only that, he's in there privately with some top brass from the US Navy and Air Force. Those guys all know each other!"

Chapter 24

Because of what we knew about General Bellamy, we had to assume they were up to no good. But what?

Just as I had to assume that my husband, George, was up to no good. I wanted to believe his explanation about coming down here with Aleksa, but I just couldn't. My trust in him just wasn't there. Not after I had learned that Aleksa had been in our apartment—*twice!* And he'd given her that video. I didn't want to *imagine* what they were doing together alone while I was out having dinner with Shelley. Without trust, a marriage is doomed.

"So what do we do now?" Aleksa asked George and me. George just looked at me the way he always did when we were stumped, expecting me to lead the way. That was George's way, but *Aleksa?* She was also looking at me to come up with a plan of action.

Her with her huge team of newshounds at CBS she orders around, and I'm her new leader all of a sudden? Well, I'll show her what one can do *without* the benefit of money and good looks, just smarts and a desire to do the right thing.

"Let's take a look at that DVD for a start. Is there sound or just images?"

"Just images, I think. It's off the video-surveillance cameras."

"Anyway, maybe we'll find something there. Next, I suggest we ambush the US Navy and Air Force guys just like we did Bellamy. We'll pretend we know a lot more than we do. If we catch them off guard, maybe they'll confirm they're co-conspirators."

"Co-conspirators in what?" Aleksa wanted to know.

"There has got to be a reason they blew up Collingwood's aircraft. Other than that, I haven't a clue."

"We'll work together then?" George wanted to know just to be sure where he stood in this triangle.

"Yes and no," I replied. "We're going to have to hit the US Navy and Air Force at exactly the same time. Otherwise, whomever we hit first is going to tip the other one off. So we'll need two teams."

"Sounds good to me," Aleksa said.

"I'd like to use your cameraman. You can have George." I had to say *something*. It couldn't be business as usual.

George just stood there with a forlorn look on his face and said nothing. After what he had done with Aleksa, what could he say?

Aleksa feigned surprise and looked at George and me quizzically. "Having a problem, you two?"

"You can have George. That's all I said."

"Okay, if you wish. I suppose you can use my guy. His name's Brian."

"Yes, I insist." And that was that. George was her cameraman from now on, and Brian would be mine, not that I minded all that much! Brian, it turned out, was a really nice-looking white guy with an agreeable, quiet manner.

"I'd like you to meet . . . um, Brian." Aleksa belatedly took the time to formally introduce us, although somewhat tentatively.

"Hi, I'm Juli." He had a firm handshake, which I liked straightaway. He was dressed conservatively for business and carried a pretty large camera that said "CBS News" on the side.

"Aleksa's told me great things about your work. It's an honor to meet you."

"Really? That's interesting." I shot a side-glance at Aleksa and caught her with an embarrassed look. "She's holding back on me," I replied with a wink to Brian.

"She wants me to work with you. Says I can use the training."

"You and I will make a good team." I really thought so, staring at his great physique. He was surely a bodybuilder, or else he'd developed those great abs by schlepping around his heavy TV camera.

"Do you have a smaller camera? We're going to be doing some stealth videos, and that thing's a dead giveaway."

"Sure, there's a tiny one in the van outside. I'll run and get it." Brian was gone in a flash.

My mood was improving! It was amazing how quickly things were turning around, although my problem with George hadn't been resolved at all. How could I ever learn to trust him again?

I tried my best to put that problem out of my mind, though without much success. It continued to fester, and it reemerged in my consciousness time and again. What really was the point of going on when my support system, my very life was so unstable?

Chapter 25

Bruce Collingwood sucked it up and entered the huge skyscraper in New York City. The building soared into the upper reaches seemingly effortlessly because of its unique architectural design with parallel vertical ribs between columns of windows. This vision of strength and stability served as a powerful symbol for the name it carried on the front facade: Transport International.

Bruce pressed through the revolving door and walked up to the imposing black marble security desk. "My name is Collingwood, Bruce Collingwood. I'm here to see Mr. Michael Snead."

"Write your name there on the sheet, and I'll call up." The guard was friendly enough but businesslike. He lifted the phone and spoke while Bruce entered his name, the date, and the person whom he was scheduled to meet.

Apparently, the guard was satisfied with whomever he spoke to because he handed Bruce a visitor's badge. "Take an elevator in that bank over there to the eightieth floor."

Alone in the elevator, Bruce had time to think and become nervous again. By the time he alighted, it was all he could do to step out of the elevator rather than ride down again and avoid this meeting altogether. What kept him moving forward was the thought that his father had made the very same trip some five years before under similar circumstances, and he had had the courage to forge ahead.

When the doors parted, he stepped out into the corporate executive suite. The reception area in front of him was beautifully appointed with a circular, cedar, secretarial desk right in the middle and with two lounge chairs, a table, and a couch forming a sitting area behind it. The sitting area was bounded by two big windows overlooking Central Park in Manhattan.

A young woman sat at a desk with an elaborate console of keypads and screens. She greeted him with a warm smile that calmed his nerves.

"You're Mr. Collingwood?" Bruce nodded. "Mr. Snead is expecting you. Won't you have a seat? I'll let him know you're here."

Bruce moved toward one of the comfortable-looking stuffed chairs by one of the plate-glass windows, but before he sat, he took in the breathtaking view of the city. He stood there a moment, looking out and feeling small, before he turned to sit and wait his turn to meet the man who had done so much harm to his family.

When he browsed the magazines in front of him on the coffee table, he noticed a copy of the annual report of Transport International, Inc. The front cover bore the logo of the company with the letters "TII."

Bruce picked up the report and started to thumb through it. The introductory pages bore a color picture headshot and a letter to the stockholders from the CEO, Michael Snead. The letter reported earnings of nearly a billion dollars the previous year on sales of twelve billion. Sales were broken down by product and service sectors of the company, with military aircraft sector, which was listed at four and a half billion, having the greatest share. The rest of the report went into some detail sector by sector and then concluded with the company's audited financial statements. Bruce glanced at the pictures for each sector, particularly the military aircraft sector, which covered the spectrum from unmanned aerial vehicles to supersonic fighter/bombers.

Surely, with all these sales to the government, there should be some funding available for Bruce to complete the development of the personal aircraft.

"Mr. Collingwood?" Bruce's thoughts were interrupted when he heard his name.

"You may go in now." Bruce looked up and saw the receptionist smiling at him expectantly. "Mr. Snead will be right with you."

"Thank you." Bruce stood up, walked toward the glass doors indicated by the receptionist, and entered a large, well-appointed conference room. Just behind him followed the man he had come to see, CEO Mike Snead. Bruce turned and timidly offered his hand.

"How do you do?" Mike warmly took Bruce's hand. "Please have a seat. Anywhere is fine. Can I offer you coffee or tea?"

"Well, thank you. I'm good." Bruce found a seat and took a deep breath. This was the moment.

Mike slid into the seat at the head of the table. "I was *so* sorry to learn about your father. I'm glad I could say a few words at his memorial service."

"It was awful," was all that Bruce could think to say.

"And it's a shame that his dream died with him. I would have liked to have seen his project come to fruition."

"Well, Mr. Snead, that's why I'm here," Bruce began. "We still have the plans and I would like to continue. If we only could get financing, we could build another prototype practically overnight."

"I'm afraid that without Carl, it will be difficult to find an investor. A project like this needs a strong champion."

"I know. I have tried. I can't raise the money."

"It's such a long shot," Mr. Snead said, "to be sure."

"It's not really. We built an aircraft, and it flew. Dad proved the concept before . . . he died. The team is still available to work together. We can do it again."

"If you have such a convincing story, why can't you find an angel investor?"

"Everyone thinks the project is jinxed. Some even think someone or some company is out to get us."

"So why did you come here?"

"I thought maybe you could help," Bruce said.

"Well, if what you say is true, helping you would be risky for us too, don't you think?"

"The project is *not* jinxed. You know that's just superstition. And the police are working on catching the guy who killed Dad. They'll eventually get him."

"Don't be too sure. They've been following a lot of dead-end leads. They even think I was involved."

"So I've heard. They say there was a bomb in that engine your company delivered."

"So you see? If my company invests in your project, that would just increase suspicion for us. People would think we killed the project and your father so we could take it over."

Bruce sank glumly in his chair. He didn't know what to say to counter this logic.

"And there's another problem. Our company is not doing very well right now. We may have to lay people off. We're fighting some very serious competition, and our sales are down. Way down. The government doesn't seem to want to buy our products like they used to."

"If you made the personal aircraft, it would sell. We know that. The US Army would have bought the aircraft if . . . if the test had been successful."

Mike Snead reached for the telephone on the conference table and picked up the receiver. He dialed a number quickly and spoke, "Shelley, could you step in here a moment? I'm in the conference room."

In less than a minute, an older man appeared at the door. Mike and Bruce stood up.

"Bruce, this is our executive vice-president, Shelley Bernstein. There is nothing that goes on here that he doesn't know about. He could run the company in my absence if he had to."

"Hello, Mr. Bernstein," Bruce said.

"Shelley. Please call me Shelley. Everyone does."

"I'd like to stay with Mr. Bernstein, sir. I . . . I'd feel . . . uncomfortable with calling you 'Shelley.' I hope you don't mind."

"Of course not. Suit yourself."

Mike briefly filled Shelley in. "Bruce would like us to invest in the personal aircraft. He says he can build a new prototype." Mike looked over at Bruce and continued without indicating what he recommended his company should do. "How long did you say it would take you?"

"Just a few months. Maybe even less if we worked day and night."

"We're cash-strapped right now, but we do have some research funds," Shelley replied. "How much do you need?"

"Five million dollars." Bruce said firmly. The venture capitalists he had spoken to had cautioned him to estimate high rather than low to avoid falling short and having to seek a second round of financing.

Just then, there appeared to be a loud commotion at the front reception desk. Bruce and the two executives turned to look through the glass doors as the young receptionist came running toward the conference room immediately followed by two tall men dressed in black suits. The doors burst open, and the receptionist rushed in, shouting, "Mr. Snead, these men are from the police!"

The two men in black barged in behind her, and one of them announced, "Mr. Snead, you are under arrest. We're here to take you down to the police station."

The other man produced a pair of handcuffs and locked them in place around Snead's wrists behind his back. He and his partner then led Snead, silent and in shock, to the elevator bank where they quickly disappeared into one of the elevators.

Shelley Bernstein, who just stood there without so much as a protest, turned to Bruce and said quietly, "We'll take an exclusive license, but you've got your money. Be sure to use it wisely."

Chapter 26

Brigadier General Bellamy was bellicose by nature—both bellicose and bold, qualities you would expect in a typical military officer. To rise through the ranks in the military, it helps to be a loudmouth and to have no qualms about pushing others out of the way to forge ahead. A contemplative "mister nice guy" seldom makes it to the top in the US Army unless one happens to have a mentor who appreciates these gentlemanly qualities. Unfortunately, such mentors like General Colin Powell for example, are rare and far between.

Suffice it to say, that David Bellamy was not the kind of person you would want for a personal friend.

Vice-President Rick Chernoff and his chief of staff, Armin Brodsky, didn't much like Bellamy for this very reason. Notwithstanding his obvious loyalty to VPOTUS and their secret Project Alpha, they just couldn't warm up to this coarse and common soldier. Useful as he was to them, and probably would be in the future, they kept him at arm's length and paid as little heed to him as possible.

After he waited for what seemed to be an interminable length of time, Bellamy was finally ushered into the hospital room. As he entered, he saw the vice president propped up in the hospital bed. "The man" was surrounded by several standing staffers, including Brodsky, who stood the closest to him on the opposite side of the bed, obviously in midconversation. Rick Chernoff nodded in greeting but, without saying a word, simply motioned for Bellamy to take a seat and turned his attention back to Brodsky.

Bellamy did so, dropping into an empty, straight-backed chair near the side of the bed and waited to be heard. During the next few minutes, he kept his eyes on Chernoff, looking for signs of the precarious health condition that both the president and the media had reported the previous day. Astonishingly, Chernoff appeared to be his old self, without any outward sign of disorder or impaired ability.

Eventually, Chernoff wound up the particular business discussion he was engaged in with Brodsky—to Bellamy seemingly in some kind of code—and again acknowledged Bellamy's presence.

"Glad you came, general," the VP began. "Don't be put off by all this hospital paraphernalia. I'm really not sick."

"But the news reports . . . and the president's speech yesterday? Aren't you—"

"No, I'm fine. But not even the president knows. We came here to get away from the scrutiny at this point in the eleventh hour." Chernoff eyed Bellamy carefully to gauge his reaction. You couldn't be too sure about those in the inner circle.

"I . . . uh, think I understand. The media's all around, snooping."

"That's right. We have to be extremely careful. We're only about a couple of months away from VP-Day."

"What about the doctors here? And the hospital staff? Don't they know you didn't . . . uh, have a heart problem?"

"No, they were all told that I brought in my own medical personnel. Only the president of the hospital knows, and he's not telling. He's one of us."

Bellamy reflected for just a brief moment and then responded, "So this will be your headquarters?"

"Will be? *Is*. We have all our communication systems in place here at GU Hospital. We're up and operating right now as we speak."

"That's brilliant!" was all Bellamy could think to say. He was indeed impressed.

"This way, we keep the world at bay until we execute. And then we move into the White House."

"You had me worried, sir. When I heard about your heart attack—"

"'Enough said. Let's get down to business. Is everything ready?"

"Absolutely, sir. You heard about Collingwood, I'm sure. It was all over the news."

"Yeah, I couldn't believe it! How about the bomb? Where is it?"

"It's on the way. InterMil came through just like they said."

"You can trust Borisnikoff," the VP said. "He runs a first-class company."

"I'll arrange for pickup at the port."

"Don't have to. Borisnikoff has his own men for that."

"Okay. I heard they have their own special car they can place on the track at any time."

"You heard that? Where?"

"From Brodsky here," the general said.

"Oh, okay. You know I'm relying on you."

"Yes, sir. I'm on your side. You can count on me."

"That's good, Bellamy. The plan is in place. I'm telling you it's a go."

"Thank you, sir. Uh, by the way—"

"Yes?"

"Will you be giving me a . . . a promotion when you're president?"

"We'll welcome you at the White House," the VP said.

"I'd like that very much, sir."

General Bellamy saluted smartly and withdrew from the room. On the way out, he thought he heard the vice president say to Brodsky sarcastically, "In your dreams, Bellamy."

Chapter 27

Aleksa and George, and Brian and I, working as teams, spent the rest of the day planning our attack on the US Navy and Air Force brass. We watched the video surveillance footage, but it didn't yield any clues. Just that a guy named Brodsky seemed to be involved in the plot, whatever it was, big time!

As our plan eventually emerged, we decided to go as separate teams to the Pentagon and try to reach the top guys in charge of procurement, Brian and me for the US Navy and Aleksa and George for the US Air Force. We needed to find out how and why they seemed to be working in lock step with General Bellamy of the US Army.

Brian and I walked out through the hospital lobby and climbed into a taxi that was standing outside at the front of the taxi line. Aleksa and George were to follow a few minutes later, as we agreed in advance, so that our teams would appear to be completely separate and independent. As a precaution and also to share any information we uncovered, we also agreed to keep in periodic touch with each other by text messages and tweets.

We zipped across the Potomac River on one of the bridges. (I was paying attention to sexy Brian at this point and definitely not to the route our taxi took.) And soon, we pulled up to the visitors' entrance at the Pentagon. On the way, I briefed Brian on our plan of attack. He nodded politely and didn't say much, just a pleasant "sounds good" every so often. I couldn't figure out if he really agreed with the plan or if he was simply going along as a good soldier, but I didn't care. He was a great-looking guy who would do his job well. That was all that mattered.

Inside, we walked past a myriad of MPs to reach the main guard desk. There were a lot of people both coming and going, most of them in uniform. The hubbub reminded me of rush hour in the lobby of Grand Central Station. There was a line of people in front of the guard desk, waiting to speak with the main gatekeeper, who, as luck would have it, happened to be an officer in a naval uniform. When it was our turn, I stepped forward with Brian and spoke up for both of us. As we had arranged previously, Brian kept his video camera in a backpack slung over his shoulders so the officer couldn't see it, at least not yet. I was concerned about the possibility that our intention to record an interview on video would get in the way of my getting some basic information. For this reason, I also didn't want to reveal that we were journalists.

"Hello, I'm Juli Gables, and this is my colleague, Brian," I began, holding out my New York driver's license with a photo of my face. "I'd like to speak with someone in naval procurement."

The officer, whose nametag read "MILKTOAST" in large capital letters, compared my face to the photo on the driver's license and then looked over at Brian inquisitively before he answered, "You lookin' to be a vendor?"

"Not, exactly. We want to discuss contracts with a particular vendor. Transport International."

"What kinds of contracts?"

"Sales contracts for US Navy ships, helicopters, and stuff."

"Okay, just a minute." Officer Milktoast looked down at his keyboard and pressed a few buttons. He then looked at a screen in front of him that was unfortunately under the marble slab surface I was leaning on, so I couldn't see. "It's on the fourth floor, E Corridor. Room E 4-2956."

"Can we just head on up?"

"Security starts there," Milktoast said, jamming his thumb toward to the security checkpoint off to the side, "The answer is yes after you get through that."

I almost caught traces of a smirk when he said that, as if to add, "I defy you to do it, though."

Brian and I walked over to the checkpoint. We were each given a form to fill out with our name, address, date of birth, social security number, that sort of thing. When we completed them, we gave them to the guard on duty together with our driver's licenses. The guard clipped them together and filed them in a box, waving us through to the next station, which was the bag and body scanner. Brian placed his backpack on the conveyer as innocently as you please, along with his shoes and the stuff in his pockets, and I did the same. We proceeded through the magnetometer and waited, fully expecting the woman viewing the X-rays to complain or at least say something. She may have been momentarily distracted by her own thoughts, I don't know, but she merely stared blankly at the screen as the backpack sailed through.

We then each entered the body scanner, first Brian and then me, and to our great surprise, we were cleared and free to move about the building.

Room E 4-2956 was not hard to find. The five legs or segments of the Pentagon are labeled with letters A, B, C, D, and E, and each segment is organized like its own separate building.

We simply walked around the loop to segment E and took the elevator to the fourth floor. As we followed the corridor and counted down the numbers, we easily found the right door. The words "DEPT. OF THE NAVY—PROCUREMENT" were painted in black on the frosted glass. We opened it, walked in, and practically ran right into the US Navy admiral in charge.

Chapter 28

I had formulated a plan for this interview, but when confronted with the right man to speak to, I suddenly lost all confidence that my plan wouldn't result in our arrest or at least in getting us unceremoniously kicked out the door of the Pentagon. My plan was simply to pretend we knew more stuff than we did and to let the interviewee fill in the gaps. I started by being upfront and explaining who we were and why we were there.

The admiral bore the name "WEST" on his nametag, so I addressed him by name.

"Admiral West, sir, my name's Juli Gables. I'm a journalist, and this is my cameraman, Brian. We'd like to ask you a few questions about a recent navy procurement contract."

Brian was unbelievably fast in getting his camera out of the backpack, stepping back and letting the big glass eye capture the scene, almost from the moment we had opened the door.

The admiral put his hand in front of his face, palm out, and tried to press through us to reach the hallway. We blocked his path.

"Why are you buying helicopters from the Russian company, InterMil, when you can get them cheaper from the American company, Transport International?"

There, I punted and held my breath. I didn't even know whether the navy had contracted to purchase anything from InterMil, much less helicopters. I could have chosen jet aircraft or even ships, but I thought that would be pushing my luck.

The admiral, God bless him, stopped in his tracks and stared at me. Brian's camera was rolling so no matter what he had to say, it would be on the record.

"How did you know about that?" he asked sharply.

"We have our sources, admiral. Could you please explain? The US taxpayers would like to know the reason."

"Well, Miss—What is your name?"

"Gables. Juli Gables." I quickly pulled out one the business cards that I carried in my jeans back pocket at all times and presented it with a respectful bow of the head. He took the card and briefly stared at it.

"Well, Ms. Gables, you can explain to your readers that, as between the offerings of both Transport International and InterMil, the InterMil equipment must have been better."

"Is there any truth to the rumor that you were *told* to buy from InterMil by someone higher up?"

At this point, Admiral West turned slightly white and then red and tried desperately to push past me again. I stood my ground and held the microphone up to his face. He was a big man, both tall and broad-shouldered, but I had the feeling he'd be a gentleman, as most navy officers are, and wouldn't think of harming or even trying to intimidate a young woman reporter.

"You need to answer this question, admiral. You won't want to appear evasive." I tossed a nod in the direction of Brian's camera. It was aimed in his direction with its little red light on.

"I can't tell you that. It's classified."

"*Classified*? The name of the person who told you to buy from InterMil is classified?"

"No, I mean it's *confidential.*"

"Confidential? How could that be? We just want a name here. The public is entitled to know who's running the government."

I knew I could get the admiral to come clean. He was too much of a straight shooter not to respond to a legitimate question with a truthful answer. Leave it to the US Navy, when pressed, to take the path of forthrightness and honesty.

"The name is Brodsky." West mumbled, almost too softly to hear. "He's the man you should speak to."

"Brodsky? Who's Brodsky?" *Who the heck is he?* I wondered.

"Armin Brodsky. White House staff."

"You mean, like the *president?*" I almost lost it when I heard this.

"No, the *vice* president. Rick Chernoff. Now, if you don't mind, I'm in a rush. I have to get to a meeting."

The admiral again pressed forward, and I stepped aside; however, as I did so, I shot one more question his way.

"By the way, admiral, what is your first name? For the record, you understand."

"Oliver. Admiral Oliver West."

I couldn't help remembering that it was a naval officer named Oliver North who would do anything, even to the extent of breaking the law, to follow orders from the White House.

Chapter 29

I called Aleksa on my cell phone, and we agreed to meet back at the Georgetown University Hospital. She said she had uncovered some startling news from the US Air Force Procurement Office, and I just couldn't wait to tell her what I had found out.

Brian and I returned to the entrance of the Pentagon, and I asked that nice MP Milktoast at the guard desk to call us a cab.

"Where are you headed?" he wanted to know.

"GU Hospital."

"No need for a cab. Just go downstairs and catch the Metro. Take the blue line three stops to Foggy Bottom."

Wow! I couldn't help thinking how user-friendly the Pentagon was. The *Pentagon*, which is ground zero and headquarters for the most powerful military force the world has ever known. They could kill every man, woman, and child on earth several times over or very easily kill any particular person you could name, if just a few determined military brass wanted to do so. It's just another stop on the subway!

So down we went to the underground, and twenty minutes and a short cab ride later, we came up near the front entrance of the hospital. As we walked in the lobby, there stood George looking forlorn, with attractive Aleksa standing next to him. I ignored George and approached Aleksa.

"What have you got?" She had piqued my interest, big time.

"The US Air Force has placed some huge orders with this InterMil outfit. Jet fighter-bombers, really advanced and sophisticated. Cost over a hundred million bucks apiece. They were developed here in the United States. But the detailed plans and specs have been sent overseas, and the Russkies are going into production with it. And there's more—"

"InterMil is moving into the unmanned aircraft business in a big way," she continued. "They have a contract with the US Air Force to develop the next generation, following the UAVs that are presently up there. They'll fly higher and faster and be more versatile."

"How come a Russian company gets all this business?" I wanted to know.

"They weren't too clear on that. Seems to be really hush-hush. But get this! I saved the best for last. InterMil is going to be the source of small atomic bombs for the US Air Force. They call them "tactical" weapons, could you believe. They're supposed to be five times bigger than any conventional explosives. They can practically blow up half of New York, but they think of them as useful weaponry and intend to buy a lot of them. Unbelievable!"

I was astounded. "Is this on the record? Can we go public?"

"Yes and no. They said they would deny anything we said about this A-bomb program, and they wouldn't let us record any of this." I shot a look at George, who just stood there sheepishly. Poor guy, he wasn't even needed on this interview with Aleksa. "But the people I spoke to really wanted to get the word out. They're scared shitless themselves about this whole thing."

"We can get the word out, all right. That's our specialty! But before we do, I've got some news for you, too." I relayed what I had heard from Admiral Oliver West, this time on the record. "The pieces are starting to fit together, and I don't like what I see."

"Me neither. It all seems to be coming back to the VP Rick Chernoff and those guys on the floor upstairs."

"Maybe we can get some more intel from the security cameras. Want to try again with your friends in the security room?"

"Might yield something—you never know. Like all dumb-ass men, they're suckers for the old sex appeal. It works every time."

We took the elevator down to the subbasement and found room SB29. To our great surprise, everything was different from earlier in the day, just a few hours before. There was an entire construction crew down there, apparently building an entranceway to the security room. We quickly looked around and saw they had cement blocks, a couple of heavy metal doors, wiring, and half a dozen large cardboard boxes. From the labels we could make out, they contained new electronic equipment.

Two MPs were on duty, and they promptly stepped in our direction. "You can't come down here," the older one said.

"I'm a friend of one of the security guards here. I'd just like to speak with him a moment. It's . . . uh, *personal.*" Aleksa leaned her head to one side as if to say, "Won't you give a poor girl a break?" but it appeared to have no effect on the MP. He said politely but firmly, "All the security guards here have been relieved. Check with the man's security agency. He's ether been let go, or they found him another job. Now I have to ask you to leave."

Something very strange was going on. This was another piece to a very complicated puzzle.

Chapter 30

Bruce Collingwood couldn't help himself. In spite of his father's tragic death, he felt psyched and *joy* for the first time since his father had died. He had inherited the complete plans for his father's personal aircraft, which he knew could and would, fly. He had a knowledgeable team of people his father had brought together to build it. He had prime manufacturing space to build it in, and now he had the money to make everything happen.

When he telephoned his father's employees one at a time to ask them to assemble together on this day at the airport hangar, he could literally feel their relief over the phone. They, too, had some unfinished business to attend to. They wanted—they *needed*—to build that aircraft anew and watch it fly. It was something they had to do, and Bruce was giving them the opportunity to do it. Most of them even had ideas for improving the aircraft design, and Bruce was entirely receptive to incorporating these improvements into the prototype.

They would gladly give Bruce their all to bring this new aircraft to life. They respected this bright young Collingwood who had more than paid his dues in supporting his father, and they would make him proud.

When Bruce pulled up to the hangar, he saw the entire development team standing in front of the wide-open hangar door, waiting for him. He stepped out of his SUV and, as if on cue, they broke into spontaneous applause. Bruce stood there a moment, stunned but pleased. Whatever concerns he might have had about taking over the leadership of this project and of these men softly melted away. He approached the waiting group of men and said simply, "Thanks, guys. Let's go to work."

Bruce shook hands all around, and they walked into the open hangar together.

Constructing an aircraft, even from proven plans, is a complicated task that requires great technical knowledge and years of experience. It also requires a number of special materials that are not available at any store or over the Internet. Because of Bruce's father, both the manpower and materials were available. Because of Mike Snead, the money was available, too.

Bruce began by bringing the entire team into the office conference room for the initial briefing. After he connected his laptop computer to a projector on the conference table and booted up, he walked his men through a series of Gantt scheduling charts and explained his plans for constructing the prototype. After thorough testing of the prototype and making whatever adjustments that were necessary, the next step would be the production of a small, versatile, two-place personal aircraft for the military.

Bruce was convinced that the military would buy the aircraft if it performed as expected because it was much less expensive to make and maintain than the equivalent, current VTOL aircraft, principally the helicopter. The personal aircraft was also extremely fuel-efficient because it had wings, and perhaps most important of all, it was designed to be extremely quiet. The PAC could fly search-and-rescue missions without alerting the enemy.

Bruce also had an idea for still another advantage that, he knew, no other aircraft could offer. Bruce had modified his father's design to use a new kind of engine called a "barrel-type" engine that could run on any type of fuel, ranging from vegetable oil to fuels derived from animal waste, kerosene, bio-diesels, ethanol, and any conceivable blend of these fuels. In addition, these engines were lighter and smaller than conventional internal combustion engines, incorporated considerably fewer parts, and had an extremely high power-to-weight ratio. And finally, they were much quieter than any other known engine, except perhaps for an electric motor.

Following a trial period of operation in the military, the personal aircraft would be released, slowly at first and then in mass production, to private industry. In so doing, the personal aircraft had the potential to revolutionize personal transportation.

The team of men listened intently and grew even more enthusiastic by the minute as they came to realize the implications of what Bruce was saying. Back in the early days of aviation, especially during World War II, Long Island had enjoyed a thriving industry of aircraft manufacture, but little by little, this industry had fallen onto hard times and had eventually almost died away. If their project proved successful—and they had every reason to think it would—they would breathe new life into the aircraft industry. This would be good for the local community, Westhampton—good for Long Island, good for New York, and good for America. Each and every one of the members of Bruce's entrepreneurial team was excited and highly motivated to complete this project. They all believed in the project and were ready to make history.

Following this discussion, the team set to work in earnest to build the new prototype. The schedule called for the first flight test in less than a month. This time, there would be no interference or sabotage by any outsider. The team would operate with the utmost confidentiality to make sure that their project was secure. No one would even know what they were doing until they were ready to announce to the world the successful test of the new aircraft.

Chapter 31

Gavin's evidence was grounded principally upon the signed statement of a new hire in Snead's company, Transport International, Inc. The man seemed genuinely interested in helping him get at the truth, which was a good thing, but a tiny cloud of doubt kept floating in and out of Gavin's mind. The cloud would appear in his consciousness from time to time, but whenever he looked closely at it, it dissolved like a wisp. Gavin couldn't help thinking about that doubt.

The employee, Andrei Gershuni, had presented himself at just the right time. It was almost as if Gershuni had known about the investigation and had wanted to participate. Gershuni had explained that he'd seen some suspicious materials in the plant, apparently plastic explosives, which were kept under lock and key by a supervisor on the engine assembly line.

When pressed for details, Gershuni had asked not to be involved in the investigation and had exacted a verbal promise from Gavin that he would not be named as a source of information before he would cooperate. Gavin regretted this promise now, but at the time, he was desperate for clues, any tiny tidbits that would link TI and Mike Snead in particular to the crime. He thought Mike had the motive and the type of personality that would stop at nothing to get what he wanted.

These top executives were all alike: mean-spirited and *vicious*. Everyone knew that big companies were run for the benefit of top management. The shareholders were thrown their bones by the way of dividends each quarter, and the employees received their pay every week or two for the work they did—boring jobs usually for meager pay and no benefits to speak of—however, it was the executive suite that looted the company week in and week out, month after month. Names came to mind: Dennis Kozlowski, former CEO of Tyco International who was convicted for receiving $81 million in unauthorized bonuses, the purchase of art for $14.725 million, and the payment by Tyco of a $20 million investment banking fee to his buddy, former Tyco Director Frank Walsh; Ken Lay, former president of Enron, and Andrew Fastow, the former treasurer, who lied about the company's profits and were accused of a range of shady dealings, including concealing debts so they didn't show up in the company books. As a result, thousands of small shareholders who thought their money was secure lost their hard-earned savings they had invested for retirement. And then there was Jack "Neutron John" Welch, the former president of GE who proudly explained in his autobiography how he ordered each of his managers to fire one employee on his team every year to increase the share price of GE stock. Could you imagine how a loyal GE employee must have felt after he or she had worked for the company for fifteen years, going home to his spouse and children to announce he or she had been let go?

No, these top executives were walking around committing mayhem every day, making decisions that affected people's lives and hurt society much more than a petty thief with a gun ever could. Gavin had no sympathy for Snead. He had probably done the evil deed, but if he hadn't, he probably should have been in jail anyway, the bastard.

But there was still that little cloud of doubt.

A police officer's job is never what it seems like on the hour-long TV shows. Crime investigations don't have a beginning, middle, and end that wraps things up. They just pass quietly into memory where they fade slowly away. Unless—

Just then his cell phone peeped. He looked at the incoming number and didn't recognize it, so he took the call. He opened his phone and barked, "Inspector Gavin." He recognized Juli's voice in an instant.

"Inspector, it's Juli. Juli Gables. We need to talk."

Chapter 32

Inspector Gavin and I agreed to meet at Gavin's office in Westhampton the very next day. I flew back to LaGuardia, rented a car, and drove east on the Long Island Expressway to Exit 58, where I stayed overnight at the Islandia Marriott. At exactly 9:00 a.m. the next morning, I walked into the Westhampton Police Station.

The desk sergeant recognized me straightaway. "Inspector Gavin is expecting you," he said matter-of-factly. "You may go right in." He waved me forward toward an open office door down the little hallway.

I stepped past the sergeant and peeked in the doorway to make sure I was at the right office. I saw Dan Gavin sitting comfortably at his desk, smoking a pipe, and staring blankly out the window. The pleasant aroma of tobacco smoke wafted in my direction.

"It's a long time since I saw man smoke a pipe," I announced as I stood in the doorway, waiting to be invited in.

Gavin immediately stood up and bowed slightly while he motioned for me to take a seat. "Hello, Juli," he said humbly. "Thank you for coming." His former antagonism had seemingly melted away. "Your call couldn't have been more timely because I'm at a standstill. I just know we haven't locked up this case. Everyone thinks we have, but we haven't. I'm hoping against hope that you've got something to tell me."

"I don't know if what I have is something or not. I was hoping against hope that you could tell *me*. I'm stuck, too."

"That's got to be a first for you. From what I've heard, you've never been stumped before."

"From what I've been able to gather, this crime may be much bigger than we could ever imagine. The only way we can possibly solve it is to work together."

"I'm intrigued, so try me."

I proceeded to do just that, explaining every last detail with the exception, of course, of my suspicions of George's infidelity. These circumstances were of no one's business but my own, and I'd deal with them later all by myself, thank you very much.

It took a half hour to relate what George and I had gathered from the video and what had transpired at our meeting with General Bellamy at his office. I finally launched into a complete report of my trip to Washington. When I finished, Gavin whistled and shook his head.

"I'll be damned!"

"Well? What do you think of all this?"

"What do I think? You want to know what I think? There is definitely something going on that doesn't pass the smell test, something involving the highest echelons of government. As a matter of fact, I think that you just might be on to the biggest crime of the century. Something like this could make your, and my, career!"

"You really think so? We don't really have any evidence and—"

"Of course not! You think the smart guys at the top are going to leave any evidence lying around? They must have been planning this for months or even years. They know exactly what they're doing, and you can be sure they're being very careful about it."

"So what do you think we should do?"

"I know one thing we can do, and we'll do it right now. We'll bring in one man for questioning, a guy named Andrei Gershuni, an employee of Transport International who pointed the finger at Mike Snead. If he's in on this conspiracy, he'll give us the goods. He's out there all alone and, with a little . . . uh, prodding, he'll talk."

Gavin lifted the phone and asked that Gershuni be picked up and brought to the station. When he was halfway through explaining what he wanted, he stopped mid-sentence and listened. "Oh, my God!" he responded and put the phone down.

I stared at Gavin, who appeared to turn a bit white. He looked back at me and said, "Gershuni was found dead in his apartment this morning."

Chapter 33

Peter Bradley slept fitfully, his mind repeatedly bordering on waking and then plunging briefly into a dream sequence before rising to the surface again, close to consciousness. Actually, Peter had not slept soundly through the night for at least the past three years, not after he had embarked upon his quest to lead the country as POTUS, president of the United States. Now at two in the morning, he was wide awake, and his brain was buzzing again.

Now, with the responsibility of the nation weighing foursquare on his shoulders, he was bearing up amazingly well during the daytime. Only at night did the many strident voices around him invade his private space and do battle in his brain.

His mind was a jumble of thoughts, none completely formal and clear, which flickered in and out of his subconscious, one on top of the other, as his brain tried to make sense and order out of the chaotic events of the day. So many people, all pressing to make their voices heard, so many human needs tugging at his emotions, calling for priority and remedial action, so many political issues, challenges to his leadership, unending pressure, moment after moment, to solve countless urgent problems that presented themselves through his enormous cadre of advisors, ministers, agency heads, and ambassadors throughout the world.

Tomorrow would come all too soon, and his day would be overflowing from eight in the morning until midnight. Convinced that he could not sleep without some chemical assistance, Peter turned on the light and reached into his night table drawer. As he groped around in the drawer, his left hand felt the familiar cylindrical shape of the pill bottle he kept at the ready, and he grasped it. After he retrieved it from the drawer, Peter glanced at the label just to be sure. "Zolpidem," the generic form of the sleep aid originally marketed as "Ambien," would work its wonders again as it had so many times before. He opened the lid, eased a single pill into his palm, and popped it into his mouth. In an emergency, he would take two pills, but one should be enough tonight, he thought.

Sure enough, within fifteen minutes, the buzzing in his brain subsided. His eyelids grew heavy, and he dropped off into a gentle and eventually a deep, albeit uneven, sleep.

As the night transitioned into morning, which for Peter was 6:00 a.m. sharp, his mind lit up with an image of a long freight train pulled by two huge diesel locomotives, wending its way along its rails and heading straight toward a single bump of green mountain in the distance. Peter wondered where the train tracks led, whether they would turn right or left to go around the mountain, or if they would ascend the steep grade in switchbacks, back and forth, to go over the top. As the train approached the sharp, tree-covered slope, he became more curious and also increasingly worried about an unseen danger until, just when he thought some sort of catastrophe was almost certain to occur, the lead engine plunged into the dark opening of a tunnel.

At this moment, Peter's mind flicked into consciousness and the mental image disappeared.

Peter kept his eyes closed and tried to remember what he was dreaming—something about a train pulling freight cars—but why? Something in those freight cars? Where had this image come from?

Peter had already begun the preparation of one of the most important speeches of his presidential career. About three months hence, on the third Wednesday in June, his schedule now called for a breakfast meeting with his national security team from 8:00 to 10:00 and then some routine meet-and-greets with several of his supporters in the late morning. At precisely noon, he would walk out onto the south lawn and board Marine One for an airlift to Andrews AFB, where the waiting Air Force One would whisk him north to Stewart Field in Newburgh, New York. Upon arrival, he would step out on the tarmac at a remote corner of the airport and climb aboard another Marine One helicopter to fly south a few miles to the US military academy at West Point. After meeting briefly with the military cadre, he would deliver this speech to announce his "peace initiative," a theme and a strategy that, he hoped and prayed, would point the world in a new direction.

Since the beginning of history, the human race could not seem to rise above its power struggles and disputes that simmered constantly in the background and then frequently erupted and flared into violence and devastation. There had been talk of "peaceful solutions" to human problems, and over the years, countless organizations were founded on the promise of bringing the human strife to an end. The travails of World War I brought the League of Nations into being with absolutely no effect at all on human behavior. Only twenty years later, the "civilized world" was embroiled in the greatest war it had ever known, World War II, which, in turn, led to the formation of the United Nations. Wars and violence continued unabated, notwithstanding the fact that democratic systems were developed and established in many countries to resolve the countervailing forces and opinions of the citizenry that can, and frequently do, break down the extremely soft and delicate social web that connects the citizenry together.

Peter had often been criticized for his views as being "naïve," but he was not. He was fully aware of what degradation humans were capable of and drawn to, as if the "normal" condition of equilibrium was a state of eternal and violent strife. The elevated state of peaceful co-existence could only be achieved briefly and sporadically, it seemed, by suppressing the violent tendencies through the respect for and strict enforcement of the rule of law.

Peter had been an avid student of the sciences all of his life. He was also fascinated by what motivated a relatively few individuals of history to achieve truly amazing things, what motivated the vast majority of individuals to cope peacefully, if not fretfully, with life, and what motivated the remaining few to cause the violent eruptions that breached the peace. If only one could civilize and pacify this small percentage of people who seemed to be at the root of most, if not all, of the problems of society, one could remake the world into a much safer and satisfactory place for all mankind.

Because of his well-known general interest in science and the life sciences in particular, Peter had been notified of a recent and significant breakthrough in understanding the human neurological origins of aggression. This discovery had been made independently and almost simultaneously by three great scientific minds: a woman physician working with patients at a research hospital in India and two male microbiologists located respectively in Switzerland and in California. They had conducted the research and, at virtually the same time, had submitted their scientific articles for publication in the same prestigious *New England Journal of Medicine*. The editors of the journal were in a quandary as to who should be credited with the discovery, so they held back publication until they could carefully establish priority. Meanwhile, however, the word had been quietly passed to the president of the United States, and so it occurred that Peter was one of only a handful of people on the entire planet who knew of this discovery and its potential to promote peace.

Couched in scientific speak, the articles revealed a way to ameliorate aggressive tendencies in humans and thus provide a possible path to world peace. True, a "plan for peace" using the discovery would have to be implemented, and this might prove politically difficult; however, Peter was up to the challenge and was eager to try. With such a plan in place, Peter would leave a legacy as the president—ending the immense human suffering caused by the violence of man against man—that had eluded every president and every national leader in the world since the beginning of recorded history.

Chapter 34

InterMil's headquarters occupied a nondescript cement building on the outskirts of Moscow. It was built in the Soviet era in Soviet style—gray and drab. The whole idea of building design back then was to create interior space for a particular purpose. Any non-utilitarian embellishment, no matter how simple or how beautiful, was considered not only nonessential and wasteful, but extravagant and bourgeois. From this premise, it followed that most, if not all, Soviet-style buildings appeared forlorn and even depressing to the human spirit. In the period following World War II, the Russians had forgotten how much a building's design could affect one's personal well-being, and they had definitely lost the art of architecture.

The workers at InterMil were not a happy or even a pleasant lot. Those at headquarters who filled offices off both sides of the long, impersonal corridors in the building were counted among the lucky ones as compared to the workers in the manufacturing plants that were scattered throughout Russia and the CIS countries, but they considered work to be a distasteful necessity and expended only the minimum effort during the long hours from 8:00 in the morning to 6:00 at night with an hour off for lunch. Yes, work was drudgery, but everyone was expected to put in the time. That was what they learned and inherited from the "good old days" when the Soviet government had reigned supreme.

Only members from the top echelon of the company were truly motivated and felt they had a purpose in life—a purpose which, unfortunately, was not to create something new or help the less fortunate in any way but to control the old. It was a purpose fueled solely by their ambition to increase their power over others and become wealthy doing so. It was a purpose recognized and understood by the small group of "directors" that managed the company as they vied for the coveted leadership positions, and no one knew and understood this ambition better than the company's chairman, Nikita "Nikki" Borisnikoff.

Nikki understood power and the ways and means to increase it. One could never have enough power, he knew. There were always opportunities to achieve greater power over an ever larger power base—an organized constituency over which one exercised one's authority—and Nikki had risen rapidly to the top position at InterMil by forming alliances with other like-minded and ambitious power seekers and then, when they were no longer useful to him, ruthlessly undercutting them through fair means and foul. It did not matter how he got there. What mattered only was that Nikki succeeded in his race to the top. And succeed he did.

Nikki was now the undisputed ultimate authority at InterMil—so much so that his opponents and detractors, no matter how ambitious, no longer attempted or even dared to unseat him. If you were on a rung in the ladder just below the top, that was where you stayed. You weren't going anywhere until Nikki moved on to an even more lofty position, if there was any such thing, and there probably wasn't, because InterMil was the biggest, most politically influential company in Russia.

As the major military and commercial supplier of equipment to Russia and its allies, InterMil manufactured everything from atomic weaponry and nuclear fuel for power plants to Zamboni machines for resurfacing the ice for Olympic skating rinks. InterMil's headquarters were located near the famous Kurchatov Institute for nuclear research, the organization that startled the world by designing, building, and testing the most fearsome weapon that has ever existed: the hydrogen bomb. Little known was the fact that InterMil took over the manufacture of all bombs for the Soviet military, not only conventional firebombs but also uranium-based fission bombs and hydrogen-based fusion bombs.

Partly because of their parallel interests in research and partly because of their close physical proximity in Moscow, InterMil and the Kurchatov Institute had developed an extremely close relationship over the years—so close that sometimes it appeared that the two organizations were really one. Indeed, the atomic secrets of Kurchatov were shared with InterMil and *vice versa* so that both organizations remained world leaders in the field of atomic energy.

Not to miss an opportunity, Nikki Borisnikoff kept a close eye on their joint developments in this field. His company was currently developing the world's smallest atomic bomb with more "bang for the buck" and "wallop for the weight" than the world had ever known.

The idea of a "suitcase-sized" nuclear bomb was, of course, fiction. It was scientifically impossible to achieve. It took fifty kilos of highly enriched, fissile uranium or about one hundred and ten pounds of 85 percent U235 to create a nuclear explosion. It took far less plutonium, about twenty pounds or so, to do the same thing, but unlike uranium, which was enriched through well-known, gas-centrifuge techniques, plutonium had to be extracted through complicated reprocessing. Weapons-grade plutonium was thus much more difficult and expensive to produce, but for InterMil, which ran the reprocessing facility for Russia, it was a piece of cake.

Nikki had at his disposal the means to terrorize and control the world, and he intended to use them.

Chapter 35

It had been a long time since Bruce had experienced the upbeat feeling that came with successful accomplishment. He was not one to feel much emotion at all, especially after all the sad things that had happened in his brief, twenty-seven-year life. But on this day, he felt buoyed by this feeling of joy as he drove himself to work.

He and his team had been constructing the new prototype airplane for weeks now, and it was beginning to take final shape, both in metal and in his mind. On that day when he first met with his engineers, he had been weighted down by the daunting challenges he faced in moving forward and recreating his father's work. There were so many things he did not know at the beginning, and his father had not kept good records. He had found scale drawings of the aircraft in the company files, but many important details were missing. Some areas like the aircraft's electrical system had not even been documented at all.

But now it seemed that most of the difficult issues had been resolved. As far as he could tell, nothing could stop him and his team from completing the prototype and making it ready for its first test flight. This time, the initial flights would be conducted in private, with himself as the test pilot and the members of his team as the only witnesses.

And all of this had been done within the budget he had set for himself. Shelley Bernstein had been true to his word in making the money from TI available to Bruce as he needed funds. Thus far, he had used only three and a half of the five million dollar investment, leaving a substantial cushion to solve the problems he knew would inevitably appear during the first and following test flights.

As he approached the hangar of Hummingbird Aircraft, however, his emotional feelings evaporated as his thoughts returned to the day-to-day business at hand. He was in the mood for work until he drove up and saw a strange car parked in front of the hangar, with a woman apparently waiting for him.

"What the—" Bruce jumped out of his car almost before it had stopped and strode purposefully toward the intruder. With every step, he felt increasingly annoyed by the interruption in his daily routine.

"Who are you?" he demanded of the strikingly beautiful African-American woman. By this time, he had become so upset his voice was hoarse and on the brink of cracking.

"Hi," came the reply in a soothingly pleasant tone. "I'm Aleksa. My friend Juli Gables suggested that I stop by." Aleksa batted her eyes just a bit, not to seem too forward with this man she wanted to interview.

"Juli never mentioned your name to *me*. I'm sorry, but you'll have to leave. Right *now*. This is private property."

"She said you're a terrific guy and that you're working on a new kind of airplane," Aleksa said, ignoring the brush-off. "She's too busy to come by herself, so she asked me to take a look."

"Is that so? Well, now I know you're lying. Juli would never have sent someone else in her place. And as a matter of fact, I told Juli she couldn't come to see us right how. We're not going to have any outsiders at our test flights."

"Test flights? You're going to start test flights?" Aleksa quickly morphed to her interview mode but didn't forget to use her sex appeal.

"Eventually. Now go!"

"You ought to get the word out," Aleksa continued pleasantly. "Most people think your aircraft project is dead. It would make a great story, telling how you brought the aircraft back from the brink of extinction. Like a Phoenix rising from the ashes."

Exasperated, Bruce finally took out his cell phone and started dialing a number. "I'm calling the police. If you're not gone by the time they arrive, they'll carry you off the property."

"You really are a difficult man to deal with. Would it help if I told you I have some information about the day your father died?"

Bruce stopped dialing and pressed a button on the face of the phone to interrupt the call. "*What?*"

"Did you hear what happened to Bellamy?"

"Bellamy?"

"General Bellamy. The guy who was here at the first test flight."

"No, what about him?"

"I just learned this morning. His car overturned on the highway between Washington and Baltimore, and he died on the way to the hospital."

"I don't believe it. You're lying . . . *again!*"

"No, it's true. It just happened a few minutes ago, and it's just now going out as breaking news."

"Does Juli know that?"

"I doubt it. I'm a TV news reporter and got it from the raw feed. So why don't we go to your office and call Juli together. I'm sure she'd like to know. I'll bet this wasn't an accident and has something to do with your father's death."

"Uh, yeah, I guess that's a good idea. What did you say your name was?"

"Aleksa. Aleksa Williams, Channel 2 News. Very glad to meet you." Aleksa held out her hand, and Bruce took it. "I have a feeling that I can be of service to you."

Chapter 36

Bruce walked Aleksa to the side door of the hangar, the one with the sign "Hummingbird Aircraft" directly above. His mood had changed slightly from feeling totally self-reliant to feeling more open and receptive, for he had begun to realize he would need all the assistance and support he could muster if he wanted to let the world know about his new aircraft. He opened the door for Aleksa and held it for her as she stepped inside the dark, cavernous space. Bruce followed her in and reached over to snap on the overhead hangar lights.

Aleksa found herself gazing at an ordinary-looking, single-engine airplane standing alone in the middle of the hangar floor. There were no other aircraft or vehicles to be seen, but the back wall of the hangar had a cluttered look, lined with various tool cabinets, file cabinets, and a long workbench that extended nearly half the width of the building. The workbench was covered with airplane parts and tools. Plans and blueprints lay atop two drawing boards that stood near one end.

"*That's* the airplane you're working on?" Aleksa asked, somewhat unimpressed. "I thought it was supposed to go up and down *vertically.*"

"Well, yes, it does. That's the trick!"

"I'll bet it's a trick, all right. Smoke and mirrors."

"Don't you notice anything, uh, special or *different* about this aircraft? Look carefully."

"Well, let's see. There's no paint on it, so it's a little plain-looking. Pardon the pun."

Bruce smiled. "Anything else?"

"Looks like a regular private plane. Low wing. Hmmm, the wing seems a bit fat compared to what I've seen before."

"You're getting very warm," Bruce said encouragingly. "The vertical lift—it's all about the wing."

"Well, duh. That's what wings are for, to lift the plane. But how does this thing go straight up?"

Bruce's eyes lit up as he began to speak. He launched into an explanation about Bernoulli's Principle and how the air speeding over the top surface of the wing would literally suck the plane up into the sky. As he spoke, Aleksa noticed the passion in his voice and marveled at his dedicated commitment to this project, a commitment that clearly sustained him through the tragedy of this father's death. Aleksa couldn't understand. Nor did she care about how the aircraft managed to lift itself up by its bootstraps, but she did feel an empathy and admiration for this bright and quite good-looking young man who was just about her own age.

"When's the first test flight?" she asked after Bruce finally finished explaining how the wing worked.

"I really don't want to say. This time, we're not allowing anyone but our own employees to view the test flights. When we work out the kinks and everything checks out, we'll have a public demonstration."

"I think that's wise. You always have to count on Murphy's Law. If anything can possibly go wrong, it will."

"In the meantime, please don't say anything or write anything about this project. We're just not ready yet."

"You have my word. I won't even tell Juli I was here."

"Oh, *that's* okay. She's one of us."

"Frankly, it's best she didn't know," Aleksa said.

"I thought she told you to come here."

"I'm sorry, Bruce. I have to tell you I lied about that." Aleksa bit her tongue and hoped against hope that this admission wouldn't get in the way of a future relationship with Bruce.

"Oh, I thought so. At least you're honest about it."

Aleksa leaned forward and gave Bruce a kiss on the cheek. "I like you," she said simply and left.

Bruce stood there a moment, thinking about what had just happened this last half hour, and then went about his daily business as his engineers began to arrive for work.

Chapter 37

It was all over the news. I'd just gotten back to our apartment in New York and had gone online to catch up with my email and to work on the Gables Report. It was there on Google, AP News, AOL, MSN, and Yahoo. A US Army general had died tragically, and they suspected foul play. Well, la de da. I did, too, but I didn't know where to start on that one. In the end, I just hoped the police could figure out who had done it. Once I knew that, I could start putting two and two together and maybe make some headway in my investigation of Carl Collingwood's murder.

Right now, I had problems of my own right here at home with my husband, George, to be exact. I couldn't believe he'd allowed himself to be sucked in by that sexy bitch, Aleksa, but I was sure that was just what had happened. As an investigative reporter, I have a nose for these things. The question was what to do about it now.

It was difficult to formulate a plan, short of hiring some gumshoe detective to shadow George and catch him in the act. But I didn't want to confront him without being able to tell right away if he was lying.

And anyway, he'd already said that "nothing had happened" between him and Aleksa. He couldn't very well fess up now without admitting he had previously lied to me, and I didn't know which would have been worse: the dirty deed itself or the cover-up lie. Either would be a betrayal.

The trouble was that there was no way George could prove to me that he was innocent, if he *was* innocent, which I doubted. It was up to me to prove he was guilty, if he *was* guilty. I must admit that I still had a glimmer of hope that he was true blue—wishful thinking perhaps—but I really wasn't sure. If I was going to find out one way or another, I needed to set a trap.

Where was George right now? I must admit I was getting worried. I hadn't seen him since all of us had left Washington, DC Aleksa, who was on an expense account, left separately by plane, leaving her cameraman, Brian, to drive the news van back to New York. I had flown back alone, leaving George to find his own way. At that point, I didn't care where he went or how he got there, but things looked a bit clearer to me now. He didn't come home—that I knew—so I just assumed he was bunking with Aleksa.

I was just about to call Aleksa when the phone rang. The caller ID said "Hummingbird Air." It was Bruce!

"Bruce? It that you?"

"How'd you guess? Oh, caller ID I bet."

"Works every time. How *are* you? It's been so long. I should have kept in touch, but I've been really busy working on . . . well, you know what. Progress is slow—that's all I can say."

"I've been hunkered down myself here with my engineers, focused on building the new prototype."

"How's it coming along?" I asked.

"It's getting more exciting now. We're getting close."

"I wish I had the time to stop by. I'd like to see it."

"Actually, the reason for my call is to ask about a person who just came by for a visit. Do you know a really good-looking reporter called Aleksa?"

I froze. "Uh, you mean Aleksa Williams? From CBS?" I could barely get the words out. She was *there*!

"That's her. At first, she said you sent her over, but then she admitted that wasn't true. I just wonder what kind of person she is. She seems really nice."

"What did you tell her?"

"I showed her around. She wanted to come to our first test flight, but I told her we're not inviting any outsiders. Just Hummingbird employees this time."

"Was she . . . alone?" I held my breath.

"Alone? Sure, why?"

"She usually brings a cameraman."

"No, she came by herself. She said she could help me get the word out about the plane—when it's ready, that is."

I could feel my jaw relax and now didn't mind putting in a plug for her. "She's pretty smart, and sure, you will need all the help you can get on that score. You can count on me to help you too, you know."

"I know that, Juli. I don't know where I'd be if it weren't for you and George. Probably in jail for stealing that train."

"You don't happen to know where George is right now, do you?"

"Sorry, no."

"Aleksa didn't happen to mention him?"

"No. Is he missing or something?" Bruce's voice reflected his sudden concern.

"Not missing. Just . . . well, missing," I said blandly.

"Why would Aleksa know about George? Was he with her?" I noticed a slight change in Bruce's voice. He was ever-so-slightly saddened, but I chose to gloss over it.

"No. No, nothing like that."

"Well, like I said, Aleksa seems nice. Why don't you call her?"

"That's a good idea. I think I will." I tried my best not to show any perceptible feeling of jealousy that kept coming up.

"Oh, and by the way—"

"Yes?" I said.

"Do you have her number?"

Chapter 38

Where could he be? If he wasn't with Aleksa, where would he go? Then it hit me. He's gone back to his mother! I still held the phone in my hand, so I did a search for her number and pressed "call." Rose answered after two rings.

"Yes, he's here. Right here." She was expecting my call. "He's so sorry, but he says he didn't do anything wrong. You've got to believe him." I could hear the despair in her voice. She was pleading with me to take him back and give him another chance.

"I wish I could."

"What happened?"

"He let another woman into our apartment. I don't really know what happened, but he ended up giving her the video of the Hummingbird Aircraft test flight, when that plane blew up. He must have gotten a pretty big treat from that girl."

"He says he didn't, and I believe him."

"You're his *mother*, Rose. Of course you believe him."

"It's not like that. If I smell a rat, I kill that rat. I've had to keep him in line more than a couple of times. Why do you think he's such a good kid?"

"You're a good mother, and he *is* a good kid. Why do you think I married him?"

"Take him back, *please*. I'm begging you. This breaks my heart!" She really got to me now. How could I not take him back, at least until I could prove he lied to his own mother and me.

"Put him on," I said.

"Be gentle. Here he is."

"Hello, George?" I was on the verge of forgiving him, whether he did it or not, but I had to be sure, one way or another.

"Yes?" His voice was so soft and sheepish.

"Are you all right?"

"Yes, I'm okay. How are you?"

"Not so good right now. Do you want to come home?"

"Yes, I do." I could hear the relief in his voice.

"Well, come on over. Let's talk."

"I'm on my way."

He hung up, and I sat there, thinking about what to do. How could I prove he was telling the truth? This was not going to be easy. I would start by drilling him about that day with Aleksa. Why had he given her the video? I decided to record my interrogation so I would have his answers on record and so I could then carefully examine his face as I asked my questions.

I needed to make the video without his knowledge. I looked around and found our belt that had the video camera built into the belt buckle—the one we used to capture the scene with General Bellamy at Aberdeen Proving Grounds—and found a place for it on a table in the corner of the room. Before I arranged it on the table, I pulled out the flash drive and plugged it into my computer just to make sure that whatever was stored there had already been downloaded and there was enough room for about an hour of recording. I saw one video file on the disk and clicked on it. To my great surprise, it was a recording, taken in our apartment, of Aleksa's visit with my husband, George, while I was having dinner with Shelley Bernstein.

Chapter 39

The belt had been set on the corner table, the very table where I was thinking to place it, and had a good view of the entire room. The audio, too, was not too bad, maybe because the corner walls behind the belt buckle collected the sound. Anyway, it was almost like being there myself as a fly on the wall.

The video started with an image of George's belly, as he leaned over and switched on the device. Then George turned and walked away, heading for the door to our apartment, which was in the hallway just outside the living room.

The living room doubled as our office. It had a long bench with two computers on it, George's and mine. This was our desk—two desks really—and it was nearly covered with phone equipment and papers organized in little neat stacks. George and I each had a desk chair, a wooden, hard-backed chair for him and a secretary's chair for me. They didn't match, but we had our preferences.

Off to the right and toward the rear near the window was our living room set: a couch, an easy chair, a coffee table, and a big screen TV. That was pretty much it—just the bare essentials.

As I watched, George led Aleksa into the room. She halted at the entrance from the hallway and looked around with a big friendly smile on her face, and then she started purring like a kitten. "What a big lovely room! Is this your office too?"

"Yup, that's where we do all our work on the website." George waved his hand at the huge desk in front of her.

"Well, it's very comfy and cozy. If you're offering drinks, I'll have a glass of wine. Chardonnay." That assertive bitch.

"I'll see what I can find. Maybe not Chardonnay, but I know we have white of some kind."

"Whatever."

George left for the kitchen, and Aleksa showed herself around. She went right to the desk and quickly perused the stacks of papers. Not finding anything of interest, she checked out the computers, but George was too quick. She heard him coming, so she walked over to the window and looked out.

"Great view! You can see all the way to New Jersey. Kind of like that *New Yorker* cover which showed the view from New York City all the way west to California."

"Hope you like this," George said and held out a long-stemmed wine glass. "It's not Chardonnay, but Juli likes it. I prefer red."

"You're not having any?" Aleksa put on a pouting face and gazed into his eyes inquiringly. I could hardly resist the urge to switch off the video, but I needed to know what came next. This bitch!

"I'll have a soda." Attaboy, George. You're doing just fine so far.

"Join me in some wine. I don't want to drink alone." You don't? I wonder why.

"Okay, I'll get another glass." George headed for the kitchen again, leaving Aleksa standing there with a glass in her hand. She quickly put it down on the table and went back to the desk to take another peek at the computers. Luckily, nothing important was on their screens, but it was clear the Aleksa was looking for something. A second later, she was back near the window and picked up her wine glass as George reappeared with his own glass in his hand.

Aleksa raised her glass and clinked it against George's. "To investigative reporting! It's a great field, isn't it?"

"Sure beats being a security guard, which I was just a couple of years ago," George replied.

"Security guard? Where'd you work?"

"At Channel 8. Where Juli used to work before she got fired."

"Oh, so that's the connection. You two go way back, don't you?"

"Yes, Juli picked me to be her cameraman when Carl Collingwood hijacked that commuter train."

"Good choice," Aleksa said. "I wish you were mine. My CBS guy, Brian, gets on my nerves."

"I'm sure he tries his best. Give him a chance."

"He's a letch."

"You're a beautiful girl." Oh, oh! George, you're crossing the line.

"Look but don't touch. Unless, of course, I want it." I was *sure* that Aleksa batted her eyelashes as she said that. Double bitch!

George, to his credit, ignored it and tried to change the subject. "How long have you worked at CBS?"

"Long enough to get the lay of the land. Everyone is running scared of the Internet. Me included. I think we 'talking head' reporters are on the way out."

"There's always room for a beautiful girl on TV." Damn it, George! Where are you going with this?

"You think?" Aleksa took this as a cue and stepped in closer, looking up admiringly.

"Uh, sure." George was suddenly a bit flustered, but he held his ground. Yes, I *know* it's hard for a man to resist a pretty woman on the make. It's in their genes for God's sake.

"So what are we going to do about it?" As she said this, Aleksa reached down quickly and started to unbuckle the belt on George's pants.

I could feel the steam streaming out of my ears and tears streaming out of my eyes as I watched. I could hardly stand to look at the computer screen I was so livid, but I also couldn't bear to tear my eyes away.

Aleksa leaned over and spoke into George's left ear, her whisper hardly audible at the video-belt in the corner: "I know how they can meet. Cindy can invite Charlie to come inside her home."

Chapter 40

I could feel my anger rising so rapidly I was about to explode! But then—God bless him, George—came to my rescue. George brushed Aleksa's hand away, gave her a gentle push back, and rebuckled his belt. "No, Aleksa. I don't do that. I'm married, remember?"

In the briefest of instants, my anger evaporated into clear air, and love took its place. Love for my husband, George. I also suddenly felt ashamed of myself. How could I have doubted him?

As I continued to watch, fascinated now, I saw Aleksa quickly compose herself, but not without a telltale flush in her face. Was it embarrassment? I could hardly think she was capable of that.

But as George charged out the door to the hallway to order her out, she made a quick, stealthy movement over to the desk, reached over, grabbed a computer disc, and then followed him out.

I was stunned. He hadn't given it to her after all. She had *stolen* it! That *bitch!* When I confronted him, he must have been so embarrassed about the theft that he had covered himself by saying he had given her the disc.

I sat there for a moment, wondering what I should say or do when George arrived. I had no clue at all at first, but in a flash, as if from heaven, just the right idea popped into my head. I would give him a present, a present of *love*.

I took off my blouse and let it drop. Then I took a step in the direction of the bedroom, took off my bra, and let it drop. I took a couple of steps farther and took off my sneakers. As I approached the bedroom door, I took off my pants and let them drop. Finally, off came my panties and, well, you get the idea, leaving a trail!

I lay spread out on the middle of the bed, stark naked and waiting. My anticipation was rising—I can tell you. It was a strange and unusual feeling for me because I'm normally focused on work, but it actually felt pretty good. I was getting more and more aroused by the minute.

Finally, in what seemed like a very long time, I heard the sound of a key in the lock at the front door. George was finally there and trying to get in. I couldn't wait to see his reaction to my little love surprise. And I was *so* ready.

But George didn't come in. I heard more sounds of metal against metal, but then . . . silence. Oh, my God, I had changed the locks, and George's key didn't work! I jumped out of bed and raced to the door, but by the time I opened it a crack and peeked out, he was gone. In the distance down the hall, I saw the elevator doors closing, leaving the corridor empty. Damn!

I ran back to the office and grabbed my cell. After I pressed "contact info," I located George's number and speed-dialed. A second later, his familiar voice came on. "Hello, Juli." It sounded awfully sheepish and contrite. How could I tell him that it was me who should be contrite right now? And tell him so that he understood.

"George, I'm sorry. I've been wrong, and I need to make amends."

"Sorry?"

"Come on up here, you big teddy bear. I need to make love to you. Right now!"

A minute later, he was at the door. When I opened it and he saw me in my birthday suit, his sad face morphed instantly into a happy one, grinning from ear to ear. He followed me into our bedroom and closed the door behind him.

Chapter 41

The POTUS, Peter Bradley, scanned the rough draft in his hands of what he thought could be, hoped would be, and knew should be, the most important speech of his presidency. This was more important than any speech of any past president or even of any other leader of the free world, because he had at his disposal the means to end all future wars and, with that, the horrible suffering and death of countless millions of people. His was truly a plan for peace.

The draft needed work, but all the essential elements were there. It read like a proclamation:

> Commanding General Dickson, officers, faculty of the US military academy, officer cadets, and my fellow Americans, 235 years ago, our forefathers brought forth on this continent a new nation, conceived in liberty, and dedicated to the proposition that all men are created equal.
>
> Since that great moment in history, our nation has engaged in war, not once but many times, testing whether that liberty and that proposition so conceived and so dedicated might long endure.
>
> We met our enemies on the battlegrounds of those wars, and our sons and daughters suffered unspeakable pain and even offered up their lives so that these principles might prevail.
>
> It is altogether fitting and proper that we fought those wars, for had we not done so, the light of our nation and the lights of so many other nations that

look to us for leadership and guidance would have been extinguished, perhaps forever.

We have come here today to remember those wars and to dedicate those battlegrounds in honor of those who fought so heroically for all of us.

But in a larger sense, we cannot dedicate, we cannot consecrate, we cannot hallow the ground upon which they fought. The brave men and women, living and dead, who struggled there have consecrated it far above our poor power to add or detract.

And whatever honor we can bestow cannot hold measure against the suffering endured by these men and women, much less against the lives they gave for our cause.

The world will little note, nor long remember what we say here today, but it can never forget what these soldiers did for our country. It is for us, the living, rather to be dedicated now to the principles that they who fought have thus far so nobly advanced. It is rather for us to be here dedicated to the great task remaining before us—that from these honored soldiers, we take increased devotion to that cause for which they gave the last full measure of devotion, that we here highly resolve that those who fought and especially those who died shall not have fought and died in vain.

Those of you before me, who are prepared to follow these soldiers who have gone before and who are prepared to dedicate your lives for our nation and for the principles upon which it stands, I want you to be the first to hear this news.

Science has just now handed us the ultimate gift: the possibility to bring an end to war and violence forever.

No, this is not an impossible dream that we cannot ever reach or realize. It is, rather, the answer to every soldier's prayer.

In the next succeeding days and weeks, you and your fellow citizens of our nation will be hearing more about this discovery and how it can and will change the course of human events.

Each of you will have an important part in the work that this discovery requires. You will be our nation's hands in forging the process, for without your service, without your dedication, we could not implement this plan for peace.

We will rely on you, our military, to secure our future, to ensure that this nation under God shall have a new birth of freedom—and that our government of the people, by the people, and for the people and the cherished principles upon which this government was founded shall not perish from the earth.

Chapter 42

Holed up in the hospital, VP Rick Chernoff wasted no time in making preparations for "the day." He drafted and redrafted his speech to be delivered at precisely the same time that the POTUS was to have delivered his speech at West Point. In between telephone calls to trusted members of his staff and private discussions with his personal assistant, Charles Brodsky, he repeatedly revised the language of the speech to make it as "presidential" as he could.

Brodsky also took a turn at tweaking the text, although his ability to write "presidential" was no better than Chernoff's. Although both were college graduates, neither had the ability, much less the interest, to write a good English sentence. However, such minor disabilities had never stopped them before.

The draft was deficient in tone; however, all the essential elements were there, and that was all that really mattered. Chernoff was also pleased that it read much like a proclamation:

> My fellow Americans, it is my sad duty to inform you that, this afternoon, a huge explosion occurred in our military academy at West Point, New York. This tragedy has resulted in the death of our president as well as many army officers and the entire corps of military cadets at West Point.
>
> We do not know how this explosion occurred, but I assure you the cause is under intense investigation. If it is determined to be an act of treason or terrorism, the perpetrators will be identified, chased down, found, and brought to justice.
>
> President Bradley was delivering a speech at the military academy when the explosion occurred.

The entire building, known as the Eisenhower Hall Theater, was destroyed and incinerated along with everyone else who was present at the time.

Not a single person in the theater survived this tragedy. In fact, their bodies have been burned beyond recognition. In some cases, it will not even be possible to identify these bodies by their dental records.

With our president dead, I will assume the office of president effective immediately. I have summoned the chief justice of the United States to come here with his Bible to administer the oath of office and install me as president of the United States.

As your vice president, I have prepared for this possibility and stood ready to take over the presidency at a moment's notice. President Bradley having passed away, I am now the next in line, and I will take charge of the country just as soon as I become your president.

My staff has prepared a number of executive orders at my direction. With these orders, which will be issued later today, I have accepted the resignations of all members of President Bradley's cabinet and have replaced them with secretaries of my own selection. I am sure you will find these men to be fully qualified for their respective positions of authority and power.

I fully expect the US Congress to approve these actions as well as such further actions as I must take for reasons of national security. I will be declaring a national emergency and will place this government on alert and under martial law. This state of emergency will remain until such time as we are confident that all threats to our established order have been eliminated.

This afternoon, I telephoned Mrs. Bradley to offer my condolences on the death of her husband. I have also asked her to vacate the White House as soon as possible so that my wife and I may move in with our staff and our household furnishings. As i speak to you today, a moving van is already heading for 1600 Pennsylvania Avenue.

I look forward to serving as your president for many years to come.

Thank you for your attention, and God bless America.

Chapter 43

Inspector Dan Gavin wasn't satisfied he had nailed the right guy, not by a long shot. Deep down at the pit of his stomach, he knew there was more to this crime than the greed of one man, the CEO of Transport International, Mike Snead.

Although Mike was safely incarcerated and would probably be staying in jail for the rest of his natural life, Gavin knew in his gut there was more to this story, this coincidence of events, than he now knew and perhaps would ever know.

When he first heard of the "accident" that befell General Bellamy, his sixth sense as a detective sounded an internal alarm. How could his car have gone off the road on the Baltimore-Washington Expressway?

Gavin's first instinct was to call Juli Gables to find out where she stood in her investigation of the Collingwood aircraft and get her take on this latest death, but he didn't have anything more than a hunch and a theory. He didn't have any real evidence to contribute, so he decided to pursue this thread on his own.

As he made that first call to the Maryland Police, he felt a bit out of his comfort zone. Why was he doing this? Before he could hang up, a female voice came on the line and said, "State police."

"Uh, this is Detective Dan Gavin from Long Island, New York. I'd like to speak with someone about an auto accident that happened about two days ago in Maryland."

"Well, you called the right place. What accident was that?"

"It was, uh, a General Bellamy. David Bellamy. I saw it in the news. It happened on the Baltimore-Washington Expressway."

"Oh, yes, I know the one you mean. Truly unfortunate, it was. He must have fallen asleep at the wheel. Ran right off the road."

"Can I talk to the officer on the scene? It's kind of important."

"Sure, that would be Officer O'Gonaughy. Kevin's out on patrol right now. Can I have him call you when he gets in?"

"Any possibility that I can have his cell phone number?" Detective Gavin asked.

"Who did you say your name was?"

"Detective Dan Gavin. I'm with the New York Police."

"Okay, I'll put you through."

A moment later, Gavin heard a deep, gruff voice superimposed on automobile engine and traffic sounds "O'Gonaughy," the man said. The voice was nearly drowned out by the background.

"I'm Detective Dan Gavin. New York Police." Gavin instinctively shouted into the phone, as if this would help O'Gonaughy hear him better. "Were you the officer on the scene at the auto accident of General David Bellamy a couple of days ago?"

"Yeah, that was me. What can I do for ya?" There was the barest trace of an Irish brogue in the officer's voice.

"Can you tell me what happened?"

"Who wants to know?"

"I'm investigating a murder up here in Westhampton, New York. General Bellamy was on the scene when it happened."

"Well, I'll tell ya. This was a strange one, it was. Car just went off the road in broad daylight. We assume the driver, Bellamy, fell asleep at the wheel."

"No evidence of foul play?"

"Nope. Nothing. The car just hit a tree. End of story."

"Where is the car now."

"At the impound," O'Gonaughy said. "It's going to the junkyard for destruction tomorrow."

"Don't let it go."

"What?"

"Don't let the car be destroyed."

"Why? It's a wreck. It's gonna go where wrecked cars go."

"It might be evidence," Detective Gavin said.

"Evidence of what?"

"I'm not sure. I just want to have a look at that car."

"Well then, you'd better get down here. By this time tomorrow, that car'll be history."

Chapter 44

Chairman Nikki Borisnikoff was in a sour mood. He was sick and tired of the grind, the routine sameness of going to work day after day, the drab details and the minutia of running his company, the endless industry reports he had to read and react to, all of which were wearing him down. The daily life of a powerful and politically connected industrialist wasn't as interesting and exciting as it might have seemed to an outsider, especially one of the vast army of "little people" who actually did the work at InterMil.

Nikki couldn't wait for the time when his friend and compatriot, Rick Chernoff, took over the presidency. Long ago, they had made a blood commitment to each other to scratch each other's back, and now was time to scratch good.

How the two leaders, hailing from two different countries and two different cultures, came to know each other and become blood brothers was the stuff from which legends are made.

Rick Chernoff, the son of white Russian immigrants and escapees from the Stalinist Soviet Union, had journeyed back to "the homeland" in the late 1960s to find his roots.

On that first and fateful visit, traveling on a tourist visa, he stomped his way back and forth through Stalingrad, looking for the family homestead. In his pocket, he had a photograph that was carefully preserved, one of the house his parents had vacated when they had fled St. Petersburg so long ago. Every so often, he took it out to study and compare the image to the houses he saw, but after he had walked the streets for three days, he had pretty much given up hope of finding that beautiful, beckoning homestead. For all he knew, the house had been destroyed to make room for the drab public housing that was so ubiquitous in that otherwise handsome and historic city.

At the end of the third day, dejected by his lack of success, he wandered into a local bar and grill for a beer and a hearty Russian meal. He found a table near a quiet corner and surveyed the crowd. Most of the people there seemed to be only going through the motions of life, without feelings of hope or even feelings at all. The strange Soviet economic model, where everyone was to work for the common good, which translated into everyone working for the government, had so sapped their motivation and creativity that it had sucked their emotions dry, too. Only one person, a man about his own age with a full beard and penetrating eyes, seemed to have any *joie de vivre*.

After all, it was quitting time, and this was as good as it was going to get in the Soviet Union, right?

Chernoff watched the man as he tried his best to dispel the foul smell of depression in the pub. He worked the room, joking and laughing first with one person and then another. He seemed to know and like everyone. As he came near, every person he approached perked up and became more animated, as if brought in an energy field. Then, as the man passed on, the person reverted to his former, closed-in self, as if the jail door slammed shut again on the person's own private hell.

Finally, after he completed the meet-and-greet with everyone in the room, including the bartender in whose company he seemed to enjoy the most, this mystery man came over, sat right down at Chernoff's table, and addressed him in English, as if they had known each other for years. "You're American, right?"

"That's right. How did you know?"

The man brushed the question aside. It was too trivial even for small talk. "You're here on some kind of quest. I know it. What is the reason?"

"My parents came from here. I'm trying to find their home."

"Aha! A *landsmann*. I knew it! Do you know Russian?"

"Never learned it. I should have, I guess. They didn't teach it at school."

"Never mind. You Americans are lucky. Everyone speaks English now."

"Does that bother you?"

"Bother?"

"I assume if the Soviet Union had its way, everyone would be speaking Russian."

"Whoa!" The man squinted, crinkling the sides of his eyes above his beard. "You have to be careful there. Live and let live, I always say."

"I'm sorry," Chernoff said. "I—"

The man's face changed again, this time into a winning smile. "No offense taken. You Americans act just like we would like to act someday—cocky and arrogant. The brightest and best. We are number two right now, but like you say in your Avis commercials, 'We try harder.'" He flashed Chernoff a pretend grin.

"Hey, nobody's perfect."

"*Shhh!* The walls have ears. And there are some guys upstairs who think they are."

"Oops." Chernoff grimaced. "Sorry again!"

"Just joking. Things here aren't that bad—"

"Oh?"

"Yet."

"You're really being watched?"

"Everybody watches everybody. It's our national pastime."

"That's no way to live."

"Well," the man said with a resigned sigh, "it does keep people on the straight and narrow. We Russians like to misbehave. You really can't give us too much rope, as you say in your westerns. We'll end up hanging ourselves . . . and everyone else too, if you give us a chance."

"I don't believe that."

"Ever hear of the hydrogen bomb?"

"Sure, everyone has."

"We'd try it out if we thought we could get away with it."

"So you're saying you can't be trusted," Chernoff replied, dubious.

"Quite the opposite. We Russians have a much more developed sense of loyalty than you Americans. Our word is our bond. You'll have trouble getting us to agree, but when you do, we stay with it to the end. It's deep in our character, not just done for commercial advantage."

"I like that. It's the way I work."

"See! That's because you're Russian. We're both cut from the same wood."

"Well, that's just why I'm here. To find my branch of the tree where that wood came from."

"It would be my pleasure to help you find it. My name's Nikki Borisnikoff." Nikki offered his hand, and Rick Chernoff grabbed it.

So began a relationship that continued over the years and eventually became one of the two men's most valuable assets—an asset that would serve them well in their respective careers in both industry and politics. Over the years, this relationship inspired them to be bigger and bolder than they otherwise could have possibly dreamed. In a word, theirs was a relationship that *worked*.

Chapter 45

Things were finally looking up for Nikki Borisnikoff. The nasty threat by Transport International's CEO, Mike Snead, had come to an end when they had blown up that new VTOL aircraft, leaving Snead on trial for murder. Rick Chernoff was now only a heartbeat away from the presidency of the United States, and the plans were in place for that heartbeat to end in less than a month. When Rick ascended to the office of president, Nikki would have untold influence in the two most powerful countries of the world: the United States and Russia. Who knew where this could lead?

Nikki's life was about to become a lot more interesting.

As he leaned back in his chair, Nikki swung his boots onto the polished, Italian marble slab he had had installed as a desktop and contemplated his next move. In true Bolshevik fashion, he was dressed all in black. In Bolshevik fashion too, his mood verged back and forth between gray and black, and right now, it was as black as a night in the Russian forest.

After a moment, he reached for the phone and barked into the receiver. "Get me Chernoff on a secure line." He held on nearly a minute as the call was placed and went through to the Georgetown University Hospital.

"Hello, Nikki. I thought we agreed not to speak until after . . . after West Point. Can't be too careful."

"Hey, comrade. Good to hear your voice, too." Nikki ignored the cautionary remark. "I want to schedule a meeting." There it was, floating out there—Nikki's next move.

"When?"

"Right after . . . West Point."

"Okay, we can do that. Where?"

"Either your place or mine. You'll be very busy, so I'll come to you."

"Public meeting?"

"Yes."

"What about?"

"Working together," Nikki said. "You're already making your influence felt in Russia. That sort of thing."

"Okay. Anything else?"

Rick was probing, but Nikki was not about to reveal his real agenda. "No, just a courtesy call. Promoting world peace."

"Just one day?"

"Yes, that'll be fine."

"My first state dinner?"

"You got it." *Perfect, as a matter of fact,* Nikki thought. *We'll announce our alliance with an after-dinner speech just in time for the New York morning news cycle.*

"I'll tell Brodsky to schedule it. He'll be in touch with your chief of staff."

"Done. Oh, and by the way, Rick?"

"Yes."

"How'd you like what happened to Bellamy?"

"He was a bit of a problem, but I don't think much of it. He wasn't a threat."

"He had knowledge that could sink us."

"Cops called it an accident," Chernoff said. "How're you doing at West Point/"

"My people are professional. They're working on it now."

"We're counting on them."

"It's coming together. See you very soon." Nikki returned the receiver to its place on his marble desk and sat back.

Yes, his plans were coming together very nicely so far.

Chapter 46

The brothers Alexander and Mikhail Muranov arrived at the gate at Port Elizabeth, New Jersey, in an extended-bed, dark blue Ford Super Duty 350 pickup truck. Alex, who was driving, smiled at the man in the window of the guard booth and handed him a bill of lading.

"Here to pick up a big wooden box," he said casually, as if he had visited the port to pick up parcels every day that week. Alex had a slight trace of Russian accent, but otherwise he was indistinguishable from the thousands of other truck drivers that arrived at the port each day. Wearing jeans and faded flannel shirts, the two men in the truck appeared as normal as an American breakfast of bacon, eggs, and hashed browns.

The guard turned his attention to the paperwork, ignoring the two unshaven men in the pickup while he punched some numbers into a computer keyboard. He squinted at the screen. It wasn't the usual clearance he expected.

"There's some kind of problem with this," he told the men. "Just pull your truck over to the right there and wait." He pointed to a parking lane. "I'll see what's the matter."

"The box isn't here?" Alex queried, seemingly unconcerned.

"Oh, it's here all right," the guard replied. "There's just . . . some kind of problem with it. Just wait there." He waived the two men off.

Alex drove the truck forward and parked to the right just as he had been told. Then he and Mikhail stepped out and walked back to the guard booth. Mikhail tried the door in the back but found it locked. In one move together as if on cue, the two men reached behind to the back of their belts and drew snub-nosed pistols. After they lowered the weapons to partially conceal them, they walked forward, one man on each side of the booth, and approached the guard's windows.

"What seems to be the problem?" Alex's Russian accent was stronger this time. He elongated the "E" in "seems" and sounded the Russian "O" in "problem." The guard appeared startled and worried at first but quickly composed himself.

"I've called my supervisor. He'll be here any moment."

"Listen to me." Alex's tone turned suddenly serious as he brought up his pistol and pointed it straight at the guard's head. "I *vant* you to open the door to this booth now."

"Oh, my God!" The guard jumped out of his seat, almost bumping his head on the low ceiling. "I . . . I will. Just don't shoot, *please*. Why do you want to get in here? This booth is empty."

"Just *do* it!"

"Okay, okay," he said, holding his hands up to show he was unarmed.

As the guard slowly turned around and stepped back to unlock the door at the back of the booth, Alex followed suit outside and waited momentarily for the door to open. The instant he saw the doorknob move, he grabbed it and yanked the door open with his left hand and fired point-blank with his right. As the guard doubled over, Alex pushed him out of the way, forced his way in, and pulled the door closed behind him.

Mihhail, who still stood by the window of the booth during his brother's action, now returned to the truck and climbed in on the driver's side so that he would be ready to leave at a moment's notice.

Alex, taking the guard's position in the booth, looked carefully at the computer monitor. The report of their shipped item still filled the screen as entries on a form. Alex scanned them as quickly as he could. What initially caught his attention was a warning in bold red letters: "Radioactive shipment. Do not release without proper credentials."

Scanning further, Alex found what he was looking for—the location of the shipment. The box was housed in a particular port, Warehouse No. 356, which was segregated from other incoming shipments at numbered coordinates D52. Without knowledge of the port, however, this information was useless.

Alex looked around inside the booth to find a map but came up empty-handed. He jotted down the number of the warehouse and the coordinates of his shipment and then used the mouse to click on the X in the upper right corner of the screen. The computer returned to the main menu, and after some searching, Alex was able to pull up a map of the port. Warehouse 356 was about a quarter mile away, one of a series of warehouses that lined the main thoroughfare through the facility. Alex clicked "print," grabbed the single sheet of paper that issued from the machine, and then headed back to the truck to join his partner.

Alex navigated as Mikhail negotiated the labyrinth of roads in the port facility. Numerous trucks and vans were parked along the way, receiving goods being loaded by port employees. Occasionally, a white sedan with "Security Patrol" painted on the side passed by the other way, but none of the security personnel paid any attention to the intruders.

Eventually, they found the warehouse with the number 356 on the side, and Mikhail pulled up in front. The two brothers could see at a glance that the overhead door at the entrance was padlocked shut. Alex stepped out of the cab and climbed onto the back of the truck, where, toward the front of the bed, it carried a ribbed, stainless steel toolbox. After he opened the lid and reached inside, he grabbed a large bolt cutter with which, upon jumping down, he used to attack the padlock on the door. With one "click," Alex severed the lock and lifted the door. Mikhail quickly drove the truck through the open entrance, and as soon as they were inside, Alex pulled down the door and closed it behind him. Now for the box!

Chapter 47

Warehouse 356 was relatively small as port warehouses go. As Alex and Mikhail drove slowly down the aisle with storage bays C and D on either side, they couldn't ignore the thought of stealing a few of these interesting-looking shipments. They could easily load some items onto their truck after they had taken the box they had come for. They assumed that all of the items in that warehouse were some kind of contraband that couldn't be released to their addressees for one reason or another, so no one would notice them missing, perhaps for weeks.

As soon as they saw their own box, however, they forgot about stealing any such items. The box was huge! So large and obviously heavy, in fact, that at first they had no idea how they would load it onto the truck.

The box was fabricated of unpainted wood boards, apparently oak, nailed and bolted together. A bill of lading, a copy of the document Alex had handed to the guard, was visible through the clear plastic window of an envelope, stapled to one side of the box near a corner.

Mikhail parked the pickup close to the box and alighted to assess what to do next. The box lay on a long pallet on the floor. Alex, who had walked directly from the warehouse door and had reached the slot D52 first, pushed against the box to test its weight. It lay there like a cold stone in the ground.

"Rats! It's heavy."

Mikhail joined him, and together, they tried to lift the box; however, it wouldn't budge.

"We'll need a lift of some kind," Mikhail said absently. For the moment at least, they were stymied.

The brothers stood there, looking first at each other and then at the box. As they pondered their next step, they heard the faint sound of a police siren from far in the distance. That galvanized them into action.

Alex and Mikhail took off on a run in opposite directions to look for something they could use to lift the box. Mikhail headed toward the front of the warehouse, and Alex toward the back. After he found nothing in the area of the door, Mikhail ran to the other, parallel, aisle that provided access to bays A and B. As he turned the corner to enter the aisle, he saw a forklift truck.

"I got it!" he screamed as loud as he could so Alex could hear.

Mikhail clamored up onto the operator's seat and scanned the controls. They had left the key! He turned the key and cranked the motor, but it didn't start. When he looked down, he saw the choke and pulled it, still turning the motor over and over, until it coughed and sputtered to life. After he pushed the choke in, Mikhail was able to bring the motor up to a smooth, loud roar and, even before this occurred, set the machine in motion.

Mikhail drove the forklift at top speed to the site of the box and lowered the prongs to just above floor level. After he took aim, he moved forward slowly and slid the prongs under the box through the openings in the pallet.

By now the siren sound outside had become much louder—so loud that Mikhail and Alex, who had returned to the box and was giving hand signals to Mikhail, could easily hear it over the engine noise of the forklift truck. They heard not only one siren but several, and they seemed to be just outside the warehouse door.

Alex opened the tailgate of the pickup while Mikhail lifted the pallet with the box and backed up to draw the load out of the slot D52. As he swung around expertly as if he had done this many times before, he lifted the pallet to bring it to just the right height and drove forward to place the pallet and box on the bed of the truck. The truck sagged with the weight.

After he backed up again, Mikhail pulled the prongs out of the pallet and out of the way while Alex slammed the tailgate shut and locked it in place. With their objective accomplished, the two brothers scrambled to mount the cab and make their getaway.

What happened next occurred so quickly that none of the policemen outside had time to react. Alex, who had taken the wheel of the pickup, gunned the engine and headed straight for the closed warehouse door. "Here goes!" he said as the truck slammed against the door and pushed it forward in front of them.

Taken completely by surprise, the police just stood in place and gaped as the truck, momentarily pressing the warehouse door forward in front of it like a giant shield, roared by them. The truck dodged to the right to let go of and maneuver past the door while they avoided two police cars that stood in its way and kept going.

Alex and Mikhail quickly reached the guardhouse at the front gate, where two more police vehicles sat blocking the exit, with a posse of police standing nearby, weapons at the ready. This time, the police knew what was coming.

Alex, the driver, feigned heading for the exit and then, at the last minute, swerved toward the other side of the guardhouse to leave through the entranceway. At the same time, Mikhail leaned out of his side window and aimed a missile launcher in the general direction of the policemen who, seeing the business end of the missile tube, scrambled to take cover behind the two cars. Mikhail squeezed the trigger and unleashed a streamlined bomb that blasted toward one of the cars and, upon impact a split second later, exploded and blew apart the car, hurtling shrapnel in all directions and instantly killing all the policemen.

"Got them!" Mikhail shouted with satisfaction as his brother drove around the guardhouse and accelerated into the clear. Within a few minutes, they were speeding north on the New Jersey Turnpike, just another anonymous blue truck among the multitude of vehicles on the East Coast's most traveled thoroughfare.

Chapter 48

Blending in with the traffic, Alex drove along the Turnpike to the end, paid the toll, and continued toward the George Washington Bridge on Interstate 95. Just before the tollbooths for the GWB, he turned off onto Route 9W and followed it north along the Hudson River. With the help of his GPS navigator, he turned off on Route 340, switched over to Route 303, and then, when he reached Central Nyack, turned left onto Route 59 and headed west. Finally, after he crossed over a railroad bridge, he turned right onto a side road and entered the small village of West Nyack. A couple of quick turns later, Alex slipped the truck quietly into a bay of a dilapidated garage on Benson Road and pressed a button on a transmitter to close the garage door. Both he and his brother, Mikhail, who hadn't spoken during the entire trip, climbed out of the cab on opposite sides, walked back to the rear of the truck, reached out, and embraced each other with great emotion.

"We did it. Nikki will be pleased," Mikhail muttered under his breath in Russian.

After a few moments for the tension to subside, Alex and Mikhail set about their business of attending to the big box. After they grabbed prey bars from a workbench in the garage, they climbed aboard the truck and began preying boards off the top and sides of the box. As they worked, they slowly revealed an ominous-looking mechanism inside that was bolted to the bottom of the oak box frame.

Also bolted to the floor of the frame and to one the side of the main mechanism was a separate cylindrical-shaped device that was painted red with a yellow, radiation-warning symbol on its side. Stapled to the frame was an envelope marked "Instructions."

Alex detached the envelope, took out a thick instruction booklet, and began to read aloud from the booklet in Russian. As he read, Mikhail executed the step-by-step instructions.

Mikhail first went to a metal cabinet in a corner of the garage, opened it, and took out a heavy overcoat and pair of gloves. Donning the overcoat and gloves, an activity that took several minutes because of the stiffness and weight of the material, he climbed back up on the truck again and worked with a wrench to unbolt the red cylinder. When he freed the cylinder, he picked it up with his gloves, brought it carefully down off the truck, and placed it on the workbench.

Alex, who had watched from a distance with the instructions in hand, went to the cabinet, removed an electrical device with a large dial on its top face, and flipped a switch at the side. The device immediately began to emit ticking sounds at random intervals. Alex carried it over to Mikhail, who was standing near the workbench with the red cylinder, and as Alex came closer, the ticking sounds became more and more frequent. Alex glanced down at the dial and saw the needle had moved to the right into a yellow region and was approaching a red zone. He stopped and held up the device so Mikhail could see the dial. Mikhail shrugged, but he moved away from the workbench just the same.

Alex and Mikhail next turned their attention to a strange-looking pickup truck in the other bay of the garage. The truck had four rubber tires, but immediately next to each tire was a metal wheel with an enlarged rim on the inside, resembling the rolling stock on a railroad car. The metal wheels did not touch the floor, but instead were elevated, compared to the rubber tires, and seemed to have no purpose.

The two men cleared some tie-downs off the back of the truck and placed two heavy planks lengthwise on the flatbed, side by side. With a tape measure from the workbench, they measured the width of the box frame and then moved the planks apart so that the distance between their outer edges was the same as the width of the box.

As a last step, Alex went to a box on the wall and pressed a button. Above them, a motor hummed, and a three-quarter-inch cable unreeled and lowered itself with a hook on the end. Mikhail climbed onto the bed of the pickup once more and grabbed the hook as it came down, signaling Alex to stop the motor when the hook was about two feet above the naked frame of the box. He then assisted Alex, passed two chains under the box frame, and looped the ends of each chain over the hook.

Alex returned to the box on the wall and pressed another button. The motor hummed again and reeled in the cable, lifting the hook and tensioning the chains. Slowly and carefully, Alex operated the controls under Mikhail's guidance to raise the box frame with its contents off the back of the truck. Once clear of the truck bed, Mikhail signaled Alex to stop the motor. Alex complied and then pressed another button to move the winch slowly along a rail on the ceiling to the other bay, carrying the box as it went. When the box was eventually over the other pickup, Alex lowered the load onto the planks on the back. With the box frame safely on this truck, Mikhail disconnected the chains and pulled them away, while Alex pressed buttons to lift the hook clear and out of the way.

With all that accomplished, the two men finally relaxed and almost cracked open a smile while they gazed at their handiwork. After a moment, Alex quietly walked over to a small refrigerator in the corner and took out a bottle of Russian vodka.

"I've been saving this for the right time," he said, pouring generous amounts into two drinking glasses. He gave one glass to Mikhail, lifted his own, pointed it at Mikhail, and gave a cheer. "To us!"

Alex and Mikhail downed the liquor, but before it took effect, Alex stated proudly,

"We're right on schedule. We even have two weeks more to get everything just right."

Mikhail responded, "Nikki will be pleased."

Chapter 49

Robert "Rob" Sapinsky, professor of neuroscience at Caltech, sat in his office and studied the articles submitted to the *New England Journal of Medicine* by Dr. Indira Agarwal of the Hospital for Mental Health in Bangalore, India, and Professor Dr. Klaus Selmeier, an institute professor with the Neurologisches Institut in Bern, Switzerland. Both articles missed the mark in Rob's estimation. At the very least, they failed to show how the solution to the problem of aggression was derived and failed to suggest how the solution could immediately be put to use to end aggression, both in the daily mundane lives of individuals and, on the world stage, to bring an end to violent crime, terror, and even war.

All of that was now possible.

What the articles did do to Rob's satisfaction was to validate his own research. When his article would eventually be published, as he was confident it would be, the criticisms of his peers would start coming in. He and the authors of the other two papers could expect a strong "peer review" process that might even turn ugly, reflecting the deep rivalry that existed among the researchers in the field.

It was helpful whenever there were two and even better when there were three articles by different sources that reported the results of research and confirmed a scientific theory, especially a theory as controversial as this one of mollifying aggression in humans.

Rob's thoughts were already beginning to extend beyond the laboratory, considering the vast implications of his discovery, when "the call" came in from President Peter Bradley. As best as he could recollect later, the phone conversation went something like this:

When Rob's desk phone rang, he picked it up and said the usual, "Hello, Rob Sapinsky speaking."

"Hello, Professor Sapinsky, this is Marlene McDuff from the office of the president. President Peter Bradley would like to speak with you."

"The president of the United States?" Rob sat abruptly upright and almost tipped over his chair.

"Yes." Rob imagined that the secretary, McDuff, must have received this reaction quite a few times. "Do you have a few moments to speak with him right now?"

"Yes, of course."

"I'll transfer you. Just a moment."

A second later, President Bradley's well-known, authoritative voice came on the line. "Hello, Professor Sapinsky?"

"Yes, it's me. This is quite an honor."

"I'm the one who has the honor. I have just learned about the paper you submitted to the *New England Journal of Medicine*. It's an amazing work. I'd like to ask you a few questions about it, if I may."

"I'm at your service, sir."

"Is this what I think it is? The answer to controlling aggression?"

"Well, quite modestly, yes, it is."

"I haven't read your paper, you understand, but I intend to when I have a bit more time."

"Would you like a quick summary?"

"Yes, exactly. That's just what I want right now."

"It boils down to one word."

"Really? What's the one word?"

"Amygdala," Rob said.

"What?"

"Amygdala. It's all about the amygdala."

"That's a pretty ugly-sounding word, if I may say so. What does it mean?"

"It's a part of the brain. Everyone has two of them—one in the right brain and one in the left."

"What does it do?"

"It controls the entire body. Sends out neurological signals that give us emotions."

"You mean there's just this one thing, the 'amygdala,' that makes us happy or sad?"

"Yes, it brings us joy or depression or even both at the same time. It's really complex."

"I still don't like the name," the president said. "Can't we call it something else?"

"No. I'm sorry. That's what it's called."

"Then I'm going to call it 'Amy' for short, if you don't mind. That's a nicer name."

"Okay with me. You're the president."

"Well, if this 'Amy' is so all-important, how do we influence it?"

"That's what my paper is about. I found a good answer to that question."

"Could you explain it to me? I may not understand it all, but I'm willing to listen. I'm fascinated by science."

"So I've heard. We scientists appreciate your taking an interest. Like you, we're also trying to make the world a better place."

"Don't flatter me, professor. I've been around too long for that. Just give me the facts."

"All right, I'll do my best," Rob started. "Very briefly, the brain processes stimuli by having the thalamus direct sensory information to the neocortex, the "thinking brain." The cortex then routes the signal to the amygdala, the "emotional brain," for the appropriate emotional reaction. The amygdala triggers a flood of peptides and hormones to create an emotion and a call for action in the body. That is the normal way it works.

"Perceived potential threats, however, can disrupt this smooth flow of information. The thalamus bypasses the cortex and routes the signal directly to the amygdala, which is the trigger point for the primitive fight-or-flight response When the amygdala feels threatened, it can react irrationally and destructively. Emotions make us pay attention right now—like saying, 'This is urgent'—and give us an immediate action plan without having to think twice. The result, unfortunately, is often inappropriate aggression.

"In our evolution, the emotional component evolved very early to deal with 'Do I eat it, or does it eat me?' This emotional response can take over the rest of the brain in a millisecond if it feels threatened. We've inherited this system. That's both good news and bad news for us. It protects us on one hand, but it causes us to strike out without thinking, often with tragic consequences.

"The amygdala is also involved—in fact, central—to what we think of as 'evil' thought processes, but I won't get into that. It's even more complex than the reaction to threats. Suffice it to say that, if we can regulate and maintain the smooth flow of information to and from the amygdala, we can avoid all kinds of aggressive activity.

"So how do we do that? How do we maintain what we call this 'emotional intelligence' on an even keel?

"Emotional intelligence is the ability, capacity, skill—or, in the case of a particular emotional intelligence model, a self-perceived ability—to identify, assess, and control the emotions of oneself, of others, and of groups of people. Different models have been proposed for the definition of emotional intelligence, and there is even disagreement about how the term should be used. But everyone agrees that we should keep the amygdala running smoothly and properly. Until now, though, we didn't know how to do this."

"I think I'll interrupt you right there," the president said. "This is a little more than I need to know right now. Just tell me: How do you control Amy to keep her happy and satisfied?"

"Glad that you asked, Mr. President. After years of research, I got lucky and found the answer. It's with a particular aroma."

"Aroma?"

"Yes, our most primitive sensory organ is the nose with our sense of smell. The neurological signals from these smell sensors go straight to the amygdala without passing 'go.' If you maintain even a trace of this aroma in the air, the amygdala functions as smoothly as it should and won't trigger any aggression or even any evil thoughts. So we now have a way to eliminate violent crime, all the way from spousal abuse to gangland crime to waging war."

"That's just amazing, professor! You mean you just have to spray the air with a little of this . . . this aroma?"

"That's right, and you don't need much. Just a few molecules per cubic foot will do. The nose is so sensitive."

"So what is the aroma?"

"I can't describe it to you exactly, but it's a very familiar smell. I'm sure you know it. It's derived from mother's milk."

Chapter 50

George and I had a glorious reunion, the kind they write romance novels about. I'm a journalist, not a romance novel writer, so I won't even try to describe our lustful twenty-four hours, but you know what I'm talking about. Just use your imagination.

When our relationship was completely back to normal and all was well, we came up for air and went back to solving crimes, and one crime in particular, namely the murder of Carl Collingwood.

Unlike the police, we couldn't interrogate people, which put us at a disadvantage. However, working as private investigators does have its advantages. You can use a whole bag of tricks that are not available to the police like breaking and entering, for example. But I'm getting ahead of myself.

After our romp in bed, George and I sat up and took stock. Had we really made any headway toward solving this crime? Not much, it appeared. Our only real progress had been in finding the connection with General Bellamy, but now he was dead. And just as we feared, Mike Snead, chairman and CEO of Transport International, had been arrested and charged with the crime.

We decided to give Inspector Dan Gavin a call.

I dialed the number, and he answered on the first ring.

"Hello, Juli. I was just about to call you. Believe it or not, I could use your help."

"*My* help? Last I heard you didn't want any help from me."

"Well, I've become a bit humbled by this Collingwood case. We managed to get an indictment of Mike Snead, but in my bones, I'm not sure he's the perp."

"I don't think he is either."

"Well, we're on the same page at least. Anything new?"

"We're pretty much stalled. That's why I'm calling *you*."

"Normally I wouldn't share this with anyone outside the department, but this isn't a normal case. I've got only one open lead, and it's a weak one. Wanna hear it?"

"Yeah, if there's anything—"

"Okay, here goes," he interrupted. "I suspect Bellamy's car was sabotaged. I'm about to go down there to Baltimore to check it out before they trash it."

"Makes a lot of sense. We think Bellamy was working for the vice president, Rick Chernoff."

"*Really?* I thought he had a heart attack and almost died."

"Maybe he did, and maybe he didn't. One thing we know is that he's holed up in the Georgetown University Hospital, running his office from there. Bellamy went to see him."

"So *that's* where he was. We wondered what he was doing in Washington."

"They have a really secure system there. No media allowed. The VP's office has gone dark."

"That's weird. Those politicos usually *want* the media to follow their every move, and the media obliges. It's a big fishbowl."

"Not now. Chernoff's found a way to get out of the fishbowl. He set himself up in a little cocoon all his own."

"I'll be damned," Gavin said. "Out of sight, out of mind."

"So what can we do?"

"Care to join me on a field trip to Baltimore?"

That took me aback. Dan was inviting George and me along on official business. Of course, I jumped at the opportunity. "Right now, I can't think of anything else we could possibly do."

An hour later, Inspector Gavin picked George and me up in the city on his way from Long Island to Baltimore. George sat in the back like a gentleman and let me have the front seat. I kept the conversation friendly and light all the way down. When we got there, we found the office of the Maryland Police that had jurisdiction over the Baltimore-Washington Expressway and reported in.

"I'm Inspector Dan Gavin, and these are my associates," Dan told the male desk clerk, waving his hand in our direction. "We have an appointment with Officer Kevin O'Gonaughy."

"He's here. I'll get him." The desk clerk pressed a button and spoke briefly into the intercom. "He'll be right down. Have a seat."

We did as we were told and waited a good half hour before O'Gonaughy walked into the waiting room. It must be a rivalry thing between cops.

Dan jumped up and extended his hand. "I'm Dan Gavin. I spoke to you on the phone."

"About that car—"

"Yes, I brought some colleagues along. We'd like to see it."

"I'm afraid that's impossible. You see, two feds came in this morning and towed it away."

Well, wouldn't you believe that the names the feds were nowhere in the database. Why was I not surprised! Here we were with another dead end, and all our leads had petered out.

Chapter 51

Mike Snead, who was about to begin the fight for his life, entered the courtroom through the side door. He had been brought up via elevator from a holding cell in the basement of the building. Supreme Court Justice Hon. Kathleen Davis had scheduled the start of jury selection for the trial, which, the attorneys involved had estimated, would last about two weeks. The trial would be short because there simply wasn't that much evidence on either side.

The courtroom was located in the Arthur M. Cromarty Court Complex on Center Drive in Riverhead, New York. Riverhead, a sprawling suburban township, was at the geographically unique mouth of the Peconic Estuary, which divided the twin forks at the end of Long Island, New York.

As Mike walked in, he looked for and quickly saw the two persons whom, he hoped against hope, could and would release him from living this nightmare, namely his lawyers, Burt Crowe and Derek Taliz.

Burt Crowe had been both his corporate and personal attorney for some twenty years now, and Mike had come to rely on his expertise and judgment in matters of ethics as well as the law. Burt seemed to know just where the line was at the very edge of what was permissible behavior in the ever-changing undercurrents of the social norm. What was an acceptable activity one day could be *malum prohibitum* the next and vice versa, as social mores and the law constantly adjusted to the popular climate.

But providing advice and counsel as an attorney was not at all the same as serving as defense counsel in a court of law. Although membership of the state bar, the license to practice law within the state of New York, allowed an attorney to represent clients in virtually any capacity, the two types of activity were vastly different from each other and required totally different skills. Unlike the medical profession, where physicians' practices were sliced like bologna into licensed specialties, attorneys had free reign to do pretty much anything professionally they wished to do within the bounds of the canons of ethics.

Burt knew this, and he knew his client would be better served by an attorney who specialized in criminal law, criminal defense in general, and the subspecialty of white-collar defense in particular. And for white-collar criminal defense, there was only one attorney of choice. His name was Derek Taliz.

Derek Taliz was a well-recognized name in the field, not only among the practitioners of the law but also among politicians and corporate CEOs and managers who had an all-too-frequent need for his services. Name a political scandal, and the name Derek Taliz came to mind. Name corporate overreaching and fraud, and the name Derek Taliz came to mind. Most recently, he had defended Carl Collingwood in a high-profile prosecution for hijacking a commuter train. Now he was defending someone accused of killing this very same man. Derek was absolutely certain his client was innocent of this crime because he, Mike Snead, or more specifically his company, Transport International, *had paid his enormous fee for defending the Collingwoods, father and son.* If Mike Snead had had any reason to eliminate Carl as a competitor in the development of a new, advanced aircraft, he could simply have left the fate of this destitute man and his son, Bruce, in the hands of the public defender and seen them sentenced to life in prison.

Having an innocent client and creating a reasonable doubt in the minds of a jury were two different things, however. Mike's financial support in the Collingwood case was confidential, and for good reason. The company would surely have reported the payments as deductible legal expenses, but as equally surely, legitimate business expenses they were not. Money laundering and tax fraud are not far behind murder and mayhem as a very serious offense. That aside, such payments would be probably inadmissible anyway as evidence in this case, as they were only marginally relevant in the eyes of the law.

Derek's chief defense could only be that the prosecutor's case was weak too, being buttressed solely by circumstantial evidence. That is not to say that the local prosecutor, a woman no less, had nothing to go on. With Mike's consent, Derek had attempted to play this card in reaching a plea bargain, but the Suffolk County district attorney, Helen Meisner, would have none of it. She insisted on going to trial to "settle the matter once and for all." The press was primed for this high-profile case, and she would be their star performer. Hey, it wouldn't hurt a lady to ride the white horse on the side of law and order, especially in this hurly-burly man's world. And it just might be good for her career.

From long experience, Derek was sensitive and attuned to the implications of a hidden, personal agenda.

As Mike entered the courtroom, all eyes turned in his direction. Not one to be shy, Mike nevertheless felt a shiver of embarrassment and even slightly of fear. Accustomed as he was to being completely in charge, this was a new and uncomfortable experience for him. He just wanted this whole thing to go away, and the sooner, the better.

"Have a seat, Mike." Burt stood in a gesture of greeting and offered the chair between him and Derek. "We're just waiting for the judge."

Before Mike could settle himself between his two counselors-at-law, the bailiff called, "All rise. The honorable Kathleen Davis presiding."

An attractive older woman with white hair and a black robe entered the courtroom through a door in the back and took her seat at the bench. "You may be seated," the bailiff announced before he continued, "The people of New York State against Michael H. Snead."

Mike and his attorneys drew a collective deep breath and prepared to proceed. The trial they had anticipated and prepared for these many months had finally begun.

Chapter 52

"I'll be asking you questions, and I want you to answer truthfully," Judge Davis addressed the potential jurors in the courtroom. "If I do not dismiss you, the attorneys for the prosecution and the defense will have a chance to ask follow-up questions. By the end of the day, I want a jury empanelled for this case."

It was clear that Judge Davis would not be just a referee but would take an active part in the trial. Her hands-on style was known throughout the tenth judicial district.

The prospective jurors who were filling the benches in the back of the courtroom fidgeted and waited for the questions to come. Although most just wanted to be excused to go back to their jobs and their normal lives for various reasons, a few of them wanted desperately to be selected for the jury. It was the judge's intention to identify and to disappoint the people in both of these categories.

The bailiff looked at his list and read the first name, "Jason Bartok."

A gray-haired man who appeared to be about seventy years old stood up respectfully to be questioned.

"Have you ever heard of the accused, Mr. Michael Snead?" Judge Davis began.

"No, ma'am . . . I mean your honor. Can't say as I have."

"Have you ever heard of Carl Collingwood?"

"No, ma'am . . . sorry, I mean your Honor. I apologize for—"

The judge cut him off and pressed on. "How do you get your news? Newspaper, radio, TV . . . what?"

"I don't much follow the news. I . . . I watch reruns of old shows like *Gilligan's Island* and—"

A light titter of chuckles emanated from those around him, but the judge ignored it. "It says here that you are retired. What did you do before you retired?"

"I was a super in an apartment building. I got my full pension last year, so I retired."

"Do you live in the apartment building?"

"Yes, ma'am, I do."

"So I assume you know everyone in the building, and they know you?"

"Yes, I'm friends with most everybody. They all know 'Jason.'"

"In talking with people, no one has ever mentioned the names Mike Snead or Carl Collingwood?"

"Can't say as they have."

"Well then, you'd make an acceptable juror in this case. Ms. Meisner, you may question the juror."

Helen Meisner stood briefly at her counsel table and said, "Your honor, I have no questions."

"Mr. Taliz?"

Derek got slowly to his feet and acknowledged the invitation to speak. He took his time as if getting the lay of the land, but in truth, he knew that the prospective jurors, from whom would come the panel of jurors, would be gaining their first impression of *him*. "Thank you, your honor," he began cordially.

He then turned and addressed Jason Bartok. "Mr. Bartok," Derek began, his voice warm with tact and respect. "Have you ever heard of the famous composer Bela Bartok?"

"Yes, I have."

"Any relation?"

"I wish. No, no relation."

"He was from Hungary, I believe. Is that right?"

"Yes, he was born there but came to the United States to get away from Nazi Germany."

"Is your ancestry Hungarian?"

"Yes, my grandfather emigrated in the early 1900s. Came through Ellis Island."

"Are you Jewish?"

"No, I don't really practice a religion."

"This apartment building where you were the superintendent, where is it located?"

"It's on the North Shore," the man said. "In Port Jefferson."

"That's a pretty upscale neighborhood, isn't it?"

"It's mixed, I would say."

"What's the average rent in your building?"

"The range is from three thousand to about nine thousand dollars."

"A *month*?"

"Yes, of course."

"That's pretty pricey, isn't it?"

"Well, the building is pretty classy. It overlooks the harbor."

"How long did you work there?"

"Twenty-six years."

"And you still live there?"

"Yes, I got to keep my apartment in the basement, rent-free. It's part of my pension."

"That's a real benefit, I would think, especially in a building like that."

"I like it there," Bartok said blandly.

Derek looked at him quizzically for a moment, as if he were going to follow up and then took another tactic. "Just one or two more questions, Mr. Bartok. Are you looking forward to being on the jury?"

"Very much so. It's a civic duty to serve."

"Civic duty?"

"That's what they say."

"Have you ever served on a jury before?"

"No, I've had to work up to now, so I managed to get off whenever I was called."

"Thank you, Mr. Bartok. You have been most helpful." Derek turned and faced the court again. "No further questions, your honor."

"Do you have a challenge?"

"Not at this time." Derek sat down and made some notes on his legal pad while the bailiff called out the name of the next prospective juror.

Chapter 53

One by one, the names in the jury pool were called by the bailiff, and the prospective jurors were subjected to *voir dire* questioning by Judge Davis and the two opposing counsels. The judge asked questions that went to the heart of the issue: Did the candidate for jury have any prior knowledge of the case, and if so, had he or she formed any opinion as to the guilt or innocence of the accused?

The opposing counsel's questions went deeper. Assuming the juror would gain all knowledge of the case through the evidence and arguments presented at trial, opposing counsel pried into the candidate's characteristics, attitudes, and experiences to identify any possible bias in favor of the prosecution or the defense.

The DA, Helen Meisner, looked for civic-minded jurors who had no reason not to trust the government and be amenable to subjecting the accused to a long prison term or possibly even the death penalty if he were found guilty as charged. It would be a plus if the person was eager to bring the perpetrator of the crime to justice.

Defense counsel, Derek, peppered the candidates with countless innocuous questions, all calculated to elicit telling personal information without seeming to pry. The questions appeared random, so they continually caught the candidates off-guard, but in Derek's mind, they fit in categories and painted a picture. Who was this prospective juror? He needed to know.

Derek's questions, which were drawn from his years of experience, poked and probed. Was this person a leader or a follower? Sensitive or impervious? Humble or arrogant? Idealistic or cynical? Emotional or logical? Sociable or shy? Trusting or suspicious? Pro-establishment or individualistic?

All of these issues were relevant in some way to the person's expected performance on a jury.

Sometimes when the potential jurors were reticent and didn't freely respond to his direct questions, Derek shifted to more general questions so as to establish rapport and get them talking. To get a better sense of a juror's personality, he asked questions like the following:

- What radio station do you usually listen to in the car?
- What is your favorite television show?
- What television channel do you watch most often?
- What is your favorite movie of all time?
- What sports do you watch?
- Do you have bumper stickers on your car?
- What do you do in your spare time?
- What is your religion?
- Is there anything about your religious beliefs that would affect your decision of guilt or innocence?
- Is there any reason you do not want to be here today?

Judge Davis became repeatedly annoyed with Derek for the length of time he spent with some of the jury candidates and urged him to "please move on," but Derek was undeterred. He knew he was entitled to ask as many questions as he needed to get to know the juror and gather enough information to make a "go" or "no go" decision.

By the end of the day, after both the prosecutor and the defense counsel had exercised their challenges for cause and their allotted number of peremptory challenges, twelve jurors and two alternate jurors sat in the jury box, ready for trial. Jason Bartok was not among them, however. Derek had exercised one of his peremptory challenges to strike Jason because, Derek thought, it was highly likely that a person who was so close to and yet so far from rich people carried a class bias against them. And his client, Michael Snead, president and CEO of a multinational corporation, was quite wealthy indeed.

Judge Davis asked them all to stand.

"I thank you all for serving on this jury. The trial will start at 9:00 tomorrow morning and is expected to last about two weeks. At the conclusion of this trial, you will be asked to make a decision as to the guilt or innocence of the accused, Mr. Michael Snead. You may take as long as you like to make this decision, but you *must* make it. And the decision must be unanimous. If your decision is that accused is guilty as charged, you must all agree on this. Now, if you would all please raise your right hands, the bailiff will swear you in."

Chapter 54

By a quarter to nine the next morning, the courtroom was filled to overflowing. A security guard posted at the door let someone in only if they either had court business or if one of the spectators that crammed the room had just left. One person had to come out before he would let another person in.

Among the spectators were countless members of the local and national media. Juli Gables and George White had to absent themselves from the courtroom because they were on the prosecutor's witness list, but Aleksa Williams had come early and snagged a front seat in the section right behind the defense counsel table. Brian cooled his heels in the Channel 2 News van outside, waiting for Aleksa to come out and give a report.

By quarter to nine, the DA and assistant DA had arrived and were setting up their laptop computers on the prosecutor's table. Burt Crowe and Derek Taliz were there too, fishing papers out of their briefcases. Precisely at nine, a side door opened, and Mike Snead was ushered into the room by two prison guards. He looked smart in his expensive, pinstriped suit and regimental blue tie, but if one looked carefully, one could see he was not at all his usual confident self.

At ten minutes after nine, another door opened on the opposite side of the courtroom. The members of the jury filed into the room and took their places in the jury box.

And finally, about five minutes later, the bailiff announced the entrance of the judge. "Hear ye, hear ye! All rise. This court will now be in session. The honorable Judge Kathleen Davis presiding."

Everyone rose expectantly and respectfully with a great deal of rustle and bustle and remained standing while Judge Davis strode up to the bench and made herself comfortable in the leather chair. She banged the gavel, and everyone sat down, too.

"Is the prosecution ready?" The judge looked squarely at the DA, Helen Meisner.

"We're ready, your honor." Helen stood briefly for this statement and then sat down.

"Is the defense ready?"

Derek rose and reported, "We are, your honor."

"Well then, you may present your opening statements."

Helen came to her feet again, stood momentarily behind her counsel table, and then came around to the front of the table and took a position in front of the jury. She paused to gaze in the face of the jury members, one by one, for just an instant to make a personal connection with each, and began, "*Res ipsa loquitur*. That will be the guiding principal in this case. It's a Latin expression that means literally 'the thing itself speaks.' In a court of law, we say, 'The thing speaks for itself.'

"The legal principal is that where a certain instrument is in the exclusive control of one person or even a group of people, provided they are under the control of that one person, and where that instrument causes the death or injury of another person, that first person is automatically responsible for the death or injury and should be held accountable.

"'The thing speaks for itself.'

"In this case, we will show that the accused, Michael Snead, acted with malice aforethought to cause the death of an aircraft developer, Carl Collingwood, to squash his competition for military contracts.

"We will show that Mike Snead's company sold an aircraft engine to Carl Collingwood's company to be installed in a remarkable new prototype aircraft and that this engine blew up during the initial flight of the aircraft, killing its pilot, Carl.

"The thing speaks for itself. The aircraft engine blew up. Why? We don't exactly know, but we do know it shouldn't have. Where did the engine come from? A company called Transport International.

Who was in control of Transport International? The president and CEO is sitting right there." Helen held out her open hand in the direction of the defense counsel table and waited until everyone in the jury had taken a good look at the accused.

"Mike Snead." The way she pronounced the name, with such disgust, one would have thought that she was speaking of the devil incarnate.

"This case is that simple." On that note, Helen returned to her seat at her counsel table.

"May it please the court." Derek Taliz stood dramatically and glowered at Helen for a moment, as if to shout out with outrage, "How *dare* you," and then strode over and took up his position in front of the jury. Like Helen, he paused for a moment to connect with his audience and announced authoritatively, "This case is *not* so simple!"

Chapter 55

"*Prima facie*. It's another Latin term that means literally 'at first sight.' In a court of law, it means that the prosecutor must present at least a minimum amount of evidence, or we should not even waste our time in conducting a trial."

Derek grinned and remarked, "Looks like you're going to be learning a bit of Latin today." Most of the jurors cracked at least a small smile at the bit of humor.

"So what have we here? The prosecutor has charged my client with murder in the second degree, a very heinous crime, but as you will soon see, she has no proof to support this charge. Already, she has started to obfuscate and try to make up for this lack of evidence.

"We'll go through this *ad nauseum*—another Latin expression, by the way—during this trial, but just to get you oriented, let's look at what the prosecutor has to prove. There are just three things:

"First, a homicide, the killing of a human being. Yes, the prosecutor can and will prove to your satisfaction that Carl Collingwood died in an aircraft explosion. We are all terribly sorry for Carl's tragic death.

"Second, the physical element, the *actus reus*, another Latin term meaning 'the unlawful killing of one person by another.' The prosecutor won't have a shred of evidence to show that my client's conduct resulted in Carl's death.

"And third, there is a mental element called the *mens rea*—Latin again! To establish a *prima facie* case, the prosecutor has to prove that my client had the *intent or knowledge* that his conduct would result in Carl's death or at least *someone's* death. The prosecutor won't be able to present any evidence of this because—" Derek said and then paused briefly for emphasis before he continued, "there is none, not a shred."

"Don't let the prosecutor fool you. This is not a simple case at all. No indeed. The prosecutor does not have a *prima facie* case, which means evidence of all three elements of the crime with which she has charged my client. As you will see shortly, she cannot even prove two out of the three.

"Now let me talk to each one of you about your role as members of the jury in this case. Under our US Constitution, any person accused by the government of committing a crime is entitled to a trial before a jury of his peers, members of the community like you. This means that you and only you will decide the guilt or innocence of my client, Mike Snead.

"As jurors, it will be your responsibility to hear and weigh the evidence presented by the government's prosecutor and decide whether the crime has been proven beyond any reasonable doubt.

"A trial by jury is a sacred right in our country. Thomas Jefferson called the jury system 'the only anchor yet imagined by man by which a government can be held to the principles of its constitution.' All I ask—all my client can ask of you—is that you take this responsibility as a juror seriously and that you make your decision based solely on the evidence. Don't be fooled by what the prosecutor says. She will try to convince you she has proven her case against my client when, in fact, there won't be evidence to support what she says.

"After all the evidence has been presented, I'll go over it with you and explain what it does and does not show.

"So will the prosecutor, Ms. Meisner, but listen carefully and with a critical mind. It is not her role to weigh the evidence on the even scales of justice. That is yours. She will be an advocate for conviction of my client, no matter what the evidence may show.

"Now, before I sit down, I want to put an end to the use of this legal gobbledygook like *res ipsa loquitur*. Let me tell you one more Latin term. It's *lex*, and it means the 'law.' I'll bet you knew that one, but if you didn't, it doesn't matter. Latin is a completely dead language, and nobody speaks it anymore. We lawyers have a lot of fun dropping Latin phrases here and there, but there's an English term for everything. I'll stick to English from now on, I promise, and I hope that the prosecutor, Ms. Meisner, does too."

Having thus dealt with and neutralized the prosecution's opening statement, Derek gave a conspiratorial wink to the jury and walked back to his table.

Chapter 56

"You may call your first witness," Judge Davis said.

Helen Meisner stood and announced, "The prosecution calls George White."

George, who had been waiting outside in the hall, was requested by a bailiff to enter the courtroom. All eyes in the room turned toward him as he appeared in the doorway and walked the few steps up to the bar that separated the inner sanctum of the courtroom from the gallery. Helen opened the gate and greeted him warmly.

"Hello, George. Won't you please take the witness stand?"

"Okay." George mounted the stand and was sworn in by the court clerk while he stood. When the clerk was finished, George sat down in the witness chair, and Helen began.

"George, please state your full name for the record."

"George B. White."

"And what is your occupation?"

"I work with my wife, Juli Gables, to research news and report news on our website."

"Your website? What's your website?"

"We call it 'The Gables Report.' It's at www.gablesreport.com."

"Does 'The Gables Report' specialize in any particular type of news?"

"What do you mean 'type of news?'"

"You know, local entertainment, Hollywood celebrities, sports, that sort of thing."

"I guess you'd say we're into breaking news on corporate and political corruption," George said. "We find it, research it, and tell about it on our website."

"You're not concerned about getting sued for libel?"

"No, ma'am. We just tell the truth. They can't sue us for that."

"Do you get a lot of hits on your website?"

"Let's just say that people are fed up. They love it when we expose the bad guys."

"So a lot of hits?"

"Yeah. A *lot* of hits."

"Okay, that's good. Now did there come a time when you went to the Suffolk County Airport to watch the first test flight of a new kind of aircraft?"

"Yes, ma'am. I went with Juli."

"When was that?"

"About nine months ago now," George said. "Can't remember exactly."

"Could it be in October of last year?"

"Yeah, that's about right."

"October 23rd?"

"Could be."

"Can you relate what happened?"

"Well, we got there at about 9:00 in the morning. Juli started interviewing everybody while I stayed in the background, shooting video. Pretty soon, the military arrived to watch the demonstration, and Mr. Collingwood, Carl Collingwood, he climbed into the cockpit and started up the aircraft to give it a test drive."

"What type of aircraft was this?"

"Looked like a regular airplane except—"

"Except what?" Helen asked.

"Except the wings looked funny. The plane was supposed to go straight up in the air."

"Did it?"

"Yes, it did. Everyone was amazed."

"So the test was a success?"

"No, ma'am. There was this explosion, and the airplane just sort of blew up and burned right there in front of us."

"You were taking a video of the flight, right?"

"Yes, ma'am. I even had to step back a bit because the heat was so intense."

"What happened to the video?"

"I brought it back to our apartment, and Juli and I watched it there."

"Did you put it on your website?"

"No, the images were so horrible we thought that it would be disrespectful to Mr. Collingwood and his family to put it on. We have never showed it to anyone."

Helen Meisner went back to her counsel table and picked up a diskette. "At this point, your honor, I would like to mark this diskette of Mr. White's video as the prosecution's Exhibit 1."

Derek jumped to his feet. "Objection!"

Helen wheeled around. "On what grounds could you possibly object?"

"Your honor, I assume that if this video is entered as an exhibit, the prosecution intends to show it to the jury." Derek glared at Helen as he said this.

"Well, of course. This video is the best evidence of the crime committed."

"Showing it would be prejudicial. It would inflame the jury!"

"We have to prove the homicide occurred," Helen replied calmly like a parent teaching a child. "It's an element of the crime of murder two, as you yourself told us in your opening statement."

"We'll *stipulate* that Carl Collingwood died during the test flight. End of story."

"That won't do it, I'm afraid. Mr. Collingwood could have died of anything. Even a heart attack."

"We'll stipulate to his death due to an explosion of the aircraft," Derek said.

"No good. The explosion could have been due to any number of causes, even accidental."

"All right then, we'll stipulate to a homicide. Caused by a bomb."

"Still no good. The video will show that the bomb was located in the engine."

"Whatever!" Derek shouted, exasperated. "We'll stipulate to that too."

Helen smiled. "We accept the stipulations. But we still need to show the part of the video leading up to the explosion."

"Objection! Relevance!"

Judge Davis finally broke in. "What's this about, Ms. Meisner?"

"May I ask the witness just a few more questions?"

"All right. Proceed."

Helen again addressed George. "Was there any indication prior to the test flight that a tragedy might happen?"

"Well, no. Not such a tragedy, but there was something, uh, strange about Mr. Collingwood's behavior."

"And what was that?"

"I can't really explain it. You'll have to see it for yourself."

Derek sat in his chair glumly, as if black smoke were rising from an invisible chimney on top of his head.

Chapter 57

The bailiff rolled out a cart from the corner of the room that carried a television set and a DVD player. After he positioned the system in front of the courtroom so all could see, he switched on the electronics and inserted the disc marked as Exhibit 1. The video image sputtered to life on the screen.

The opening was a wide-angle shot of a cavernous aircraft hangar with an enormous open door. The camera zoomed in on Carl and Bruce Collingwood, who were standing in the right far corner of the interior space, holding coffee cups, and apparently chatting with five other men, employees of Carl's company.

Carl and Bruce were locked in a heated exchange while the employees looked on with amused smiles on their faces.

"You've got to be kidding, Dad. You're twice my age! Pardon my saying, so but your reflexes are a bit *slow.*" Bruce dragged out the last word for effect. "The PAC's going to act more like a bucking bronco than an aircraft."

"But I know all the different twists and turns it can make," Carl said. "I've done the math. It won't make any moves I can't keep up with."

"Why don't we let our people decide?" Bruce turned to the others for assistance.

"Yeah, right," Carl said sarcastically. "If they choose you, I'll be pissed at them, and if they choose me, you'll be pissed at everyone, including me."

"Okay, here's Juli!" They all turned their attention to a young woman as she walked up to them. "Maybe she can settle it."

Both Bruce and Carl broke into wide grins and took turns giving Juli bear hugs. "Welcome stranger!" Carl held her face between both his hands and looked at her squarely in the eyes. "How've you been?

Survived that Bermuda honeymoon? Where the heck's the lucky man?"

Juli nodded in the direction of the camera, and the entire crew walked straight toward it. As they came close, the image cut to the next scene, a long shot of the aircraft and the people around it.

After a brief exchange, the camera panned to focus on a black SUV that pulled up and stopped just outside the hangar. Three men in uniform got out. The driver had master-sergeant stripes on his sleeve while the other two wore military hats with gold graffiti on their visors proclaiming their elevated status. All three headed toward the assembled group near the aircraft.

Carl just stood there, staring blankly without moving, as if the arrival of the military had triggered something, and he froze.

Sensing his father's difficulty, Bruce quickly stepped forward to greet the visitors, "Hi, I'm Bruce Collingwood." He held out his hand. "Thanks for coming."

"I'm General Bellamy, and this is Major Hendricks and Master Sergeant David Schulz."

They shook hands all around, and Bruce introduced his father, still standing silently, and the other members of his team. Again, the image cut to another scene.

"We still haven't decided who will fly it, Dad or me," Bruce said, while Carl still seemed to be tongue-tied. "We'll have to flip a coin or something."

"Is that a problem?" the general asked. "It's *your* invention," he said, turning to Carl. "*You* decide who flies it."

Without a word, Carl reached for his flight jacket and put it on as he walked out to the aircraft on the tarmac. Bruce followed and helped him climb in through a side door above the wing.

At Bruce's signal, Carl opened a side window of the cockpit and shouted, "Clear prop," finally finding his voice. The front propeller cranked a couple of turns and awakened the engine, which sputtered briefly before it settled into a smooth, comfortable-sounding hum. Then, a moment later, a second engine started up with a muffled, high-pitched whine. The combined sound was something like a sound from a bagpipe.

The wheels of the craft were blocked, keeping it from moving forward or back. Bruce moved in and grabbed little ropes that were attached to each chock and then pulled the chocks away, at first from the front wheel and next from the main landing gear under each wing. He backed off to a safe distance, carrying the chocks, and watched the aircraft vibrate as its propeller and rotating blades in each wing churned the air.

The aircraft shuddered slightly as its engine sound increased in pitch and then moved forward a bit as it slowly lifted itself, seemingly by its own bootstraps, off the ground. The landing gear extended downward at first, leaving the wheels on the tarmac beneath, and then held firm and picked the wheels up off the surface. The craft was airborne.

Helen, who had walked over and stood next to the TV, signaled to the bailiff to switch it off. "I have no more questions of this witness."

"Cross-examination?" the judge queried.

Derek rose slowly and approached the witness. "George, earlier in your testimony, you characterized Carl Collingwood's behavior on that day as being 'strange.' Can you elaborate on what you meant by that?"

"Not really. When you run a video camera, you're concentrating on getting the best shot, not on what the people are actually doing. I only noticed it later when I watched the video."

"You mean all you can tell us is what you saw in the video?"

"Yes, I assume you saw it, too?"

Derek ignored the question from the witness and pressed on. "Did anyone else notice this 'strange' behavior that you know of?"

"Well, Juli was there. She was paying close attention. Why don't you ask her?"

"Perhaps we will hear from her later. Thank you for your testimony, George. I have no more questions."

Chapter 58

Detective Dan Gavin had testified at trial many times but never in such a gruesome murder case as this. He was visibly nervous as he sat in the witness chair, and Helen noticed. More importantly, everyone in the jury noticed, too.

After quickly going through the preliminaries for the record and for the jury, Helen got to the reason she had called him as a witness. "Did there come a time that you were called to investigate the explosion of an aircraft at Suffolk County Airport about nine months ago?"

"Yes, I'll never forget it."

"Would you tell the court what happened when you arrived on the scene?"

"There was an aircraft there or what was left of it, all crumpled up, still hot and smoldering. It was *awful.*"

Derek squirmed in his seat but didn't make an objection to this statement of opinion, preferring not to call the jury's attention to it.

"The local police had cordoned off the area, and I started by finding out who was there at the time. After that, I interviewed everyone before letting them go."

"Who was there?"

"Carl Collingwood's son, Bruce, nine employees of Collingwood's company, three military personnel who had come to witness the test flight, and two media people, George White, who just testified, and Juli Gables."

"What did you find out when you interviewed them?"

"Pretty much nothing. Everyone except the military people knew and liked Carl Collingwood. They all were clearly devastated by the disaster. No one had a motive for killing Carl or blowing up the plane. In fact, everyone had a stake in the successful outcome of the test flight. The military was going to invest in the development and buy hundreds of these aircraft if it could really take off vertically."

"You said 'everyone *except* the military people.' Didn't they know Carl Collingwood?"

"Apparently not. They just came to view the test. They were from Aberdeen Proving Grounds, the army's base for testing and procuring military equipment."

"Did there come a time in your investigation that you came to understand how this crime was committed?"

"Objection! The prosecution knows better than to ask a question like that!"

"Sustained. Just stick to the facts, Ms. Meisner." the judge ruled.

"Okay, I'll break it down. Detective Gavin, were you able to determine what caused the explosion?"

"From examining the video, it was pretty clear that the explosion started in one of the engines. However, the aircraft was too badly burned for our forensics to find residue of a bomb or anything like that."

"So you really don't know what caused the explosion?"

"We know it came from the engine—that's all."

"And where did this engine come from?"

"We learned that it was manufactured by Transport International and delivered to Hummingbird Aircraft two weeks before the test."

"Hummingbird Aircraft. That's Carl Collingwood's company, is it not?"

"Yes, that's his company—or was."

"So it is your testimony that Transport International delivered the engine that caused the explosion?"

"That's correct, yes."

"How can you be sure the engine wasn't tampered with after it was delivered?"

"We interviewed everyone who could possibly have had access. There were always at least three or four people present at Hummingbird Aircraft from the time the engine was received to the time of the test. They were working around the clock. And besides, no one had motive."

"So the reason for the explosion, whatever it was, had to have come from Transport International?"

"That's our determination, yes."

"No further questions, your honor." Quite satisfied with the testimony, Helen Meisner returned to her seat at the counsel table.

Derek remained seated for a moment, scribbling on a legal pad, and then rose, taking the pad with him.

"Detective Gavin." Derek paused and looked squarely at the witness to lock eyes and connect for a moment. "Did you interview people at Transport International about the manufacture of that engine?"

"Yes, we did."

"Were you able to determine if a bomb or any other kind of incendiary device had been installed?"

"No, we weren't. Everyone we talked to said the engine was fine and running perfectly before it left the factory."

"Everyone? Everyone who had access to the engine?"

"No, there was one person who we weren't able to talk to."

"Oh? Who was that?

"It was a recent hire. He had some kind of funny name. Andrei, uh, Gershuni or something like that. He came forward himself and said he had some information, so we talked to him. He explained that he'd seen some suspicious materials in the plant, apparently plastic explosives, which were kept under lock and key by a supervisor on the engine assembly line."

"A supervisor? Who was that?"

"A guy named Joseph Santucci. We talked to him, of course, but he denied there were any such explosives. We couldn't prove anything."

"About this Andrei Gershuni? Did you look into his background?"

"Yes, but it seems he had just emigrated from Russia. We couldn't check his record any further back than a few months."

"Did you consider him a suspect?" Derek asked.

"Everyone's a suspect until we find the right guy, but we weren't able to follow up."

"Why is that?"

"He died before we were able to bring him in for questioning."

"So you dropped the lead."

"What could we do? It was a dead end. Pardon the pun." The courtroom twittered.

"All right, let's turn our attention to these military personnel that were at the flight test. You interviewed them?"

"Yes, we did. They appeared to be just what they seemed. There were three of them that came up from Aberdeen Proving Ground to watch the flight test."

"Who was in charge?"

"A guy named David Bellamy. A major general."

"That's a pretty high rank for someone just to come and watch an airplane fly, don't you think?"

"I wouldn't know."

"Are you aware that the reporter at the test flight, Juli Gables, has a website?"

"Of course," Gavin said. "That's how she gets her news out."

"Were you aware that she accused General Bellamy of triggering the explosion?"

"I was aware of that, yes."

"That she put up an ambush video of General Bellamy on her website?"

"Yes, she told me."

"Did you ever watch it?"

"Sure, but he didn't admit to anything."

"Did you ever follow up?"

"No, we figured that, after being ambushed like that, Bellamy would be lawyered up and refuse to answer our questions."

"Now let me get this straight. You had a lead with this Mr. Gershuni, but you didn't follow up—"

"Couldn't."

"Couldn't follow up. And you had a lead with this General Bellamy, but you didn't follow up. Yet you still arrested the accused, Michael Snead, who probably didn't even go near the manufacturing floor for that engine. Is that right?"

"That's right, but—"

"Don't you think it would be wise to question this General Bellamy under oath even now?"

"We couldn't, even if we wanted to."

"Why is that?"

"General Bellamy was killed last month in an auto accident."

Derek turned on his heels in disgust and informed the court, "I have no further questions."

Chapter 59

"The state calls Sheldon Bernstein to the stand," Helen announced loudly.

It was the start of the third day of trial. Everyone had settled into the routine by this time, and the apparatus of justice was running according to plan—Helen's plan, at least.

Shelley Bernstein was sworn in by the court clerk, made himself comfortable in the witness chair, and leaned forward toward the microphone in anticipation of Helen's questions.

"Mr. Bernstein, please state your name and occupation for the record."

"Sheldon Bernstein, but everyone calls me 'Shelley.'" Shelley's voice was deep and sonorous, so much so that it made even the most easily bored person sit up and take notice. "I'm executive vice president of Transport International."

"Do you know the accused, Michael Snead?"

"Of course. He's sitting right there." Shelley pointed to his boss, who sat glumly at the counsel table between Derek Taliz and Burt Crowe.

"As executive VP, do you report to him in the corporation?"

"Yeah, Mike is president and CEO. He runs the company."

"Now Mr. Bernstein—Shelley—did there come a time when Hummingbird Aircraft submitted a purchase order for an engine to be used on their new kind of aircraft?"

"Yes, nearly two years ago, when he was just starting the development of his aircraft, Carl Collingwood came to us to discuss the purchase of an engine. It was a special engine called a barrel-type engine where all the cylinders are arranged in parallel and in a circle like the barrels of a six-shooter pistol. Pistons go back and forth inside the cylinders to rotate a cam on a drive shaft in the center.

The whole thing is very small and light for the amount of power it puts out.

"Anyway, we decided to develop the engine for him at no cost, because we wanted to use this engine in our own aircraft. Our development was successful, and we delivered the first engine to Hummingbird Aircraft on time and under budget."

Helen picked up a piece of paper from her counsel table and brought it over to Shelley.

"Mr. Bernstein, uh, Shelley, I show you a copy of a purchase order. Do you recognize it?"

"That would be the original purchase order from Hummingbird for the engine."

"I'd like to mark this purchase order as the prosecution's Exhibit 2 for identification." Helen brought the paper to the court clerk, who placed a yellow sticker in the upper right corner and wrote, "P EX 2," in the space provided on the sticker.

After she took the marked exhibit from the clerk, Helen returned to the waiting witness and handed him the paper. "Would you please review this document?"

"Okay." Shelley looked at it carefully and then looked back at Helen, waiting for the next question.

"I notice it says 'N/C' at the bottom. Does that mean 'no charge?'"

"Yes," the witness said.

"Why no charge?"

"I guess we didn't charge them anything. Because it was a developmental engine, I suppose."

"Shelley, did Transport International make a practice of developing engines or anything else for its customers at no charge?"

"No, can't say that it did."

"Let me rephrase the question. Did Transport International *ever* develop a product for any other company at no charge?"

"No, I can't recall that it did."

"Transport International is in business to make a profit, is it not?" Helen asked.

"Yes, of course."

"Then can you explain to me why Transport International made an exception from its normal practice and supplied an engine to Hummingbird Aircraft at no charge?"

"No, I can't."

"Could it be that the defendant, Mike Snead, wanted to supply an engine that would be installed in the new aircraft so as to blow up the aircraft with its pilot Carl Collingwood to destroy this competition?"

"*No!* Of course not!"

"Transport International attempted to eliminate Hummingbird Aircraft as a competitor once before, did it not?"

"Well, that may be true, but—"

"Didn't Mike Snead testify in court that he loaned money to Hummingbird for the express purpose of placing it in bankruptcy when it couldn't pay?"

"Objection!" There's no such testimony in evidence here!"

"Sustained."

"Did Transport International loan that company money?"

"Yes," he admitted.

"Did Transport International take over the company when Carl Collingwood missed a payment?"

"Yes it did, but—"

"Did Transport International stop the aircraft development and keep the patents when it took over the company?"

"We didn't think—"

"Yes or no!"

"Yes," he again admitted.

"It stopped the development?"

"Yes."

"Did not Mike Snead, the defendant here, once state in court that it was his purpose to eliminate Hummingbird as a competitor when Transport International was sued by Carl Collingwood?"

"Objection. Hearsay!" Derek jumped up and shouted. "Your honor, the prosecution is completely out of order!"

"No further questions." Helen turned dramatically to Derek and said, "Your witness."

Derek rose to cross-examine. In his mind, he knew he should bear down on Shelley and do his best to challenge Shelley's credibility. Truly, he had plenty of material to work with because Shelley was Mike Snead's right-hand man and was as guilty as Mike of any corporate malfeasance, perhaps even more. At the very least, he could inquire deeply into the circumstances of developing the new aircraft engine for Carl Collingwood.

And what about hiring that Russian immigrant, Andrei Gershuni, or anyone else who could have planted the bomb in that engine. All Derek needed to do to establish a reasonable doubt as to Mike Snead's guilt in the minds of the jurors would be to propose another plausible scenario and motive for the crime than the one being offered by the prosecution.

But Derek was ever-mindful of who wrote the checks for his exorbitant legal fees. His invoices were paid by checks from Transport International, Inc., and because the CEO, Mike Snead, was in jail, those checks were signed by Shelley Bernstein. Derek wasn't about to press, much less destroy, Shelley on the witness stand and fatally jeopardize his attorney-client relationship. Shelley was on Mike Snead's side, but he surely wasn't willing to fall on his sword for the man. In fact, if Mike Snead were convicted, Shelley would in all probability take his place as president and CEO.

"I have no questions of this witness, you honor."

Chapter 60

Helen called her next witness, Bruce Collingwood, for one reason and one reason only: to engender sympathy for the victim and outrage at the perpetrator, whomever it might be.

Helen just wanted to get him talking about that terrible day and let the jury's imaginations do the rest.

"May I call you 'Bruce,' Mr. Collingwood?"

"Yes, please do. Everyone does."

"Bruce, you are the son of Carl Collingwood, who was killed in the aircraft explosion this past year, are you not?"

"Yes, I am."

"And you were present on that day, were you not?"

"Yes," Bruce said.

Stray noises in the courtroom evaporated, leaving an eerie silence with all eyes focused on Bruce. Helen could feel her strategy working.

"I'm sorry that I have to take you back to that time, but it is important to explain just what happened."

"I understand."

"Prior to the day of the explosion, were you involved in the development of that aircraft?"

"Yes, I worked for my father the whole time since we started building the prototype."

"The company was called 'Hummingbird Aircraft,' wasn't it?"

"Yes."

"Did this name have any significance to your knowledge?"

"The name was mom's idea, really. We were building an aircraft that could hover like a hummingbird."

Helen was at the top of her game. The reference to his "mom" was the next best thing to having the victim weeping on the stand.

"When did you start the project to build the aircraft?

"About six months before the . . . uh, accident. But we started preparations well before that. We drew plans, rented space, ordered parts, hired people, that sort of thing."

"Did you order an engine for the aircraft from Transport International?"

"Yes, my father did."

"When as it delivered?"

"About a couple of months before the aircraft was finished. We dropped it in and hooked it up right away."

"Did you ever run the engine prior to the day of the test flight?"

"Oh, sure. We ran it several times to spin the wing fans and test the system."

"And it ran well?"

"It ran beautifully. It was a fine engine."

"Did anyone in your company, Hummingbird Aircraft, examine the engine carefully after it arrived?"

"There was one employee, Bill Paley—he works for me now—who was in charge of the engine. I think he did, but you'll have to ask him."

"You say he works for you. Is Hummingbird Aircraft still in existence?"

"Yes, I took over the company, and we are building a new prototype."

"The same design as the one that your father developed?" Helen asked.

"The same plans, yes, with some minor changes. We simplified a few things."

"How close are you to the first test flight?"

"We'll be ready next week, as a matter of fact."

"Really? Have you announced this to the press?"

"No, we wanted to keep it a secret." Bruce rolled his eyes and quipped, "I guess everyone will know now, won't they?"

The courtroom, quiet until now, twittered in brief relief from the seriousness of the testimony.

"Bruce, from the time that the engine arrived at Hummingbird Aircraft until the day of that test flight when it exploded, could anyone except the employees of the company have had access to the engine to plant a bomb or something like that?"

"I have asked everyone on the team, and they all say the same thing. No one was allowed to come into the hangar except us. And there was always at least one of us there day and night, working on the airplane."

"Thank you, Bruce. I have no further questions."

Helen and Derek changed places seamlessly in front of the witness and Derek began gingerly and respectfully to cross-examine.

"Bruce, have you ever met Mike Snead, the defendant who is on trial here?"

"Yes, sure. Many times."

"When was the last time you saw him?"

"I was at his office when he was arrested."

"Really? Why were you there?"

"I went there to ask him for money to continue the development of the aircraft with Hummingbird Aircraft."

"You were sitting in his office, speaking with him when the police arrived, is that right?"

"Well, in a conference room, yes."

"Did you ever get the money?"

"Yes, we did. His company loaned us the money. They gave us a credit line of five million dollars."

"At what interest?"

"It was a favorable rate. Two points below prime."

"What were the terms? When do you have to pay back the loan?"

"We don't as long as the aircraft can fly. Transport International received an exclusive license to make and sell the aircraft. It's a royalty-bearing license, so after a few years, the royalties will have paid off the loan."

"What happens then?" Derek asked.

"What do you mean?"

"Once the loan is paid off, will the royalties continue?"

"Oh, yes. They received some stock, and I hope they'll invest more. It will be a long-term relationship with TI."

"So it was Mike Snead's company that has made it possible for you to continue. Is that correct?"

"Yes, that's right."

"And to your knowledge, was it Mike Snead's company that provided money to your father to develop the aircraft in the first place—the one that exploded, I mean."

"Objection!" Helen rose from her seat. "No foundation."

"Overruled. The witness can answer," the judge said firmly.

"My father received a ten-million-dollar investment from the company to build the prototype," Bruce said.

Derek paused a moment to look at his notes. He was quite aware that Bruce was now CEO of the company and could have had a motive to remove his father from that position. Upon brief reflection, however, Derek decided not to go there.

"Thank you, Bruce. That is all the questions I have."

Helen rose again and addressed the court. "I have a few questions on redirect, your honor."

"Then by all means, proceed."

"Bruce," Helen began softly, "was it not true that Mike Snead at one time tried to destroy your father's company by pulling the funding and taking ownership of the original patents?"

"Yes, that's true, but he later changed his mind. He made up for it by funding the company again and giving the patents back."

"Didn't he once say that he wanted to eliminate your father as competition?"

"Objection!" shouted Derek, jumping up. "The question was asked and answered."

"No, he didn't," said Bruce, oblivious to the objection.

"He didn't?" Helen asked with a sarcastic tone in her voice. "Just a few minutes ago, you testified—"

"He said he wanted to eliminate the *aircraft*, not my father."

"Thank you, Bruce. You may step down now."

Derek jumped up again. "One more question, you honor?"

The judge glared at him. "All right, go ahead, Mr. Taliz."

"Bruce, your company, Hummingbird Aircraft, is currently funded by Transport International, is it not?"

"Yes, sir."

"Thank you. No further questions. You may step down."

"Just a moment!" Helen stood again and addressed the judge. "One more question, your honor?"

Finally exasperated, Judge Davis had no choice but to agree. "All right!"

"The funding that supports your company now—that was granted *after* your father was killed in the aircraft explosion, was it not?"

"Yes," Bruce admitted

"Wasn't it possible the defendant, Mike Snead, granted this funding to make people believe he wanted to help Hummingbird Aircraft when, in fact, he wanted to stop the company from developing the aircraft?"

"*Objection!*"

"Sustained!" Judge Davis shouted, her anger fuming. "Ms. Meisner, you *will* sit down. Ladies and gentlemen of the jury, you are instructed to completely disregard that last question. It has no factual basis in this lawsuit and should not have been asked. Ms. Meisner knows this, and I am very close to holding her in contempt."

Helen sat down as instructed, but she knew the jury understood her point.

Chapter 61

"The prosecution calls Bill Paley to the stand."

Helen Meisner gave the bailiff a nod, and he opened the door to the courtroom to admit the next witness. Paley walked hesitantly down the aisle through the gallery to the bar where Helen stood waiting. Helen smiled at him, opened the gate, and led him to the witness box, where he stood for the swearing-in process.

"You may be seated, Mr. Paley. Make yourself comfortable and adjust the microphone so that we may all hear you."

Paley complied and Helen commenced.

"Please state your full name and occupation, Mr. Paley."

"William C. Paley. I am an aircraft engineer working for Hummingbird Aircraft."

"How long have you worked for this company?"

"About two years."

"Two years. So you worked for Hummingbird Aircraft during the time that it constructed a prototype of a new kind of aircraft?"

"Yes," Paley said.

"What were your duties and responsibilities during that time?"

"I was in charge of the electrical and power systems, installing the electrical wiring and the engines and generators that powered the aircraft."

"Did there come a time that another company, namely Transport International, delivered an engine for this aircraft?"

"Yes, I remember well. We were all excited to receive and install that engine."

"Why is that?"

"It was a new type of engine called a 'barrel' engine that had a wobble plate instead of a crankshaft."

"A wobble plate? What is that?"

"Well, it doesn't really wobble, but it looks like it does. It's a large, round plate that rotates about its central axis. It has sinusoidal cam surfaces on either side that move the pistons back and forth when it rotates. The pistons move back and forth in cylinders all arranged in parallel around the central axis like bullets in the barrels of a Colt revolver."

"That's way too much information, but I asked for it, I guess." Helen cracked a smile, and some of the jurors smiled with her. "Why this kind of engine? Why did you need it for the aircraft?"

"It's small and extremely light for the power it puts out. That engine could literally pick the aircraft up by its bootstraps and lift it vertically."

"Did you have occasion to examine the engine carefully?"

"Yes, I was curious about it and looked it all over. I ran it too, first on a test stand and then in the aircraft after we installed it."

"Did you see anything that might have caused it to explode?"

"No," Paley said.

"Are you sure?"

"Yes, I looked it over carefully, but I found nothing on the outside at least."

"On the outside? How about the inside?"

"I didn't open the engine up. I didn't look inside."

"Could there have been a bomb inside?"

Derek was on his feet in an instant. "Objection! This witness just said he didn't look inside."

"Your honor," Helen responded. "Mr. Paley is an aircraft engineer and very familiar with the workings of this engine. I'm sure he has expertise he can share with the court."

"May we approach?" Derek started walking forward even before the judge had given her permission. Helen followed Derek, and the two stood shoulder-to-shoulder in front of the bench.

"All right, counselor," Judge Davis said and looked at Derek. "The man has seen the engine. Why can't he give a layman's opinion?"

"Your honor, we don't even know if he's seen the engineering drawings for the engine. All we know is he didn't open it up and look inside."

"Ms. Meisner, why don't you ask him that? If he's seen the drawings, I'll allow it."

Derek went reluctantly back to his seat while Helen continued.

"Mr. Paley, did you ever see engineering drawings of the aircraft engine that came from Transport International?"

"Sure. I worked with the TI engineers as they designed the engine to our specifications."

"So you are intimately familiar with what was inside?"

"Yes," he said.

"All right then. Could there have been a bomb inside the engine?"

"Do you mean if there was room. Yes, there was plenty of extra room in the casing around the wobble plate."

"One could fit a bomb in there?"

"Yes."

"A bomb big enough to blow up an airplane?"

"Objection!" Derek interposed. "The witness is not a bomb expert."

"Sustained. Ms. Meisner, I believe you have gone quite far enough with the witness on this subject."

"All right, your honor." Helen acquiesced and said, "I have no further questions."

Derek came forward again and smiled pleasantly at the witness.

"Mr. Paley, you worked for several years for Carl Collingwood, did you not?"

"Yes, I did. I enjoyed working for him and his company."

"You would like to find out who killed Carl as much as anyone, wouldn't you say?"

"Yes, I would. Everyone in the company was terribly shocked by this, especially his son, Bruce."

"And you work for Bruce now, don't you?"

"Yes," Paley said.

"Completing a new prototype, are you?"

"We're just about done, yes."

"From what you have heard about the aircraft explosion, would you agree that it was due to a bomb on the aircraft?"

"Yes, it had to be. There was no other way that aircraft could have . . . uh—"

"Exploded like that?"

"Yes, blown up."

"From the video of this tragedy, it would appear that the explosion was initiated by that engine. Assuming this to be true, where do you suppose the bomb could have been?"

"Inside the engine."

"So someone must have put it there, correct?"

"Yes."

"You testified that from the time the engine arrived at Hummingbird Aircraft, you never opened it up to see inside. Is that right?"

"Yes, that's right."

"So the bomb must have been placed in the engine before it was delivered to your company, is that right?"

"Yes, it must have."

"So one of the engineers who built the engine at TI must have placed the bomb there. Wouldn't you say?"

"No, that couldn't be true."

"Oh? Why do you say that?"

"Because I know those men. They could never do such a thing."

"You knew them?"

"Yes, I worked with them to develop the engine. I even saw them put the engine together."

"You did?" Derek looked at the witness incredulously. "Well, why didn't you say so?"

"Nobody ever asked me."

"You saw them assemble the engine?"

"Yes," Paley said.

"And close the engine up?"

"Yes."

"And there was no bomb?"

"No bomb."

"So how do you suppose the bomb got in there?"

"Objection!" This time, it was Helen's turn to stop the flow. "Pure speculation."

"I'll allow it. After all, Ms. Meisner, you started this inquiry."

"It had to have been one of the other employees at Transport International."

Derek was wading into unknown waters and was well aware he could suddenly sink, but on a hunch, he kept going deeper, looking for something helpful there hidden beneath the water's surface.

"Could it have been the CEO, Mike Snead?"

"No," Paley said.

"Why not?"

"The president never came down to the factory floor."

"Then who might it be?"

"I'm thinking it's a guy named Andrei Gershuni."

"Oh? Why him?"

"He was there."

"Was he a member of the engineering team?"

"No, I don't know what his job was, but he wasn't working on the engine."

"Then how could he have planted a bomb?"

"He was always hanging around as we were building the engine. Then just when we were about done, he moved to the night shift when everyone else was off."

Not wishing to press his luck, Derek stopped wading further. "Thank you, Mr. Paley. That is all."

"Redirect. Ms. Meisner?" queried the judge.

Helen was not about to risk wading deeper into the unknown waters. "You may step down, Mr. Paley. I have no more questions either."

Chapter 62

"You can come in now, Juli." I had been sitting there for two hours waiting to be called as a witness.

After Bill Paley's date with the court, it was to be my turn. Helen Meisner, the prosecutor, asked me to be ready to take the witness stand at Mike Snead's trial just as soon as Bill finished testifying. It was nearing the end of the week, so I thought she might have me start the following Monday, but she told me to wait in the hallway outside the courtroom on that Friday just in case she could fit me in. So there I sat.

I arrived during the lunch break while people were away, hoping against hope that Bill Paley would finish early enough that I could testify and get it over with that day. Much as I wanted to help Mike Snead in proving his innocence, coming all the way back again to the far end of Long Island from New York City on Monday was not the way I wanted to help him. As it happened, I was called upon to do just that, but some very dramatic events intervened.

At about three in the afternoon, the courtroom doors opened, and Bill Paley stepped out. He winked at me, told me testifying was "not so bad," and headed for the elevator. Fifteen minutes later, the court bailiff came out of those doors, found me sitting there, and invited me in.

"You're next. Juli," he said. "The prosecutor would like to have you testify for about an hour before we break for the weekend."

"Will I have to come back?"

"Don't know. My guess is she'll try to finish today, but it depends on how it goes and what the defense counsel decides to do."

I entered the courtroom and walked the short distance down the aisle to the bar where Helen Meisner was waiting. She opened the gate and led me to the witness stand. There, I was sworn in and took a seat.

After the preliminaries, during which I gave my name and occupation, Helen got into what happened on that terrible day.

"Were you present on the day when Carl Collingwood was killed by an aircraft explosion?"

"Yes, I was there with my husband, George, to cover the flight test for our news website."

"So you witnessed the tragedy?"

"Yes, I did."

"And your husband, George, made a video, is that right?"

"Yes," I said.

"Following that fateful day, have you conducted an investigation as to how this tragedy occurred?"

"Yes, I have."

"Have you come to any conclusions as a result of your investigation?"

"Yes."

"What were they?"

"We believe a bomb was planted inside one of the engines and that this bomb was triggered by General Bellamy of the US Army, who was present during the test flight."

As she asked this question, out of the corner of my eye, I saw Derek perk up and lean forward. He gave no objection to the question.

"Do you know why General Bellamy was there at the test?"

"Yes, he was in charge of procurement for the army and came to evaluate whether the army should buy the aircraft."

"So if the test were successful, the army was going to purchase a number of these aircraft?"

"That's what Carl Collingwood said. He had a lot riding on the outcome of this test."

"Ms. Gables, were you aware that the defendant, Michael Snead, and General Bellamy were friends?"

"Objection! Foundation. And what do you mean by the word 'friends?'"

"I'll withdraw the question. Ms. Gables, do you know if Mr. Snead and General Bellamy knew each other before the day of the tragedy?"

"No, I don't." I really didn't. I had no idea whether Mike knew General Bellamy, although come to think of it, they must have. Over the years, the army had purchased an awful lot of equipment from Transport International, and General Bellamy must have been a factor in these purchases. I wasn't about to volunteer anything that might lead the jury to think there was a conspiracy.

The prosecutor backed off and took a different approach. "On the day of the tragedy, when General Bellamy arrived, did you notice anything strange about Mr. Collingwood's behavior?"

"Well, yes, kind of."

"How is that?"

"It's hard to explain. Just that he didn't say anything, anything at all, when General Bellamy arrived."

Just then something occurred that set in motion a chain of events that affected much more than the course of this trial. *The cell phone in my jeans pocket buzzed.*

"Uh, excuse me." I reached into my back pocket, brought out my cell phone, and looked at the screen. In bold letters, there appeared: "Admiral O. West. US Navy."

When I looked up, I saw the entire courtroom was aghast at the interruption, especially the judge. At first, there was an eerie silence, and then, all of a sudden, everyone started speaking at once, even members of the jury. There was practically pandemonium. The loudest voice, however, was that of the judge. She banged three times with her gavel, which brought the voices down to a tolerable level, and shouted, "*How could you bring that cell phone into the court building?*"

"I just brought it in. No one said anything."

"You were supposed to give it to security at the door," the judge said with a nasty tone.

"I always carry it in my back pocket. I don't even think about it anymore."

"Give it to me, now!" The judge held out her hand to grab it. Because the witness chair was right next to the judge's bench, her hand was inches from my face.

"I can't do that, your honor."

"*What?*"

"I have to take this call." With that, I slid the iPhone's screen switch to the right to unlock the instrument and placed it to my ear. "Hello, this is Juli Gables speaking."

The judge pounded her gavel again. "*Stop*, or I will hold you in contempt!"

"This is Admiral West. Oliver West of the US Navy. You interviewed me some time ago and left me your business card."

"Put down that phone!" Judge Davis was going nuts, but I had to speak to Admiral West.

"Yes, admiral, I remember. What can I do for you?"

"Bailiff, snatch that phone away. This is outrageous behavior, and I won't stand for it!" The judge pounded again, even louder this time, and it was making it difficult to hear the admiral.

"I have something important to tell you. I'd like to meet you right away."

The bailiff made a grab for it, but I ducked and turned my head away. He was coming for me now, but I managed to say, "I'll meet you in your office tomorrow at ten, admiral. Gotta go now. Bye!" before I handed over the phone.

"Young lady, you are in contempt of court, and I fine you $250! You will pay the clerk before you leave this building." Judge Davis shouted angrily at me but then quickly turned to address the jury and said with a surprisingly even tone, "Now, ladies and gentlemen of the jury, we have completed the first week of trial. Before I dismiss you for the weekend, I would like to explain a few rules."

The judge then proceeded as calmly as you please to instruct the jury to ignore my insolent behavior and to refrain from reading or watching any media that reported about this crazy trial.

Chapter 63

The next morning, I left George at home to hold down the fort and took a 7:30 flight from LaGuardia to Reagan National. Not many passengers were on that early Saturday milk run, so the trip was really quite comfortable. And heck, Delta made tons of money on the "New York to Washington" shuttle during the week, so it could afford to send some half-empty flights back and forth on weekends.

When I got off the plane, I walked over to the Metro, bought a two-dollar-and-fifty-cent pass at the vending machine, and took the next train three stops to the Pentagon. After I got off the train, I followed the small crowd upstairs, where I again found myself in the Pentagon lobby.

As I walked up to the main desk, I recognized the MP in charge. It was Officer Milktoast, but this time, I had an appointment with an admiral, no less!

"Hello. Remember me?" I handed him my New York driver's license with my photo.

"Not really."

"I was here with a friend a few months ago and asked for naval procurement."

"I don't remember. So sue me," he replied a snotty tone of voice.

"I have an appointment with Admiral Oliver West."

"Oh, really?" Officer Milktoast was not at all impressed until he made an entry on his keyboard and looked at a screen in front of him. "Well, I'll be darned if you don't!" He stared at my face with a new respect and compared it to my driver's license picture. "This picture doesn't do you justice," he remarked as he handed the license back. "The admiral's on the fourth floor, E Corridor. room

E 4-956." He handed me a badge to paste on my lapel and show the security guard.

"Can I head on up?"

"Yes, of course. Just keep your badge visible." What a difference a few months make.

At ten minutes to ten, I opened the door to the naval procurement office and walked in. There was an attractive woman in uniform at the front desk and a large room half full of both male and female clerks facing their computers. I was surprised at the activity on a Saturday, but then, on second thought, I realized this was the military. They operated 24-7.

The woman looked up and asked politely, "May I help you?"

"I'm here to see Admiral West."

"You're Juli Gables, right? The admiral's expecting you. Step right this way."

The woman smiled, got up from her desk, and led me through the maze of cubicles to a conference room in the back. As we entered, she pointed to a side table and offered, "There's coffee, tea, and Danish. Take whatever you like. I'll tell the admiral you're here."

Boy, what a difference from the last time I met the admiral! What was this about?

I took advantage of the coffee and goodies on the buffet and picked a central spot at the conference table. Within a minute, the admiral appeared in his Superman-looking, white naval outfit, his brass glinting reflections from the recessed overhead lights. He was certainly dressed to impress.

"Hello, Ms. Gables. Thank you for coming on such short notice." His voice was deeper than I remembered. You had to like this man. I could only hope that he was one of the good guys in this strange conspiracy, which I was yet to understand.

"I'm at your service, sir."

"Please sit down." I sank quickly into a conference chair. "What I'm about to tell you is absolutely confidential. You are not to ever say where, how, or from whom you received this information, do you understand?"

Yes, sir."

"If you ever tell anyone you heard this from me, I'll deny it."

"I understand."

"All right, then. The reason I called you is that I'm conflicted."

"Conflicted?"

"I don't know who is rightly giving commands. In layman's terms, I don't know who my boss is."

"The last time we met, you told me about a man named Brodsky. Charles Brodsky. He's the assistant to the vice president."

"Yes, and I have now come to wonder if the vice president is on the same team as the president."

I sat there, dumbfounded. I couldn't think of what to say, so I just listened.

"The president is scheduled to give a speech at West Point on Wednesday morning. What I have learned is that he will announce what he believes is a major breakthrough in medicine. He wants to change the way we think, particularly the way we treat our enemies. It has to do with the way we wage war.

"Now I would have liked that he would give this speech at the naval academy in Annapolis, but that's not important now. The point is that I believe there are forces that are plotting against him, forces that want to take over our constitutional government."

"How did you learn this?"

"To be absolutely honest, it is just a surmise. The speech has been announced, but the subject of the speech has been kept a closely guarded secret. Also, Vice-President Chernoff, I learned, has taken over Georgetown University Hospital and is maintaining absolute control over any and all information that emanates from there. I'm not privy to any inside information myself, but I have connected the dots, and it doesn't look good to me."

"So what can I do? Why did you call *me*?"

"Because I really don't have any solid information, and even if I did, I don't know who to be loyal to—the president or the vice president."

"Even I know the answer to that. The president is the commander in chief."

"Yes, but suppose the president wants to disband the military. I'm not sure I could support him in that."

"Our president is very smart. He wouldn't do anything that was not best for our country."

"You must understand that I have an extremely strong interest in this matter, and I also want to do what is best for our country. So I have had some loyal members of my staff quietly researching what the president is going to say. I believe that they found it, and I'm going to tell it to you now."

Again, all I could do was sit there. The admiral had sucked all the air out of the room.

"There's a man in California, a Professor Rob Sapinsky at Caltech. He's the man with the breakthrough. I'm convinced he's the key."

I continued to say nothing. It was a bit embarrassing, but I was struck dumb.

"You should go there and speak to him. Find out what's going down."

I just stared at the admiral, my mind awhirl.

"As I said, I'm conflicted, and I cannot reveal my knowledge to anyone."

I finally got a grip on myself, and I managed to utter, "Thank you, admiral."

I stood up, and so did he. I noticed his eyes were moist. He held out his hand, and I took it. He looked down at me from his six-and-a-half-foot height and said, almost sadly, "Good luck, Juli."

I felt the weight of the country at that moment—or was it the weight of the entire world? I don't know. But it was clear there was a crisis in our country, and I was now right in the middle of it.

As Admiral West turned to leave, I got up the courage to ask one final question that had been burning inside me since yesterday. "Admiral, why did you call *me?*"

"I noticed something about you when you ambushed me. You're plucky. If anyone can make sense of this, I know you can."

And with that, he was gone. On the conference table was his business card, and I picked it up.

Chapter 64

I'm sure you've seen those commercials for a cell phone where a person looks up an airline schedule and makes a flight reservation right there on the phone using nothing more than that tiny screen with the even tinier keyboard. Well, I'd never done that before, but it was high time I tried. I climbed into a waiting taxi outside the Pentagon building, told the driver to head for Dulles Airport, and pulled out my iPhone.

I'm pleased to report that I'm not a complete dunce when it comes to using that little gizmo. By the time we arrived at "departures"—the words "arrivals" and "departures" at an airport are confusing, or is it just me?—I had booked an outbound flight to LAX and a return on Sunday afternoon to JFK. I even got myself a room for the night at the Ramada Inn in Pasadena.

My next two calls were to my husband, George, and to Professor Sapinsky, in that order. I gave George my schedule and asked him to pick me up at JFK when I got back. We needed to drive out to the tip of Long Island on Sunday so I'd be there ready to testify first thing Monday morning.

The professor was next. I urgently needed to see him, but it would be a miracle if he happened to be home on Sunday and willing to see *me*. After all, who was I but a nosey reporter? I got his number from 411 in Pasadena and placed the call. He answered, thank *God*. The conversation went like this:

"Hello?" His voice, not mine.

"Professor Sapinsky?"

"Yes, that's me."

"My name is Juli Gables. I'm in Washington, DC, and have just been in discussions with Admiral Oliver West. Do you know him?" I had to use *something* to get some credibility.

"Can't say as I do, no."

"Well, he has the president's ear, and he told me about the work you have done. I'd like to discuss it with you."

"He's working with the *president?*"

"On the military side, yes." This wasn't a white lie. What military person isn't working for the president? Maybe not "with" but at least "for."

"I'm sure he has questions. What can I do for you?"

"I'd like to meet you at your office."

"My laboratory, you mean. That's doable. When would you like to come?"

"Tomorrow morning. I can be there at eight."

"Done. I'll e-mail you the address."

Whew! That was all there was to it! I gave him my e-mail address and boarded the plane.

The very next morning, there I was at the Caltech campus. The university was in session, and students were everywhere. I found my way to the department of neuroscience and located the professor in his laboratory.

I was dressed in the most businesslike outfit I owned, the same conservative suit that I had worn at the Pentagon. I hoped against hope that he would take me seriously. I need not have worried.

The professor turned out to be a delightful conversationalist who seemed to take a liking to me. I certainly did to him. We talked for four hours about his work. As a reporter, I know how to ask leading questions, and he reveled in the attention. His claim to fame was finally going to be recognized after all these years of tedious research. His star was on the rise in a clear sky over the distant horizon.

What I learned was that mankind had developed or rather "evolved" in a niche. We are neither carnivorous nor vegetarian, neither monogamous nor polygamous, neither polyandrous nor polygynous. Our schizophrenic psyche leads to unnecessary competitiveness as well as endless disputes between individuals and between groups of individuals, resulting in crimes, wars, and misery. Up to now, there has been little understanding of how the brain is wired to deal with these stressful situations; however, after much study and many failures along the way, Professor Sapinsky had eventually been able to postulate and prove a theory of how the brain works.

By noon, I had what I had come for. I knew what the president's speech would be about on Wednesday, and I knew whom Admiral West should call his boss—the real commander in chief.

Before we parted, Rob—we were on a first name basis by that time—gave me a present. It was a canister about the size and shape of a home fire extinguisher that contained what he called the "peace gas." When breathed in even in small traces, a person could no longer react in anger or even in annoyance. Any ideas that might lead to violence were no longer "logical" and were, therefore, rejected by the mind.

I could not help thinking that Rob was using the gas, because he was so much at peace with himself and with me, who had come to him as a complete stranger and was now his friend.

In the end, I could barely tear myself away. Rob called a cab for me, and I headed back to the airport with my special present. However, as I held it in my lap and looked at it, I realized, to my dismay, that I had a problem. I could never get the canister through airport security!

At first, I had no idea what to do. Then I remembered I needed to call Admiral West to tell him what I had learned from the professor. At the same time, I could ask if he could help me somehow to get past security. I fished around in my pocket to find his card and then placed the call.

"Admiral West? This is Juli."

"Hello! I've been thinking about you, Juli. How is it going?"

"I have some good news and some bad news, admiral. Let me tell you the good news first."

"Go ahead."

"I've just spent four hours in a meeting with Professor Sapinsky. His discovery is *real*. If the president announces this discovery on Wednesday, I'm convinced he'll make history."

"That's *incredible!*"

"Yes, it is, but there's also some bad news."

"Okay, what is it?"

"The professor gave me a canister of his "peace gas," but I can't get it through security at LAX."

"*That's* the bad news?"

"Yes. I can't come home with—"

"That's not a problem at all."

"It's not?"

"Not an insurmountable problem, anyway. At LAX, go to the general aviation desk. Use my name, and they'll take care of you."

It was that easy. It's not what you know but whom you know.

I did as I was told and was escorted by an agent out to the tarmac behind the building. There, waiting for me, stood a sleek Learjet that had just flown in from the naval airbase in San Diego. The pilot waved to me from inside the cockpit, and I walked over to the open door, the kind that opened downward to provide those little steps up to the cabin.

"Climb up here and let's go!" shouted an attendant in naval uniform who stood in the doorway. He didn't need to ask me twice.

It took just four hours to cross the country and land at MacArthur Field on Long Island. On the way, the attendant showed me how to use the phone, and I called George to tell him when and where we were going to land.

Boy, was he impressed as he watched me step out of that private plane!

Chapter 65

George and I stayed overnight at a cheap motel and planned our strategy for the next day. We needed to accomplish two things: First of all, we wanted to try out the peace gas to see what it could do, and second, we needed to stall for time to find the who, what, and why of the bomb that had killed Carl Collingwood.

We also planned how to go about doing that, but I'm getting a bit ahead of myself. All I can say is we suspected that our country's VP, Rick Chernoff, and his chief of staff, Charles Brodsky, were somehow involved.

Early Monday, before the morning rush, we entered the court building and waited in line for our turn to pass through security. I held in my hand the "peace gas" canister. On the side of the can, I had written "Oxygen" with a Sharpie in bold letters. In my back pocket was my cell phone. George was right behind me, his cell phone hidden, too. For some reason, my phone had passed through the metal detector before, and I was hoping against hope that it would do so again. George's too, because that was part of our plan.

"What's this?" the security guard demanded as I showed him the canister. "You can't bring that in here!"

"I've been called to testify today, and I have terrible asthma. It acts up, especially when I get nervous. I've just got to have my oxygen handy."

"Now I've heard everything! You have to turn that thing in over there." He pointed to a small window where people were handing in their cell phones and getting receipts to pick them up later.

"I . . . I just can't. I can die if I don't inhale. Have you ever had asthma?"

"Do you have a note from a doctor or something?"

"No, I never had this problem before. I've never had to enter this building."

"You're a trial witness, you say?"

"Yes," I said.

"What trial?"

"Mike Snead. He's on trial for murder. I'm a witness for the prosecution." *Now I'm sunk*, I thought. *He is going to check with the clerk and find out that I testified last Friday, when I didn't have an oxygen bottle with me.* But instead he looked at me and smirked.

"For the prosecution, eh? All right. You go on up there and nail that bastard."

Geez, I didn't know that Mike was that unpopular. The media frenzy about this case might not be fair to him, but it worked for me!

George had no problem getting through, and our cell phones made it through, too. We went straight up to the courtroom on the second floor and took front seats in the gallery right behind the bar. Being early, there were only a few other eager beavers, media people who wanted to be sure they got a seat. We saved a place for Aleksa, whom we knew would be there soon.

I whipped out my phone and called Detective Dan. I didn't want to bother him on Sunday, but I had no such reservations now. The man had to go to work.

"Hello, Inspector Gavin? This is Juli. You said to call if I had any information for you. Well, I do. I've got to see you. I'm at the court right now, and I have to testify this morning. But can we meet for lunch? Yes, that's good. I can find it. See you there at about 12:30. Oh, and I'm going to bring my husband, George. Yes, we're together again now. And also Aleksa and her cameraman, Brian. Yes, that's right. We work together now too. Okay, see you then."

Aleksa arrived about ten minutes later and spotted us. "Oh, my God, you guys!" she said as she came down the aisle toward us. "It's so great to see you together!" Was she an idiot? Didn't she know she was the cause of our problems?

I bit my tongue and greeted her. "Hello, Aleksa. We've got a lot to talk about. Come sit with us." In order to solve this crime and to do so before the end of this trial, George and I needed all the help we could get. Aleksa sat down, and both George and I went at it and gave her an earful. Aleksa's mouth dropped as we laid out our plan. "Oh my gosh, of course!" This was all we needed to know. She was on board, and we were almost good to go.

As we talked, the courtroom quickly filled up until the court clerk announced the arrival of the judge and called the court into session at precisely 9:00.

Helen stood up and called me forth to the stand. I complied, taking my canister with me.

"You understand you are still under oath," she admonished.

"Yes, ma'am." I was going for "super polite" this time around.

"All right then. When we left off last Friday, you had testified that you thought General Bellamy had something to do with the bomb that exploded, killing Carl Collingwood. Is that right?"

"Yes, he—"

Helen cut me off. "Do you know for a fact that General Bellamy planted the bomb?"

"No, he couldn't have—"

Again, she wouldn't let me finish. "Do you know who placed the bomb in that engine that was installed in the aircraft?"

"No, I'm not certain, but—"

"Could it have been someone at Transport International?"

"Objection!" Derek quickly jumped up and stood there, ready to fight.

"I think we have established the bomb was placed in the engine at Transport International."

"Your honor, puh-lease!" Derek said sarcastically. "This witness knows nothing about what took place at Transport International, if anything happened at all."

"He's right, you know, Ms. Meisner."

"Please indulge me for a moment, your honor. We are trying to get at what the witness knows."

"All right, I'll allow it. But get right to the point."

Helen turned to me again "Please answer the question."

"I . . . uh, forgot. Could you ask it again, please?" I wasn't stalling. I really didn't know the question anymore.

"Could you read it back?" Helen asked of the court reporter.

She looked back through her tape and read, "Could it have been someone at Transport International?"

"Yes, I believe so."

"Have you ever heard of a man named Andrei Gershuni?"

"I've heard the name."

"Who told you?"

"Detective Daniel Gavin. He mentioned the name to me."

"In what context?"

"I guess you would say he was a suspect in the investigation."

"Of Carl Collingwood's murder?"

"Yes," I said.

"What did you learn about Mr. Gershuni?"

"Objection!" Derek said. "Hearsay."

"Did you ever meet Mr. Gershuni?"

"No, I didn't."

"Weren't you investigating the crime too?"

"Yes, I was."

"Then why didn't you contact him?"

"I was going to, but he died."

"I have no further questions, your honor."

The people in the courtroom gave a long sigh, as if they had collectively held their breath and, altogether, they had exhaled. The judge banged her gavel and said, "Let's take a short break. Be back in your places in fifteen minutes." With that, she literally jumped off the bench and disappeared through the side door to her chambers.

Chapter 66

I had an important date with Inspector Dan and Aleksa Williams, but before we were allowed to leave for the lunch break, I desperately wanted to finish the job I had to do on the witness stand. After I came down off the stand during the midmorning break, I went over and asked Derek how long he thought he would take in cross-examination. He told me, "Not long at all. Just one or two questions, and we're done." Great!

Back on the stand, as soon as Derek commenced the cross-examination, I immediately knew where he was going. Thankfully, I was able to head him off the track and bring my examination to a close.

"Ms. Gables, may I call you Juli?"

"Of course. Everyone does."

"Juli, you have known the defendant, Michael Snead, for quite a long time, haven't you?"

"Yes, a couple of years, at least."

"Would you say that you are friends?"

"Not at all. He doesn't invite me to his home, and I don't invite him to mine." This little remark of mine got a brief rise from those in the courtroom. Nothing like a bit of dark humor to break the tension.

"I just want everyone to know that you're not here as an advocate for this man. You're not biased in any way."

"I suppose that's true," I said. "I always tell it like it is."

"Have you formed an opinion of the defendant's guilt or innocence?"

"Objection!" Helen jumped to her feet. "That's for the jury to decide!"

The judge brushed the objection off. "I'll allow it."

"Please answer the question."

"I really don't know. I guess Ms. Meisner is right. That's for the jury to decide."

Derek looked deflated. "That's all I have for this witness, your honor.'

"Redirect, Ms. Meisner?"

"No, your honor, the prosecution rests. Ms. Gables, you may step down."

Just then my phone rang in my back pocket. I pulled it out and looked at it.

"*Ms. Gables! What did I tell you about bringing a cell phone into this courtroom!*" the judge shouted, incensed, as I knew she would be.

I put the phone up to my ear. In fact, it was just George calling from the gallery, and I winked at him. I saw the bailiff running toward him to grab his phone away, but it didn't matter. He had done his job by calling me just at the right moment. I kept going as if the call were from someone else outside the courtroom.

The judge now screamed at me, "*Put down that phone . . . now!*" She was about to go ballistic, just as I had hoped.

Another court bailiff headed my way, so I held on to the phone but picked up the canister and pressed the button on top, aiming the spray in the direction of the judge. Everyone in the courtroom stared aghast, wide-eyed, and the bailiff, heading toward me, stopped short in his tracks, not believing what he was seeing and, as if I had a gun, afraid to come closer.

We all looked at the judge, who just sat there and blinked a few times. Everyone expected her to either explode in anger or fall down dead, one or the other. But in fact, as I thought she might, she cocked her head, looked thoughtfully at me, and said calmly, "What is that gas?"

"It's oxygen, your honor," I lied. "It says so right here on the bottle." I held up the canister and showed her the writing.

"Well, that was quite a surprise, Ms. Gables. But it calmed me down. I'd like another whiff of that, uh, oxygen, or whatever it is. It went right to my head."

"Do you feel all right?" I asked, suddenly feigning concern.

"Oh, yes. Quite all right. Excellent, in fact. Never better. I feel like a judge *should* feel, in complete control of my emotions."

By this time, the peace gas had spread throughout the courtroom, and everyone started looking at each other and talking at once in strangely rational tones. Pure logic seemed to have replaced biased opinion, and courtesy had replaced any arrogance in demeanor. We were all friends!

My impromptu test had just been proven to be a tremendous success. *The peace gas worked like a charm!*

Now it was time to put it to use.

Chapter 67

Judge Davis, now in a pleasant mood, called a two-hour lunch break before Derek would begin his defense. As I came off the witness stand, I walked over to the defense table to ask Derek to stall for more time.

"Is that really oxygen?" Mike Snead asked intently as I approached his table. He sat in the middle with Derek and Burt Crowe on either side.

"No, it's not. I don't have time to explain, except to say that the president of the United States is set to make an announcement about it on Wednesday and we've got to work fast. Derek, how long do you plan to take for your defense?

"A day or two, at most. Mike will take the stand tomorrow. We'll probably present final arguments on Wednesday, and then it's up to the jury."

"Can you delay it just one more day? Wednesday is cutting it close. I can get here by Thursday. I think I know what happened, but I'll need a couple of days to work it out."

"Heck, you know me," Mike said with a smile. "I can BS on the stand for days if you want."

Derek glared at him sternly. "You'll be under oath."

"So?"

"Just until Thursday. That's all I need."

"You got it!" Mike gave me the high sign. For the first time during this trial, he looked like his confident self.

We met at a diner across the street from the courthouse. Aleksa, Brian, George, and I got there first and took a round table for six. As we sat and talked about the trial, Dan walked in and joined us. Now that we had our team together, we got right down to business, and I explained the plan.

Aleksa lent her support. "It seems like a long shot, but we don't have the luxury of time."

"The way it is now, we're locked out of the information flow," I added. "This is the only way I see that could possibly work." We all looked at Dan.

"I agree. Let's do it."

"Don't you think we should bring in the FBI?" George threw out the important question.

Dan gave the answer: "The FBI could ruin everything for us. For all we know, they have a direct line to the VP, and they'll tighten security there at the hospital. They'd be waiting for us and shoot us down like sitting ducks."

"Once we have the video in the can, the FBI will have to act," Brian noted. We all nodded in agreement.

I looked at our little team, and for a moment, I couldn't help wondering if we could really pull this off. *We* were going to save our country? Come on! What was I thinking?

Yet we had no choice but to move ahead, and move fast. It was showtime!

Chapter 68

We all drove our own cars to Washington, DC—Daniel with his unmarked police sedan, Aleksa and Brian in their TV van with a roof antenna that transmitted to a satellite, and George and me with our little Honda. In the trunk of our car was the canister of peace gas and our belt buckle with the built-in, hidden camera.

We arrived at about eight in the evening and checked into the GU Hospital Hotel. We went straight to bed because we were tired and needed to get our rest for the big day.

At seven the next morning, we walked over to the hospital. I must say that Aleksa had done us proud. Our plan called for her to exude maximum sex appeal, and she exceeded our expectations. Her hair and makeup were straight off the cover of *Cosmo* magazine. She wore a fabulous, floral-pattern dress that was cut halfway down to her naval to show off her spectacular boobs, and she walked on her pink Isaac Mizrahi loafers—the better to run with in case we had to scoot. In one hyphenated word, she was a man-magnet.

She also carried a cute Coach bag concealing a small six-shooter pistol and some spare ammo. She had purchased these long ago to carry for protection when she sallied forth into dangerous areas of the city.

As we walked, I watched the eyes of passersby and witnessed an example of woman power I never even knew existed. They stared and followed her with their heads. These people—doctors, nurses, patients, visitors, whatever—they had no shame. One young guy had to catch himself before he bumped into a lamp pole!

The other members of our little party were all but invisible next to her, but that didn't bother us in the least. Dan carried his Glock pistol in a chest holster under his jacket. Brian brought his handy cam slung on a shoulder strap. George wore his video belt, and I lugged the canister of peace gas. We were locked and loaded.

The hospital lobby was nearly empty at that hour, except for a couple of security guards on either side of the entranceway and another one standing next to a receptionist behind the front desk. We passed right by the desk and walked toward the elevator bank. We expected the security guards to stop us, but like everyone else, they appeared mesmerized by the sight of Aleksa. One of the elevators stood waiting at the lobby floor, its doors open, so we all entered it and pressed "SB" for sub-basement. As the security guards just stood in amazement, the doors closed and down we went to the bowels of the hospital. We had made it in.

Aleksa, bless her little mean-girl heart, took the lead. By this time, I was getting very nervous, almost to the point of sweating, but she carried herself with all the assurance and self-confidence that only a drop-dead gorgeous babe can know. When the elevator doors parted, she headed straight for the security office, with us following like sheep. Even Dan, I noticed, was not exactly exuding mister macho-man at that point.

Another security guard stood outside the closed door of room SB29 and held up his hands as we walked up, signaling us to stop. "Whoa," he said in a frosty voice. "Where do you think you're going?"

Aleksa beamed her trademark smile and addressed him with her trademark, "Hi, honey." The guy underwent a visible meltdown right in front of us. You had to see it to believe it.

"How can I help you?" he asked her, almost politely now.

"Could you let a girl in there for just a moment?" Aleksa nodded toward the door. "I need to ask a friend of mine a question." The man hesitated as he scanned Dan, Brian, George, and me up and down.

"These guys will stay out here," Aleksa added quickly. "I need only a moment with my friend."

"What's your friend's name? I'll ask him to come out."

"No, no." Aleksa was following the script that we had prepared. "He needs to watch those video monitors. You never can tell when a terrorist will make his move to attack the vice president." She smiled at the guard again and winked conspiratorially. For that moment at least, the two of them were the only ones standing in the hallway. We weren't even there.

After he grabbed the key chain on his belt and put one of the keys in the lock, the man opened the door just enough to let Aleksa in and then closed it again. When he turned around, he folded his arms across his chest and stared at the four of us standing there, looking goofy with fake smiles on our faces.

A minute passed and then two and . . . we suddenly heard Aleksa's scream from within the guardroom. The stone face of the guard in front of us changed in an instant to reflect horror, and he turned back to the door. Dan pulled out his weapon while Brian aimed and switched on his video camera. The door opened and revealed the guard inside holding a gun to Aleksa's head.

What happened next occurred so quickly it was nearly a blur. Dan lunged at the guard in front of us and forced his body through the doorway into the guardroom, where he fell to the floor. This action so startled the guard in the room that he forgot about Aleksa and aimed his gun at Dan. Aleksa spun around and gave him a knee in the groin that bent him double, while a third guard in the room who was initially caught by surprise but now galvanized into action smashed into her and brought her down. By this time, though, George had rushed in behind Dan and had taken another crack at the guard that had held Aleksa. He grabbed the muzzle of the guard's gun with his right hand and tried to pull it away while he held the man's arm in a vice-grip with his left.

Meanwhile, when all this mayhem was going on, Brian was rolling the camera while I just stood there, dumbfounded and pretty much frozen in place. At the outset at least, it was an even match between the three guards and our three warriors, but I feared they would eventually get the best of us. So I fired my weapon into the fray, which was the peace gas.

It is difficult to do justice to describing what happened next. It was like a video that had been running in fast motion at first had now briefly frozen frame and then had continued running in slow motion. Everyone in the guardroom got a grip, slowly stood up, and looked around at each other, seemingly in a daze. It was like, "What the heck are we doing? Can't we all just get along?"

Chapter 69

"Who are you guys, and why are you here?" asked the guard who had attacked Aleksa and had brought her down. He appeared to be the boss.

Dan took over the role of spokesman, which was all right with me and everyone else in our group apparently. "I'm Dan Gavin. Detective with the Sufflok County Sheriff's Office out on Long Island. These are my deputies." A white lie, of course. "Aleksa, whom you met, and Juli, George, and Brian, who has the camera."

"I'm Billy, and these gentlemen are Sean," he said and pointed to the guard we first met outside, "and Keshawn." The last was the African-American man who Aleksa had subdued with a knee to the groin. Keshawn made a face as if to say, "Let bygones be bygones." "So what do you want?"

"We're here investigating a murder, and we think Vice-President Chernoff has some information about this that could be useful."

"Why don't you just go see him? He's on the seventh floor."

"I don't think he'll want to speak to us. You see, he's . . . um, implicated. Anyway, we assume there's the Secret Service guarding him, and we won't be able to get past those guys."

"That may be true. And they're a tough bunch, believe me. But you haven't answered my question. What do you want?"

"We'd like your help."

"Our help?" Billy was more than a bit incredulous. "What can *we* do?" He emphasized the word "we" as though he and his fellow security guards were the last people on earth who had any influence over the vice president.

"We figured you'd know a way in."

"Even if we wanted to, which we don't, we're not aware of any chinks in his armor. This place is locked down 24-7 like Fort Knox.

I don't understand it really. What's the big deal with protecting these bigwigs, but the Secret Service takes it very seriously."

"We have a plan."

"Oh? A *plan*?" Billy said sarcastically "Does it include breaking the law?"

"No, not at all, but it might seem that way. One of us needs to get up on the roof." Dan explained this as if it were the most normal thing in the world to climb around on the roof of a hospital.

"The *roof*? What's up on the roof?" Billy was on his guard and becoming more and more skeptical by the second.

"All right. We're going to have to take you into our confidence. If a word of this ever gets out, we all might as well leave this country on the next plane." Dan looked Billy in the eye. "Can you keep a secret? Just for twenty-four hours. That's all we need."

"Depends on what it is. If you're talking about attacking the vice president, *I don't think so!*"

"Nothing like that. We just want him to tell the truth to the American public."

"Well, that'll be a trick. It'll never happen." I was beginning to like the way this man thought. He knew, like everyone else in this country, that politicians never told the truth and could never be trusted. Never, perhaps, until now. Thanks to the peace gas, we finally might, just *might* have a chance to make some changes in the way the system worked.

Dan continued, "Do you realize what just happened? The first minute, we are fighting together like junkyard dogs, and the next, we're standing here, talking civilly to each other. Wouldn't you agree that's a little strange?"

"Well, yeah, that's like . . . never happened before, but why not? Seems like a good way to go."

"Yes, it seems reasonable now, but that didn't seem so reasonable a few minutes ago. What made us change?"

"I don't know. You tell *me*." All three guards were standing around Dan, listening intently to what he had to say.

"Juli here squirted us all with a special gas. It turned off our proclivity to fight and allowed our brains to run on reason. It interrupted our animal impulses."

"You sure that's a good thing?" Sean wondered aloud. "Suppose our enemies get hold of this gas and use it on us?"

"We'd just use it right back on them, and all the fighting would stop."

"Does it work against criminals?" Keshawn wanted to know.

"Like a charm." Dan really didn't know the answer, but he punted well. "No more violent crime!"

"Geez! Are we going to be out of a job?" The guards looked at each other, suddenly concerned.

"Heck no! But your job will be a lot safer. The violent crime will fade away, but there's still white-collar crime. People will always be figuring out new ways to grab other people's money."

"I guess that's a good thing," Billy quipped.

"Now I can answer your question about the roof. I want to go up there and squirt the gas into the ventilator. Everyone in this whole hospital, including Chernoff, will change their way of thinking."

"Hmm." Billy cocked his head and thought for a moment. "Now that would be a *really* good thing!"

Chapter 70

Billy went to the computer and pressed a few buttons. A floor plan of the hospital appeared on the screen. He clicked with the mouse, and four copies of the floor plan emerged from the printer.

Within a few minutes, we had figured out the ventilating system, and Billy had explained how to get up to the roof just above the section of the building where Vice-President Chernoff was holding court. What we didn't know was whether the Secret Service kept a twenty-four-hour surveillance on the rooftop.

"You don't have a camera up there?"

"No," Keshawn said. "At least we can't pick it up on one of our monitors."

"Maybe that means the roof's not covered, but we have to be sure. Could you ask someone?"

"If we do, it will tip them off," Billy interjected. "Maybe I should just go up there and see what they've got."

"Mind if I come?" Dan asked. "I'll bring the canister, and if the coast is clear, I'll get it done."

"Okay," Billy agreed. "But we'll also bring our weapons just in case we meet resistance."

Dan nodded. "That's a plan."

"Wait just a minute. You'll have the gas with you? We won't need weapons!" Billy laughed out loud. "We'll just squirt gas at them!"

"Sorry, but that won't work," I piped up. "Hate to say it, but the gas needs to be in an enclosed space, or it won't work."

"Bullets are still good?"

"Yup," I agreed, smiling inwardly. It was a huge comfort to have this man and his two fellow guards on our side.

Brian, who had been standing in the background and running his camera since we had barged into the security office, finally

239

stopped recording and came over to us. "Man, is this exciting! What a story. I'm going up with you guys to the roof, right?"

Dan and Billy looked at each other. Then both said at the same time, "No, it's too dangerous."

"But I'll stay clear and just shoot video. We've *got* to get this in the can. It's breaking news!"

Billy was a tough sell. "What are you? Some kind of warfront TV journalist? The answer is 'no.' When the bullets start flying, we want you out of the way."

Dan was more sympathetic. "We don't know what we're going to run in to, Brian. We don't want to have to worry about you."

"But I'll stay way back and use the telephoto. No one's even going to know I'm there."

"If anything happens, you'll hide—that's what you'll do. Even if it means not covering the action, right?" Dan was softening.

"Absolutely!" Brian beamed.

Billy reluctantly caved too, but not without a parting admonishment. "If we say 'go!' you go. No back talk. You just leave. Is that clearly understood?"

"Yes, sir!"

"All right then. Let's head up."

I gave Dan the canister. "Here's our good luck charm. Take good care of it."

"I will. I promise." Dan was in a somber mood.

"I know. It's in good hands." I kissed Dan on the cheek, and he gave me a squeeze. Neither of us knew what to expect next. We were just following our plan as far as we could take it.

Over to one side, I saw Aleksa do the same with Brian. She whispered something to him I couldn't hear, but I could see. A quick glimpse was all I needed. She had taken the pistol out of her purse and secretly handed it to him. I looked over and saw that neither Billy nor Dan had noticed.

So off they went, all three of them. Dan said he would call my cell after he had injected the ventilation system with a good dose of the peace gas. Aleksa, George, and I stayed in the security office with Sean and Keshawn to watch the monitors. If we saw any unusual activity anywhere in the building, we were to call Billy.

Chapter 71

What happened next was pieced together after the fact from speaking with our "warriors," who survived their altercation with Vice-President Richard Chernoff's Secret Service agents and from viewing Brian's video. It's all there in digital glory. Our objective was to inject our peace gas into the air stream that ventilated Rick Chernoff's floor of the hospital—he occupied the whole seventh floor—and then ask questions of his staff and perhaps of Rick himself to "smoke out" his nefarious scheme, whatever it might be.

It all hinged on Dan Gavin getting to the inlet of the ventilator to carry out our plan. This step was crucial. As Princess Leia once said, "Obi Wan Kenobi, you're our only hope." We just as well could have called our gas bottle "Obi Wan."

Although we knew that the plan was a bit of a stretch, we thought at the time we'd have a pretty good shot. Little did we understand who and what we were up against.

Our crew left us with our prayers for their safety and headed for the elevator bank. Billy, now their leader, noticed that the button for the seventh floor didn't work, so he pressed six. When they arrived on the sixth floor landing and looked around, they took in what appeared to be normal hospital operations except for men in dark glasses and dark suits who were stationed in front of every stairway exit. Billy tried to use one of these exits but was turned away and told to go back down on the elevator.

There were only two possible ways to reach the ventilator on the roof: First, from inside the building, either up the stairwell or via the elevator, and second, from outside the building by means of a fire escape or by helicopter. Because the building didn't have a fire escape and we didn't have a helicopter and because the elevator was locked out, we had to force our way up the stairs. Good luck to us when there were Secret Service goons with guns blocking the way!

After we took a few video shots of the SS, which was like waving red flags in front of their faces, the crew went down to the fifth floor and tried to enter one of the stairwells from there. No one stood guard at this exit, so they slipped in. With Brian's video camera rolling, our men started walking up the stairs, Billy in the lead. They were halfway up to the sixth floor when they encountered resistance. As he looked up, Billy stared into the barrel of a gun. "Hold it right there," came a voice from behind the gun.

Billy didn't think twice but lunged straight into the agent's legs and grabbed on to prevent the man from keeping his balance. The man went down, falling hard and firing a shot toward the ceiling as he banged against the stairs. Billy quickly reached forward for the man's gun and held on tightly as they struggled together. Dan dropped the canister, pulled out his gun, and jumped into the fray behind Billy.

The single shot fired from the agent's gun had sounded the alarm. It was as if Billy had stuck his finger in a beehive and awakened all the bees. Suddenly, five more black-suited SS men appeared in the stairwell, all with guns pointed at Billy, Dan, and Brian. Brian stood back at first, taking all of this in with his camera, but then put the camera down slowly, feeling "sheepish" (his own words), and raised his hands in the air.

"What is this?" Billy demanded with his bravest bravado voice. "Stand down, or we'll call security!"

"We *are* security, you idiot!" one of them said. "Put your weapons down and put your hands on your heads." The security guard who fired the shot picked himself up and trained his gun on Billy. "You bastard! Where the fuck do you think you're going?" He was borderline over the edge he was so angry.

Down in the sub-basement in room SB29, Aleksa, George, and I watched the video monitors but saw nothing of this because it all had taken place in the unmonitored stairwell. Eventually, we saw the exit door open on one of the monitors that was aimed at the sixth floor exit near the elevator landing, and out they all came, with our men surrounded by the SS agents carrying guns. The game was over, or so we thought.

Not knowing what else to do, we ran for the elevator bank and headed straight for the sixth floor. On the way up in the elevator, we looked at each other, and with unspoken communication, we agreed we only had one weapon left: It was Aleksa with her sex appeal. George had the presence of mind to turn on his video belt as the elevator doors opened, and we stepped out on the landing, Aleksa first.

Aleksa played her part like a princess or maybe even a queen. Everything about her at that moment shouted, "Look at me!" All heads turned.

The men in black were standing in the hallway, surrounding Billy, Dan, and Brian, who all had their hands on their heads. Aleksa walked up to the one who appeared to be the leader and addressed him, "Hi, honey, what's happening here?" All the others stopped and stared. You could have heard a pin drop.

"Uh, can I help you?" was all the agent could say. He was in meltdown mode.

"Is there a problem here?" Aleksa smiled innocently, not knowing quite what to do next. Meanwhile, George and I tried to communicate silently with our three hostages, who looked back at us helplessly. I noticed the canister was missing, as was Brian's camera, and I assumed they were still in the stairwell.

"No problem at all." The man tried to smile back at her but couldn't muster more than a fake-looking grin. "We're the US Secret Service." He said it as though he was trying to impress. "And you?"

"I'm Aleksa Williams. CBS News. And you're on camera." Startled, the agent looked around for a camera but found none. He dropped his fake smile and looked at her suspiciously.

"You're not who you say you are."

"Watch the CBS Evening News tonight, handsome. You might see yourself there."

"That's pretty hard to believe since you've got no camera, but I'll take that as a compliment."

"What are you going to do with those men?" Aleksa queried, nodding toward Billy, Dan, and Brian while trying to keep the conversation going.

"Police business. Can't answer that."

"Are they under arrest?"

"Yes, we have them in custody."

It was time for me to speak up. "Do you mind if I leave by the stairway?" The agents didn't know that I was associated with Aleksa, so I made my move. "I'll walk down here," I said as I took steps toward the exit door.

The SS agent looked at me for the first time and frowned. Both George and I had been pretty much invisible, standing there in the presence of Aleksa. "Go ahead," he said absently. "Just make sure you go down and not up."

"Okay, thanks." As I passed by our crew with their hands on their heads, I looked at Dan and gave a short nod. Dan winked back, confirming that the canister was out there where I thought it must have been. I quickly exited, leaving George with Aleksa to record everything on the wide-angle video in his belt buckle.

I found Brian's video camera and the canister where they had laid it in the stairwell and returned, canister in hand. I opened the door and let go with a healthy spray at all the people standing there. Eyes turned at once from Aleksa to me while I spritzed them and said brightly, "Hello, everybody! I'm back!"

The SS agent that had been flirting with Aleksa glowered at me questioningly, wondering what had just happened. Billy, Dan, and Brian dropped their hands and stood there calmly in the middle of the group of agents, knowing no harm would come to them now that they were all breathing peace gas. The tables had turned, and our saga had entered a brand new chapter.

Chapter 72

"Who the heck are you people? Why are you here?" the SS agent asked in a calm voice, realizing finally that we were a cohesive group. Dan stepped forward and spoke for all of us.

"I am Inspector Dan Gavin, a detective from the Suffolk County Sheriff's Office, and these are my colleagues. We are here on a mission of utmost urgency. It is our belief that the vice president is planning an attack on President Bradley."

There it was, out in the open. Dan's bold stroke would probably be perceived as the wild conspiracy ravings of just another crackpot, but what he said was absolutely true. We all looked at the agent and waited for his reaction. The agent's eyes grew wide as he looked us all over, apparently wondering how he should respond. He finally said, "Let's talk. I have suspected for some time there is something sinister in the wind."

I couldn't believe it! We weren't the only ones who thought this way. I breathed a silent sigh of relief as Dan continued, "We need to speak with the vice president right away. Can you arrange that?"

"He's running a highly confidential operation up there." The agent pointed upward with his finger, indicating the seventh floor. "Access is strictly controlled. What makes you think he'll speak with *you?*"

"For the very same two reasons why you are speaking to us now: The first reason is Aleksa." Everyone turned to look at her, and she beamed back brightly with a pretty smile. "And as for the second, we have a special gas that keeps people rational." I held up the canister and smiled, too. For the first time, everyone looked at *me.* It felt really nice.

"A *gas?*" The agent was shocked. "You can't bring that thing up there!"

"What if the gas made your brain smarter? Could we use it then?"

"That's not going to happen, and you're not going to use it. Full stop."

"It already *did* happen. You're breathing this gas right now. Check it out yourselves. Don't you feel smarter?"

I took a chance at this, because I didn't know what they would say, but I didn't have another way to prove what the gas could do. All six SS agents looked at one another as though they expected to see some kind of a change in their physical appearance and, at the same time, stopped to reflect a moment on their own persona and mental ability. One of the men cocked his head thoughtfully and blurted out, "I think it's working. Son of a bitch, I think she's right!"

The others were having the same reaction, and all started talking at once. "I'm totally calm and collected!"

"I've never felt so much in control."

"I can almost feel my brain thinking."

"My brain's running on all twelve cylinders!"

The lead agent looked back at Dan and agreed to help. "Okay, I can bring you up, but from then on, you're on your own. Whatever happens there will depend on you, and I'm telling you they are not nice people."

"We'll take our chances," Dan replied. "Just lead the way."

"Before we go, we'll have to search you for weapons. I don't want any foul play. Not on my watch."

"Not a problem. Be our guest." Dan stretched out his arms and legs for a security search, and Aleksa, Brian, George, and I did the same. The agents had already disarmed our warriors and were not surprised to find us clean. We walked over to the elevator bank, and the lead agent pressed the "up" button. When the elevator arrived, he stepped in, inserted a key in the control panel, and pressed the number seven. I entered the elevator with my four colleagues and my precious canister. Billy stayed back to return to his post with Sean and Keshawn.

"There you are," the SS agent said. "I'll call up there and tell them to expect you."

"Who are you going to say is coming?" Dan wanted to know.

"I'm going to tell them we checked you out," he replied. "You're clean, and you have an important message for the vice president."

"That will do just fine," Dan said.

The agent stepped out of the car, and the doors closed us in. We were on our way to the top.

Chapter 73

When the doors parted, we stepped out and were greeted by two US Marines in full military uniform. Their eyes were immediately trained on Aleksa rather than my canister, which I clutched to my chest in an attempt to make it appear inconspicuous. Like laser beams, their eyes followed Aleksa as she stepped out of the elevator.

"Hello, fellas! I'm Aleksa Williams. I and my friends are here to see the vice president." She said this with such self-assurance it seemed as if she knew Vice-President Chernoff, which she didn't, and as if she had an appointment with him, which she also didn't. The tactic worked on the marines, though. They snapped to, and one of them immediately lifted the phone to announce our presence to someone within the inner office. The man seemed somewhat taken aback, however, at what he heard in reply and looked over at Aleksa as he held the telephone receiver to his side.

"Where are you from?" he called over to her.

"I'm from CBS News," she replied in an irritated voice, implying that he should know that.

The marine repeated the information to whomever he was speaking with on the phone and listened briefly. Then, with a puzzled look on his face, he replaced the receiver in its cradle and told us, "You can't see him now. You'll have to come back another time."

"We need to see him right away." Aleksa was undeterred. "This matter is extremely urgent, I'm afraid."

"The answer is no. I'm sorry."

It's just amazing what one can do if the use of force is not an option. The other four members of our party stood in front of me, blocking the view of the marines so they couldn't see the canister.

I pressed the button on top of the can to release some more peace gas, and we stood waiting for a moment for the gas to take effect. Dan then spoke up. "I'm Detective Daniel Gavin from the Suffolk County Police on Long Island, New York. It's extremely important that we see the vice president. It's a matter of national security."

Now that we were no longer in danger of physical harm at the hands of the marines and we could proceed in a civil manner, Aleksa stepped forward to the marines while Dan moved toward the main office door.

"Hey, don't go in there!" one of the marines shouted as Dan tried the door handle. It was locked. "What do you think you're doing?"

Dan knocked on the locked door to get the attention of someone inside. Apparently, someone did notice the knock because the telephone rang on the little desk in the hallway. Dan, who was closest to the phone, picked it up. As he told me later, someone asked, "What's going on out there?"

He replied simply, "The marines have requested your presence."

The door opened a crack, and a man, whom we later learned was Charles Brodsky, poked his head out. "What's going on?"

Dan, who had his hand on the doorknob the whole time, yanked it open. It was now my turn again to take action. I sprang to the doorway and, holding the canister over my head to avoid spraying Brodsky in the face, pressed and held the button down for as long as I could, sending gas into the cavernous office space behind the door. The marines, who were at first startled but then aghast at the sight, pushed Aleksa aside and headed straight for me. Peace gas or no peace gas, they weren't going to let this happen. They rammed into me like linemen in a football game, and I went down and dropped the canister as I fell, but not until I had given the office a healthy spray. *It's enough*, I thought, *to do the job, depending on the size of the space and depending on whether or not the vice president was nearby. We would soon find out.*

Brodsky, for sure, had received an effective dose, so when our little mêlée was over and the marines and I had picked ourselves up off the floor, I probed with some critical questions. George stood nearby and looked on with his video-belt recording the scene on the plug-in flash-drive memory stick.

"We need to speak with the vice president . . . right now," I said.

"What do you want?"

"We have an urgent message for him." I really had no such message.

"You can tell me. I'm his chief of staff."

"No, the message is just for him personally." I added bluff upon bluff.

"I'm authorized to speak for him and to receive all messages."

"It's about the president." I had surmised that much at least.

"What about the president?"

"When will it happen?" I knew *something* would happen at least.

"Tomorrow, during his speech at West Point."

"With a bomb?" I totally guessed. But it had to be either a gun or a bomb.

"Yes, the atomic bomb."

"How will it get there?" I figured it had to be by airplane.

"By train."

"Train to West Point?" I knew there was no such train.

"Train under West Point."

"*Under* West Point?" *What?*

"There's a tunnel."

Just then, the vice president himself appeared, as if out of nowhere, and looked at us suspiciously. "Charlie, what's going on? Who are these people?"

"They want to deliver a message. They said it's for your ears only, but I told them I was authorized to receive it."

"So what was the message?"

"They didn't tell me yet."

"All right then," the vice president said and looked at me strangely, "Let's have it."

"The message, Mr. Vice President, is this," I told him right to his face. "Don't set off that bomb."

"Oh, yeah? And who says there's a bomb?"

"Sir, do you really want to kill all of those people?"

"Of course I don't. I don't want to hurt anybody. I just want to be president."

Chapter 74

We were stunned!

But not so stunned that we didn't all in our different ways immediately go into action. But first, we had to get out of there.

"Stop them!" ordered Vice-President Chernoff, suddenly realizing this little group of insurgents had just tricked Brodsky into revealing information that might lead to his destruction. He panicked visibly, becoming red in the face, and charged directly at Dan like an angered, frenzied bull in a Spanish bullfight.

Standing right behind Dan, I stood my ground and sprayed him again, straight in the face this time, holding the spray button down for what seemed like forever. Like in that movie *The Matrix*, time dropped suddenly into slow-slow motion as we saw Chernoff stop his blind charge and gather himself. He had been about to ram forward into a rampage of rage, but now instantly calm and collected, he had turned on a dime and presented a new face to us, the face of reason. Now it was all about damage control; however, he knew that we knew, and it was too late for him. There was nothing he could do but to stop us from reporting what we had seen and heard.

"May I invite you to join me?" he asked with an even, almost charming voice while he motioned with his hand to the door behind him. "Come on in. Let's talk about this." To his horror, we quickly but respectfully declined. It was over for him.

Detective Dan flipped open his cell phone and immediately placed a call to the FBI right there in front of everyone, including Chernoff, Brodsky, and the two marines. Dan was about to make a memorable day for whoever took the call at the other end.

The rest of us didn't wait around for the FBI to arrive.

Brian, who stood in the back with his camera rolling and was closest to the elevators, pressed the call button. When an elevator arrived, the four of us stepped in and headed downward, leaving Dan to deal with the devil and the devil's defeat. It was news time, and Aleksa, Brian, George, and I were all *journalists*, first and foremost. We had the breaking news story of the century, and we—and we alone—were going to break this story to the world. It was so incredible. You couldn't make this stuff up!

When we landed at the lobby, Aleksa and Brian rushed outside and found an open spot in front of the hospital from which to record their report for TV broadcast. Aleksa used her compact to touch up her hair and lipstick, while Brian panned around the sprawling hospital building and paused to zoom in on the Georgetown University Hospital sign. George and I observed them briefly and then quickly left, Aleksa holding the CBS microphone in her hand and starting her monologue to the red recording light on the video camera. All we heard was, "This is Aleksa Williams reporting from outside the Georgetown University Hospital, where Vice-President Richard Chernoff has secluded himself with his staff for the last couple of months."

Aleksa's report, we knew, would be uploaded to the CBS news desk and broadcast to the world within the hour. George and I had to work fast if we wanted the Gables Report to be ready with details of the story the TV broadcast news couldn't possibly provide. And we also had a video that Brian didn't have, a close-up of Chernoff saying, "I don't want to hurt anybody. I just want to be president."

Much as I appreciated Aleksa's diligence in digging the dirt—it was indispensible, I knew—in the end, this news business was and is a competition, and I wasn't about to let Aleksa get all the credit for this news story. No matter how gorgeous and glamorous she was, the Internet-based Gables Report was going to win the ratings race!

George and I hurried back to our hotel and worked with my laptop to create the text and graphics for the website. We viewed the belt-buckle video that George took while he had been standing behind me outside Chernoff's office, and sure enough, although the sound was a bit fuzzy and we would need to add subtitles, the images were amazingly clear and covered all the important action. We would probably have added subtitles to the video anyway just for emphasis.

While George prepared the graphics, I wrote and rewrote the accompanying text, going back as far as our first trip to DC, exposing Chernoff's fraudulent health problems and explaining how we suspected he was involved with at least two and maybe three murders. George left a box in the main screen area for a sidebar, and I wrote that, too. We used our standard word counts for the main story and the sidebar, leaving a number of unreported tidbits for future stories. Within an hour, we had uploaded the page to the website on the server of our service provider using our ID and password, and we finally signed on to www.GablesReport.com. There it was in all its glory!

PLOT TO ASSASSINATE PRESIDENT BRADLEY
Evidence implicates Vice-President Chernoff
VP says, "I don't want to hurt anybody. I just want to be president."

That done and with us satisfied with this first story, George and I turned on the television to watch the reports come in on CNN. Things were going so well! It was electrifying to see live footage of a SWAT team arriving at the hospital to take down the vice president. There must have been fifty newshounds standing right at the spot where Aleksa had made her broadcast earlier that day. As Chernoff was brought out the front door in handcuffs with FBI agents on either side, he was definitely not a happy camper. He scowled as the crowd surged forward and shoved microphones in his face and frantically asked questions. He refused to answer any of them but did make one short statement. As he looked straight at the camera, he shouted, "This is all just one big mistake. It's the hyperactive imagination of a crazy newswoman who is using it to draw interest to her junk news website." I knew exactly to whom he referring, of course. That was *me!*

I shuddered and looked desperately at George. Could what he said be true?

Chapter 75

Early the next morning, George and I checked out of the hotel, threw our stuff in our car, and headed north to New York City. George drove while I rode beside him in the passenger seat and took calls on my cell phone. Everybody—and I mean *everybody* including George's mom—wanted to know what had happened yesterday. It was a great therapy just to sit and talk about it. My stress level had come *that* close to my personal redline, and I was still a bit shaky from the ordeal.

Meeting the vice president of the United States would have been stressful enough for anyone, but meeting him as an adversary was over the top.

I also got call after call from fellow members of the media. They weren't so much interested in what had happened yesterday as they were about Chernoff's remark when he had been arrested. They poked and probed into the sources of my information, shamelessly unabashed. After the first few calls, I knew what they were up to. They were trying to get a sound bite from me that would prove Chernoff was right about that "crazy newswoman." They were as transparent as glass and so *competitive*, trying to bring me down because, I assumed, they were jealous of my success. They all started by congratulating me on my investigative reporting. Then some of them shifted to saying, "We're colleagues, both plying the same profession," trying to gain my trust so I would drop my guard and spill the beans.

What they didn't know was that I considered myself an outsider and that I worked independently of their closed-door fraternity of erudite wordsmiths and also that there really were no beans to spill. Other than members of my family, I gave them all bupkis—that is, until I received a call from my friend Shelley Bernstein at Transport International.

"Hello, Juli." I recognized instantly the deep, gravelly voice.

"Hello, Shelley. How's the company doing?"

"Not too well. We still have our problems selling military stuff to the government."

"Did you see my website? I broke a story about the vice president."

"That's what I'm calling about. I think there's a connection."

"Really? What have you got?" Shelley had been such an excellent source of leads in the past, so I knew I was about to receive another good one.

"Nikki Borisnikoff is coming in this afternoon on a plane from Russia."

"How'd you find that out?"

"Can't tell you that, but it's significant, don't you think?"

"Him coming in?"

"Just at this time."

"Maybe," I said. "Where's he landing?"

"Right here in New York. JFK."

"I'll try to be there. Thanks."

"Don't mention it. Oh, and Juli—"

"Yes?"

"How did you get wind of Chernoff's plans?"

"I have a contact in the navy."

"Oh, really? Who's that?"

"Admiral Oliver West."

Because he had told me what he had wanted to tell me and had learned what he had wanted to learn, Shelley hung up. I sat there in silence, thought for a while, and then switched off my cell phone. I let more incoming calls go to voice mail before I finally spoke to George. "That was Shelley."

"I know. What did he want?"

"He said Nikki is flying in this afternoon to New York."

"Should we meet the plane?"

"I don't think so. He won't tell us anything, so why bother?"

I switched on the car radio to listen to the news. I leave the radio dial set to my favorite station, a channel on XM called "POTUS," which doesn't stand at all for "president of the United States." Instead, they call it "Politics of the United States for People of the United States." That's cute, right?

The top of the hour AP Radio News, which came on at ten o'clock, was about Chernoff's arrest and his protestations of innocence. He had spent an uncomfortable night in police custody but was expected to be released today and to make an announcement at half past noon, which was the exact time the president was scheduled to deliver his speech at West Point. It was the second news story that had me riveted:

> The FBI is looking into the allegations that Vice-President Chernoff had plans to explode some kind of bomb at West Point during the president's address to the cadets. They are taking this very seriously, although no evidence of such a bomb has been found. As a precaution, the FAA has issued a no-fly zone in the airspace over the military academy, and air traffic to Westchester Airport has been diverted to overfly the wealthy estates in nearby Greenwich, Connecticut.

"The train!" I almost shouted at the radio. "We found out the bomb's coming in by *train*!" No sooner had I thought this out loud than the announcer continued:

> The FBI has also halted a CSX freight train that was scheduled to pass through the tunnel under West Point at about 12:30. They have searched every one of the seventy-six freight cars in the train as well as the two diesel engines and have found no evidence of a bomb."

For the second time in the last twenty-four hours, I was stunned. I sat there in the car, traveling north with George at seventy miles an hour on the New Jersey Turnpike, with a sinking feeling in my stomach. Maybe I *was* a crazy newswoman with a hyperactive imagination.

Chapter 76

We continued north along the Jersey Turnpike in silence for a while. At this point in our relationship, George and I were so closely in synch that we were thinking each other's thoughts and we didn't have to do more than touch base with each other from time to time. I eventually felt guilty staying out of communication with the outside world and turned on my cell phone to pull down my messages. The very first one was from Bruce Collingwood.

"Juli, I've just got to speak with you!" The excitement in his voice was infectious, and I sat up and listened intently. "I'm in the air! I'm calling from our new airplane, and it *works*! Call me back—on my cell, obviously—as soon as you get this message."

I immediately checked the push-down stack of incoming calls, found his number, and hit "call." He answered on the first ring.

"Juli, thanks for calling back. I've never been so happy and excited in my life! We conducted our first test flight this morning—you know, with the tether and everything—and the airplane went straight up five feet and hovered. I couldn't believe it!"

"That's fantastic, Bruce! Congratulations."

"Well, here's the best part. I pushed my luck and had our guys unhook the tether. I took the plane up again and then used the front engine to fly forward. I circled the field, came back, and stopped in midair! I'm amazed how well this thing flies."

"George and I would have loved to have been there."

"I really regret not inviting you guys and Aleksa, too! We had no idea it would go so well, and we didn't want to jinx it. You know what I mean?"

I felt of pang of jealousy when he mentioned Aleksa. George and I thought we had an exclusive on this one. "Where are you, anyway?"

"Right now, I'm crossing Long Island Sound, heading to Westchester Airport. I'll do a touch and go and fly back to Suffolk."

"Touch and go? You mean on the runway?"

"Yeah, I don't want to show them the VTOL stuff. I want to keep it secret until you and Aleksa take your pictures and we announce it."

There was that name again—Aleksa. I said, "I have another idea."

"What's that?"

"You can land in a parking lot, can't you?"

"Yeah, anywhere. I can go straight up and down."

"George and I are driving north on the Jersey Turnpike. We'll be at the Vince Lombardi Service Area in about twenty minutes. That's the last rest stop before we reach New York."

"Not a problem. I can find it," Bruce shouted over the background sounds of the aircraft. "It's a beautiful day up here, and I can see for miles!"

"George and I will get set up, and we'll do a full report of your landing."

"Now you're talking. See you there!"

I pressed "end" to end the call and went back to my phone messages. The next one was from Dan Gavin.

"Juli, we have a problem. Call me ASAP." His voice sounded grave, which was not like him, so I did just that. I found the number and pressed "call."

"Dan, this is Juli." I tried to sound breezy, but as soon as he came on, I lost all pretense and went straight to grave mode myself.

"Everyone's taking this thing too lightly," Dan began. "The vice president denies any plot, and everyone believes him because they *want* to believe him. The FBI has declared a "no-fly" zone over West Point and has combed the place with their bomb-sniffing dogs. They're convinced the president is safe."

"What about the tunnel?" I could feel my fear factor rising rapidly.

"Turns out there's a railroad tunnel right under West Point. The FBI stopped the trains that are scheduled to pass through there today. They also checked every train and found nothing. Nada!"

"You think our news reports scared them off?"

"No! I have a really bad feeling about this. Suppose—" I held my breath. I didn't know where this conversation was heading, but Dan was clearly not convinced the president was out of danger. "Suppose they have their own railroad car with a . . . bomb." Dan avoided saying the "A" word. "They could run right into that tunnel and *blam!*" It was too horrible to imagine.

George pointed to a sign as we sped by, signaling that we had a mile to go before the rest stop. I needed to end this call with Dan.

"Dan, I've gotta go now. What can we do?"

"They should guard that tunnel, but as far as I know, no one's paying attention."

"Can *you* do it?" I pressed him. "Can you get a police helicopter and fly over there?"

"It's too late now. Helicopters are too darned slow. It would take over an hour to get there from here in Westhampton, and the president's speech starts at noon. Those helicopters are noisy, too! Assuming the bad guys have fire power, which is a no-brainer, they'd hear us coming and shoot us down."

"Do it anyway. Meet us there!"

"What do you mean?"

"I'm going over there right now . . . with Bruce Collingwood and his new airplane!"

Chapter 77

George and I stood together out in the open on the huge parking lot of the Vince Lombardi Service Area off the New Jersey Turnpike. We scanned the cloudless sky toward the northeast, squinting to buffer the bright rays of the late-morning sun. We watched for about ten minutes but saw nothing.

"Maybe he can't find it," George said dejectedly. He had set up his video camera on a tripod, aimed northward, ready to catch Bruce's plane when it came into sight.

I stood there with him, my "peace gas" canister in hand, ready to climb on board Bruce's plane when he landed. Every minute was precious.

We focused and refocused our eyes, but we saw nothing until we heard a fluttering noise behind us. When we turned around, we were almost too late to see the aircraft settling down in an open space like a big bird alighting with its wings outstretched. George quickly rotated the camera on its spindle and grabbed the final seconds of the landing on video.

I ran over, careful to avoid the propeller in the front that was feathered and spinning nearly noiselessly, and shouted up to Bruce, "I want a ride!"

The plane was a two-seater, one seat behind the other. Bruce was in the front seat and waved for me to stop and stay put until he killed the engines. I didn't want to waste any time, but I also didn't relish coming close to all those dangerously spinning blades, so I waited for all the movement and noise to cease before I rushed forward and climbed aboard. Bruce opened the cockpit door for me, and I stepped in, carrying my canister, and settled myself in to the seat behind him. He then pulled the door shut and started the engines again.

Bruce didn't seem at all surprised to have me join him. He assumed I was in my reporter mode and just wanted to experience a joyride firsthand. He looked over his shoulder and asked me with a big grin on his face, "Where to?"

I pointed with my index finger first up and then north. "I'll tell you on the way." The engine noise increased slightly, and up we went over the parking lot like a balloon rising. I looked down and saw George following us with his camera eye and waving. I waved back.

The hum of the front engine increased slightly as Bruce cranked in the variable pitch prop, and we began to move forward as well as upward. Within a few minutes, we were moving along at quite a fast clip. Scanning the horizon, I could see practically the entire island of Manhattan off to the right, and looking ahead in the far distance, there were the twin spires of the George Washington Bridge. Back on the parking lot, I knew that George was breaking down his tripod and packing everything in the trunk of the car. As we arranged, he would head over to JFK airport and wait for my call.

"Bruce," I said finally. "I've got something to tell you."

"Okay, but where are we going?" First thing's first.

"We're going to West Point."

"No can do. I hear there's a 'no-fly' NOTAM issued for West Point today," he said, referring to the FAA's notice to airmen. "The President's there today."

"Just head in that direction. We're not going that far. When we pass over the Tappan Zee Bridge, fly straight up the Hudson along the west side of the river."

Bruce gave me the thumbs-up sign to show he understood. I couldn't bring myself to tell him that we might now be heading into a fatal confrontation with a terrible, vicious enemy on this the happiest day of his life.

As we cruised along, I took a moment to take in the beautiful scene on this beautiful day. To the right, I saw the Interstate 287 snake through the greenery of Westchester County toward White Plains in the distance. Off to the left, the New York State Thruway headed due west past the Palisades Mall in West Nyack before it disappeared in the woods of Rockland County. The thruway, I knew, would turn north toward Albany and eventually west again and pass north of the Finger Lakes on its way to Buffalo.

On land jutting into the river, a cluster of geometrically designed gray buildings slid peacefully by on the right. Ironically, I recognized the Indian Point atomic power plant, the main source of power for New York City.

Up ahead was the Hudson River, smooth as black ice as it flowed between mountains, passing beneath the miniature suspension bridge called the Bear Mountain Bridge. Perhaps the bridge was not so tiny for those who had built it, but it was small nonetheless in comparison to the mighty Verrazano Narrows Bridge, which spanned the river just before it reached the sea.

Running along the left side of the river and also passing beneath the Bear Mountain Bridge were two railroad tracks, a parallel pair with their polished steel surfaces glinting in the sunlight. I tapped Bruce on the shoulder and pointed down, directing him to follow the tracks as we flew northward over the bridge. He nodded, maintained a steady altitude, banked to the left, and followed the tracks that led us forward, bending around the mountain up ahead.

As we came abreast of the mountain on the left, I looked ahead, following the tracks with my eyes, and saw the tracks disappear into a black tunnel at the base of another mountain. This mountain rose up sharply from the water's edge and leveled off to a nearly flat area upon which jutted upward the Gothic stone buildings of the military academy.

My eyes followed the train tracks backward toward our position until, looking downward at a sharp angle, what I saw made me freeze with fear. There, crawling north along the right-hand track, was a strange-looking, self-propelled railroad car, a pickup truck with a huge load in the back heading straight for the tunnel.

"Bruce," I leaned forward and spoke quietly in his ear. "There is something you need to know."

Chapter 78

How do you ask a guy to put his life on the line, no matter what the cause?

How do you tell him what the dangers are and expect anything but "no" for an answer?

I don't remember what I said. I just remember that he looked over his shoulder at me, his eyes wide with excitement, and said, "Let's do it!"

Then he turned his attention back to flying the aircraft and made a few swift adjustments to the controls, and we sank like a stone, falling directly toward the railroad car or truck, whatever it was. If there ever was a scary ride heading toward oblivion, this was it.

We came in silently from above and slightly behind the railroad car and landed like a pancake on top of it. Our wings wobbled from side to side as we slammed in, and for a second or two, I thought we were going to tip over to the right and slip off the side. I saw Bruce frantically working the VTOL controls and heard the wing fans whirl faster, raising first the right wing and then, when we tipped too far to the left, the left wing, until the aircraft settled down and sat there steady and horizontal, riding atop the beast below us.

All the while, the vehicle was moving at a fast clip forward toward the dark tunnel up ahead.

When he realized the danger, Bruce revved the front engine. He must have reversed the pitch of the front propeller blades because I could feel them pushing back, braking both us and the vehicle below. Pushing at first almost imperceptibly, but then pushing harder and harder, the aircraft propeller managed to slow until our forward motion, holding us back against the opposite force of the vehicle's engine and drive wheels that were working hard to keep us going. The propeller eventually brought us to a halt in a pitched battle of airplane versus railroad car, and then we even started to edge backward, the airplane evidently the winner in these two forces of nature. We didn't move very far before the high-pitched sound of the car's straining engine ceased and the car's brakes stopped us both—pardon the expression, but I couldn't resist it—dead in our tracks, and I heard a scream that made my blood run cold.

From inside the vehicle came an angry male voice that said, "Whoever they are, they're dead!"

Bruce shut down the engines, and we waited there in the aircraft cockpit for a moment, wondering what to do next, when two men emerged on opposite sides of the vehicle's cab and started climbing up to the place where we sat. The one on the left side had a gun in his hand. I reached down and grabbed the only thing we had to defend ourselves, the canister of peace gas.

The man on the left reached us first and, with his free hand, ripped open the cockpit door. He tore it away like so much tinfoil. With the other, he brandished his gun.

"What the fuck?" he screamed. Both Bruce and I sat there frozen, unable to speak.

The two men on either side glared at the aircraft in disbelief, assessing the situation mentally and giving me a chance to get a grip. I held up my canister, put the nozzle to my mouth, and pressed the valve button.

The odd sight startled the man with a gun. "Hey, what's *that?*" he demanded.

"It's nerve gas," I replied bravely. "One whiff, and all fear is gone."

"*Nerve* gas?"

"Gives you *nerve*." I stared him down, and he blinked!

"Nerve gas like . . . uh, in World War II?"

Meanwhile, I saw out of the corner of my eye that the guy on the other side pulled out his gun and aimed it at Bruce's head, who sat there frozen with his hands in the air.

"Alex, hold it!" the man on the left shouted. "I got this."

He looked back at me, frenzy in his fearful face. I just looked at him said as firmly as I could, "No, nerve gas as in *no fear.*"

"No fear? Even of dying?"

"Who's going to die?" I asked with a thin grin and all the courage I could muster.

"You are. We are. We're on a suicide mission."

"You're *what*?" Nothing would shock me now, but I faked being shocked.

"See that tunnel?" He pointed up the tracks. "We're going in there to blow up the mountain."

"And *kill* yourself?" I asked incredulously.

"Kill everyone. Everyone for miles around is going to die. This is an *A-bomb*." He nodded at the load in the back of the truck.

With that I shook my head in disbelief and started to take another breath of peace gas. As I did so, the man grabbed the canister away from me, jabbed the nozzle into his mouth, and sucked in, pressing the button as he did so. Just to be sure, he did it again, breathing deeply this time.

"You're afraid to die?" I asked.

"You have no idea," was all he said. I shuddered at the thought of the wrath this man would face when he met his maker.

He stood there for a moment, motionless, and then tossed the canister out to the side. It clanked as it hit one of the metal tracks that ran parallel to ours. As I watched, I could see his face change from a deep angry red to ashen white. I looked on anxiously for a sign that the peace gas was working, but he gave no clue.

Then in one swift movement, he raised his gun and fired a shot. I heard the blast and expected the pain, but none came. I realized he had blown his partner away, not Bruce or me. The man's eyes revealed his disbelief as he stared at the shooter, teetered for a moment, and then fell off the truck onto the rocks below.

"Why did you do *that*?" I asked, aghast, believing surely we were next.

"I couldn't risk it."

"Risk it?"

"That man's *crazy*. None of this makes any sense."

Chapter 79

I had my answer. The peace gas *did* work Thank God!

I could talk to this man now. He was rational. He was *human*.

"*Who sent you here?*" That was the burning question of the minute, the hour, the day, the year, and maybe even the past ten years!

"I work for Nikki Borisnikoff. Whatever he asks me to, I do." For the first time, I noticed his Russian accent. He was about to blow up our president, and he wasn't even an American!

"Even die?"

"Maybe not die. Not now." The man thought for a moment. "No, I wouldn't die for him. Why should I?"

As we talked, I thought I heard the familiar chopping sound of a helicopter beating against the air, at first very faintly and hardly noticeable but then clearly recognizable. I looked up in the direction of the sound and saw it like a tiny black fly moving against the blue sky background. It was coming toward us with ever-increasing size and volume until it loomed large and eased down slowly in a grassy area off to our left. The helicopter was painted black and bore the word "Police" on its side in huge white letters.

The instant it alighted, the side door facing us slid open, and Dan Gavin jumped out onto the tall grass. He was followed by three other men in full police regalia and bearing arms. I could feel the tension leaving my body like air released from a balloon. Bruce and I would live to see another day.

All four of them ran up and circled the pickup truck with the aircraft sitting on top. They must have thought this a strange sight as they took up their positions and trained their weapons on the man standing next to me, who held his hands high in the air. I found it ironic that this guy, who moments ago was about to release the most awesome weapon known to man, killing himself and everyone else for miles around, was now concerned for his own life, or so it seemed.

"Are you all right?" Dan called up to Bruce and me. We still sat there in the cockpit of the aircraft, but we were quite ready and willing to get down off of this odd-looking rig. On Dan's cue, we extricated ourselves from the cockpit and climbed down while his officers kept their guns trained on the Russian. Finally, they had him climb down as well.

"I'm still shaking," I admitted as I stood there on terra firma, soon joined by Bruce, and we moved aside, leaving the Russian in the center of the circle of police with drawn guns.

"I figured we bought the farm this time," Bruce said with obvious relief. He looked a bit wobbly too, or maybe it was me who was wobbling.

Dan approached the Russian, his gun threatening. "What is *that*?" he asked angrily, pointing toward the bomb in the back of the pickup, as if he didn't know.

"Zat is an A-bomb. Vee need to be vary careful, or et vill go off, and vee all will die," he said crisply with his Russian accent.

Dan clearly didn't expect that answer. It seemed so much like the reasonable Dr. Spock of *Star Trek*, so I filled him in. "I gave him the peace gas." Dan nodded, showing me that he understood, and I continued, "But he blew away his partner. He thought he was going to do something crazy like maybe kill us and set off the bomb." I walked around the back of the truck and pointed to where the other man lay in a heap, bleeding. Dan followed me to see the dead man for himself.

"You are one brave woman," he said finally. "You saved the day."

"Didn't have much choice," I replied, "once I saw that bomb. But if it wasn't for Bruce here, we would have all been history." It was now just dawning on me how courageous Bruce had been to fly his plane straight into this point of no return. No one else could or would have done that.

Dan turned his attention again to the Russian, this time with renewed anger and indignation. "Is that bomb set to go off?" he demanded to know, very concerned now. As he spoke, one of his officers cuffed the man while the other two kept their guns trained.

"No, et is not. Vee weren't sure of the timing, so vee were going to set et off ourselves inside ze tunnel. There's a lever in the cab to trigger ze bomb on ze truck." The Russian pointed to a control lever sticking out beneath the dashboard.

The three police officers guarded the man while Dan inspected the cab and carefully closed the cab door. When we heard fluttering in the sky, we all looked up and saw another helicopter heading our way, this one from the direction of West Point. It was also black, but its only identification was a number on the side. The US Secret Service had arrived.

As the big black bug slowed and began to ease itself down toward us, Dan quickly gave instructions to his officers to pass along the Secret Service agents and ordered the Russian into the open side door of his police helicopter. Dan, Bruce, and I climbed after him. Dan reached back and closed the door, and we were off in an instant just before the Secret Service landed.

"I didn't want to lose time talking," Dan explained. "Those SS agents are a tough bunch, and we've got to get to JFK. Boris's plane lands in a half hour."

The four of us strapped ourselves in as our helicopter, floated up and over the Hudson River, and left the A-bomb threat behind us like image fragments from a bad dream. Dan and I sat facing rearward, opposite Bruce and the Russian, who faced forward.

"What is your name?" I asked the Russian, hoping to start the flow of information that I knew we needed before we reached JFK.

"My name is Mikhail Muranov," he said with surprising dignity under the circumstances.

"Who was that other man with you? The one you killed?"

"That was my brother, Alexander." He pronounced "Alexander" in the crisp Russian way.

"You both work for Borisnikoff?"

"Yes, we did, but not anymore. Alex is dead, and I am finished."

"Finished?" I said.

"I do not follow him further. He is corrupt."

"Corrupt? What do you mean 'corrupt?'"

"He is old friends with your vice president, Chernoff," he said with bitterness in his voice. "Zay work together to blow up your president."

Dan, who I'm sure couldn't believe what he was hearing, took over the questioning. "Would you be willing to wear a recording device when we meet Mr. Borisnikoff? We will need evidence to convict him."

"Yes, of course. Vee have to make zis right and put zese men avay in your prisons."

Dan reached down and pulled a small electronic device out from under his seat. "I just happen to have a mini-recorder right here!" he announced with a grin.

Chapter 80

The Aeroflot flight from Moscow to New York City arrived every day at 5:00 p.m. We had to rush to be there and catch Borisnikoff as he came through customs. It would be great if we could go there by helicopter. Oh, but wait, we *were* in a helicopter! *I could easily get used to this way of travelling*, I thought as I looked out the window and saw snarled traffic on the highways below. Carl Collingwood had certainly been onto something with his "personal aircraft" that could take off and land anywhere.

Then I remembered I needed—and wanted—to make that important call to my dear husband, George, who was also on his way to JFK. I whipped my cell phone out of my pocket and pressed the speed-dial button. He answered on the first ring. "Juli?" came the worried voice.

"We did it! We stopped them!" I shouted. I sensed everyone in the helicopter was staring at me, but I didn't care. This was my soul mate, and I was going to share this important moment with him. I gave him the short version of what had happened and asked him to wait for us just outside the doors where the passengers appeared after they passed through customs. I could just feel the joy at his end coming through the phone.

I also told him to wear his video belt and bring his camera equipment. He needed to be ready for anything. We had an exclusive on this story!

By the time we reached JFK, Mikhail had the handcuffs off and the wire recorder on. Despite all that had happened, we had to trust this guy to do the right thing. So far at least, we had a good feeling about him, but you never knew for sure. He was not exactly an Eagle Scout who was now a member of his local rotary club.

Dan's helicopter pilot descended slowly toward JFK and dropped us on the tarmac near the "terminal one" building that leased space to Aeroflot. We climbed out of the craft and hurried inside.

Dan kept flashing his badge at everyone we met to get us into the customs area so we could watch and wait for Borisnikoff when he got off the plane. Just as we arrived at customs, George phoned and said he was outside in the arrivals waiting area. Dan badged him in too, and he joined the four of us.

"There's a guy just outside holding up a sign 'Nicholas Borisnikoff,'" George said. That confirmed that we could expect him on this flight.

Our plan was to stay in the background, incognito and inconspicuous, while Mikhail greeted Borisnikoff and engaged him in conversation. George set up his video on the tripod in a far corner of the large room and let his camera roll freely as he innocuously panned the incoming passengers. Dan, Bruce, and I wandered about the area behind the customs booths, where the officers stood checking the passengers as they came through, and tried our best to blend in while Mikhail stood there, wired for sound.

Right above the double doors to the arrivals area, where passengers headed after screening by customs, was a wide sign that said, "Welcome to the United States of America." Below the sign was a huge television screen as wide as the doors, one tuned to the twenty-four-hour news on CNN. I couldn't help staring at it because the president's speech at West Point was the news of the day.

High up in the four corners of the room, one of which was above my husband's head, were monitors that listed all the aircraft arriving at terminal one. The Aeroflot flight first appeared as "on time," but that quickly changed to "arrived."

A few passengers straggled in, looking somewhat haggard from the ten-hour flight. These would be the first-class passengers, and we could expect Borisnikoff to be one of them. I didn't know what he looked like so I watched Mikhail, who stood in front of the exit doors, nervously paced about, and watched for his former boss. Very soon thereafter, I saw Mikhail stop and stare abruptly with a clutched look on his face. I followed where Mikhail was looking and saw our target. I knew it was Borisnikoff.

Nikki Borisnikoff was a big man with a large, imposing head atop a wide frame. Unlike the other arriving passengers, all of whom dressed casually, he wore a gray business suit that was cut to perfection and a bright red tie. He was pulling his luggage with one hand and talking on his cell with the other.

He walked up to the one customs booth that wasn't busy, closed his phone, and reached for his passport. As he presented the passport, he looked the young customs official straight in the eye and waited for him to speak. After a brief exchange that I couldn't overhear, he was waved through, and after he grabbed his suitcase again, he headed toward the double doors. Only now did he see Mikhail standing there in front of Borisnikoff, right in his way.

Borisnikoff paused for a moment, his facial expression remaining unchanged and not revealing a single concern or worry. He then continued toward this man, whom, as I understood it at least, he had sent to this country to kill the president of the United States and, in doing so, kill himself. I didn't know whose face to look at—Borisnikoff's or Mikhail's—as I stood there off to the side, so I tried to do both. Out of the corner of my eye, I caught George leaving his camera on its tripod, its red light illuminated, and walking quickly toward Borisnikoff and Mikhail. George, I knew, was recording and storing the entire scene on his magic belt buckle.

As Borisnikoff walked up, Mikhail brought his hand up to his face and touched his lips with his index finger, the universal sign for silence. With that, Mikhail turned around and put his right arm around Borisnikoff's shoulders, and the two of them walked quickly toward the double doors, which parted with a "whoosh" as they approached. They passed through. The doors slipped back together, and they were gone.

Chapter 81

Dan, Bruce, George, and I stood stunned for a moment and then took chase. We dashed to the exit doors, and they opened, all too slowly it seemed, revealing the relatives, friends, and limo drivers that surrounded the way out, waiting for the arriving passengers. However, Borisnikoff and Mikhail as well as the driver with the "Nicholas Borisnikoff" sign were nowhere to be seen.

Dan immediately reached for his cell phone and made a call. He looked at us nervously as the connection went through and then spoke into the instrument. Unfortunately, there was little he could do except call his office for backup, because we had no clue as to which black limousine now carried the world's greatest villain, much less where that limo was heading. All of those Lincoln limos looked alike!

For George and me, however, it was time to go. We needed to get back to the city to post the most important news story of the decade and maybe even the century on our website. Dan and Bruce would have to fend for themselves.

George hurried back to retrieve his video camera and tripod, and together, we ran for our car. In his haste to get to the terminal, George had parked just across the street in the expensive area, not in the long-term parking lot where we usually went. He had even found a convenient space on the first level of the garage. We paid at the exit and headed back to the city.

There are three ways you can travel from JFK to the island of Manhattan: the Robert F. Kennedy Bridge, still called by many the Triborough Bridge, the Queens-Midtown Tunnel, and the Brooklyn-Battery Tunnel. But all of them required you to start by getting onto the Van Wyk Expressway. As we cruised along the Van Wyk, George driving as usual, I looked out for limousines that might be carrying Borisnikoff and Mikhail. This turned out to be a problem, because the rear windows on most of the limos were tinted and you couldn't see in. Now and then I saw a limo with clear windows, but the passengers I saw in them were single men and definitely not the big man I had seen at the airport.

Finally, when we had to turn off and follow the route to the Midtown Tunnel, I gave up hope of spotting the right limo. George and I continued on in silence, knowing it was too much to ask to find that car among the gaggle of limousines moving all around us, crammed together on the interstate highway. George slowed to pay the toll with our EZ-Pass before we entered the tunnel while I stared out my side window, musing about what we would report on our news breaker website. And there, passing through the toll gate right next to ours, was a gray limousine with Russian insignia on the side!

I strained to look in but couldn't tell much, except to see what appeared to be two men in the back. Of that, I was certain. Could we possibly have had such unbelievable good luck? It stood to reason they were coming to midtown rather than the downtown financial district or the uptown residential area, and they left JFK only a short time before we did and probably drove a bit slower than George, who liked to press on as fast as the traffic allowed. *That could be them*, I thought.

"George, follow that car!" I screamed, excited in spite of the doubts I had. "That could be them!"

George looked over and saw it too. "Well, I'll be darned!" was all he could say as he slowed our car and, signaling first, edged over to the right lane behind the gray limo.

On one hand, following a car in Manhattan is easy because there are so many different kinds of cars around you won't be noticed. On the other hand, it requires a bit of luck because the car you are following might get through a traffic light and leave you to wait until the light turns green again.

Depending on the way you are travelling, the lights can be either synchronized in your favor or allow you to go just one short block before you stop you again. If someone knows how the lights work, they can make pretty good progress through the city and can lose anyone who is trying to tail them. If they don't, they will just poke along, and anyone can easily keep up.

We followed the limo a safe distance behind all the way through the tunnel and out the other side. We merged onto 37th Street and went west to Third Avenue, where we waited behind the limo for the red light to change. When the light turned green the limo took a right on Third and proceeded north one block to the next traffic light, which was red too. We followed and came up alongside on the right so George could look over at the driver to see if he recognized him from the airport.

"I think it's him," he said, "but I'm not sure. He has a hat on that he didn't wear when he was holding that sign."

We had no other choice but to follow to find out.

The lights all the way up Third Avenue changed one after another, and we were off to the races. The limo driver must have known to drive fast to see how many lights he could get through before they started to turn red again. We made it all the way to 51st, where we had to suddenly slow and stop to wait for the next green wave. We kept going like this, leapfrogging over the cross streets two more times, until we were stopped again at 19th. George changed lanes from time to time as we followed to remain as inconspicuous as we could, and this strategy seemed to work. The limo driver wasn't making any evasive maneuvers.

As we started up again, the limo's left signal light came on, and it turned left onto 91st Street. We followed gingerly behind, turning only when the light was about to turn red again and allowing another car, a blue Mercedes, to turn left on 91st in front of us. That put a buffer between us and the limo, but it also put us in jeopardy of losing sight of the vehicle if we got caught at a light. Luckily, we made it all the way across Park Avenue before the traffic lights became a problem. At Madison, the limo made it across, but we got stuck behind that blue car we let go in front. We had come this far only to lose them!

At first, I just sat there fuming at the situation and waiting for the light to change, but I couldn't contain myself. I leaped out onto the street so I could look around the car in front of us and maybe see where the limo had gone. It might have been stopped by the next traffic light, but knowing the synchronous light system in New York, I didn't hold out much hope. The limo should have made it through the next light too and turned south on Fifth. By the time we could reach that corner, it would have disappeared.

Imagine my surprise and elation to see the limo parked on the right halfway down the next block and someone getting out! Just then our light changed, and the car behind us honked loudly and startled me as I jumped back in and closed the door. The car ahead turned right on Madison, leaving the intersection clear, and George shot forward into the next block. He slowed as we approached the parked limo, and I saw who had just gotten out. It was Mikhail, and he was rushing under a green awning into the building on the right. At the entrance of the building was a brass sign that read:

RUSSIAN FEDERATION

CONSULATE GENERAL

Chapter 82

The gray limousine, which we now knew carried Nikki Borisnikoff, suddenly took off down the empty street ahead of us and raced toward Central Park. Our cover clearly blown, George sped after them and nearly caught up as we reached the intersection and turned left onto Fifth Avenue. Although the traffic light was green for us at the intersection, we could only go one block on Fifth before we both had to stop at the red light. George pulled up alongside the limo, and I tried to look at the passenger in the back; however, the tinted windows blocked my view. There was nothing we could do but follow them while I contacted Dan Gavin to tell him where we were.

I speed-dialed Dan, and he picked up on the first ring. "What's up?" came his familiar voice.

"We found Nikki! We're in New York City, following his limo down Fifth Avenue. We're at 90th now, but the light will change in a second. And who knows where he'll go? How can we get him?"

"That's *fantastic*! Follow him! Don't let him out of your sight. I'll call the NYPD and fill them in. They'll send a dozen squad cars in your direction and stop that guy. I'll call you back just as soon as I get off the phone with them to find out where you're headed."

That was easy! Now all we had to do was keep up with the gray limo through the New York City traffic. As it turned out, *that* was not so easy.

The lights all the way down Fifth Avenue turned green one after another. If there were no traffic, one could make it all the way to Union Square at Fourteenth Street without stopping, but that could never happen. Fifth was always loaded with traffic, traffic that in our case could allow the limo to surge ahead of us and disappear. It was up to George now to stay on their tail.

The gray limo sprang ahead like a stone from a slingshot, and we took chase. We quickly caught up with the cars that had stopped at the light ahead and sped past them, clicking down the blocks about one every couple of seconds, eighty-nine, eighty-eight, eighty-seven, and so forth, traveling so fast we were almost keeping up with the green wave of traffic lights on Fifth. We were going maybe forty miles per hour, but it seemed like eighty in the blur of the city. We blasted across 85th, a street that ran through Central Park, and we kept on going, wishing that the lights would turn red and stop the gray limo that seemed to be pulling ahead while George did his best to keep up.

We passed 80th Street on the left and maneuvered around cars that seemed to be standing still in the middle of the avenue because we were going so fast. The limo passed them on the right, and George and I on the left, leaving an open stretch out in front. We were just about to accelerate to close the short gap between us and the limo when the limo abruptly braked sharply and turned right on 79th into Central Park.

"Yikes!" yelled George and swerved, trying to make the turn. Our car went into a skid and slid sideways down the avenue while my heart jumped into my mouth. George did his best to keep the car under control, and much to my surprise, we ended up stopping dead pretty much in the middle of the intersection, aimed sideways on Fifth and parallel to 79th. Our engine stalled, so George frantically cranked it to get it going again. It coughed and caught on, revving up with a whine. George grinned and gunned it again, and we were off, entering Central Park in pursuit of that elusive gray limo with a driver who obviously knew what he was doing.

My cell phone chimed, and I put it to my ear. It was Dan, thank goodness!

"The NYPD are coming. Where the hell are you?"

"We're crossing Central Park on Seventy-Nine. They'd better hurry. We're doing about ninety miles an hour!"

"Keep on it. I'll let them know. Bye"

Again, it was up to us to keep that limo in sight. But right now it was gone!

We sped across the park, hoping against hope that the limo would be caught by the light at Central Park West. We couldn't see far ahead because the road curved north from 79th to 81st Street.

As we came around the corner, we saw them there to our great relief! They had stopped for that light, and I'm sure they sat in the limo with smirks on their faces, thinking we had kept on going down Fifth Avenue and were stuck because we wouldn't be able to cut across the park until we reached 65th Street. Well, hello! Here we were!

The light turned green just as they came into sight; however, by the time they started moving again, we had sailed up right behind them, and we practically hung on their tailpipe as they crossed the intersection and headed west. The city had slowed them down, and I figured now we could hang in there until the police showed up.

We tailed them for three blocks and followed as they turned right on Broadway. In the distance, we heard sirens but didn't see any police. I phoned Dan Gavin again to report where we were.

"Going north on Broadway. We're at 82nd right now."

"Got it. I'll let them know." Dan clicked off again.

This was nerve-racking, but I knew it was just a matter of time.

In fact, within a few seconds, a police car pulled up behind us on Broadway, its siren blazing and causing the traffic to part, and joined us in following the limo. We pulled over to the right to let it pass as the limo dashed ahead even faster than before. We slowed to watch what would happen and saw the lights up ahead on Broadway turning red, but the limo kept on going as police car after police car passed us by in hot pursuit. Satisfied that Borisnikoff and his driver would be caught, we turned right on 85th Street and headed back to the east side across the park.

"Whew! I'm glad that's over," George said with great relief as we rode along together at a moderate speed. "I'm not used to this stuff."

"You did good! I'm so proud of you." I truly was. George was a great driver, whether he acknowledged it or not. "Now let's go back to the Russian consulate and see if we can speak to Mikhail."

"Mikhail? Why would he talk to us?"

"I don't know. The peace gas maybe? I have a good feeling about him for some reason."

"We won't be allowed into the consulate, you'll see."

"But maybe he'll come out."

"Not a chance." George was probably right, but I wanted to try.

"Go there anyway. It'll just take us a moment. Then we can go home."

George nodded, and after we passed through the park and crossed Fifth Avenue, he turned north on Madison and then left on 91st. He pulled into the open space in front of the consulate, and we both jumped out. I ran up to the door and pressed the button on the intercom.

"Yes, please?" came a male voice.

"We would like to speak with Mikhail Muranov, who just came here a half hour ago." There was silence for what seemed a full minute, and then the door opened, revealing Mikhail.

Mikhail stood on the threshold in the doorway but didn't come out and didn't invite us in. "What happened?" he wanted to know. He was as anxious to talk to us as we were with him.

"Could we come in?" George asked.

"I'm afraid not," he said. "You need a security clearance before you can enter."

"Then let's talk out here." George and I both stepped back out of the way to allow him to exit the consulate, but he didn't budge from his spot inside the door.

"Are you kidding? In here, I'm safe. I'm in Russia. Out there, your police can grab me and put me in jail."

"You're in Russia?" I wasn't getting what he was saying.

"Sure, this building is in your country, but your police can't come inside. As long as I stand behind this line," Mikhail said and pointed to the door jam on the floor, "I'm in my own country."

Chapter 83

While we were standing there in front of the entrance to the consulate, we faintly heard sirens in the distance, hardly noticeable at first but then gradually a bit louder until I realized we might be listening to the very same police chase that we had called in. I looked at Mikhail and could tell he heard it too and knew what was happening. He stiffened slightly and retreated a bit, backing up inside away from the doorway. Then he spoke with his Russian accent, "They are after him, aren't they?"

"Yes," I said. "And they'll catch him, too."

"They can't hold him. They have no evidence."

"You told me yourself that he ordered you to blow up that mountain at West Point."

"That may be true, but you'll never make me talk. If you people violate our sovereignty and try to arrest me, I'll deny it."

"What happened to that recorder you were wearing?" George wanted to know.

"I ripped it off when I got in the car. Nikki had a big laugh about that. I gave it to our driver, and he switched it off."

As we spoke, the sounds of sirens became much louder, sounds coming from the west in the direction of Fifth Avenue, but most of it came from the east. George and I turned to look in the direction of Madison Avenue and could see the reflections of flashing red in the distance high up on some of the buildings far down the street. Something was definitely happening, and it was coming our way.

As we stood there, amazed at what we were seeing, the gray limousine raced up the street toward us from Madison and screeched to a halt right in front of the consulate. The limo was followed closely by two police cars, one behind the other, that also braked abruptly to avoid causing a chain reaction of collisions.

As soon as the limo stopped, its right door flew open, and Nikki Borisnikoff jumped out with the intention of seeking refuge in the consulate. As he did so, a police car came racing down the street from the other direction and braked to a stop directly in front of the limo, blocking any possible attempt by the driver to flee the scene. As the police cars, both in front and in back of the gray limo, arrived, uniformed policemen climbed out with their guns drawn and ran in our direction in an attempt to catch Borisnikoff, who by this time was nearly upon us as he ran toward the entrance we were standing in.

I instinctively stepped out of the way, but George bent forward in the stance of a football lineman and charged toward Borisnikoff! Both of them collided with a loud "crunch" and went down onto the cement sidewalk. Borisnikoff, the bigger man of the two, started grappling with George while I just stood there frozen, unable to move a muscle, as I saw the scene unfold. Borisnikoff tried to pick himself up and move toward the consulate but kept getting pulled back down by my husband.

"Help me!" Borisnikoff shouted, seeing Mikhail standing there in the doorway, and held out his arm so that Mikhail could grab it. His reach was almost across the threshold into "Little Russia," and Mikhail could easily have grabbed his hand and pulled him in, but to my great surprise, Mikhail just looked at him, with distain in his eyes, and slowly closed the door of the consulate. With disbelief on his face, Borisnikoff stopped struggling and succumbed to the police as they held him down and cuffed him.

Amidst all this activity, an unmarked black SUV pulled up and stopped in the street behind the police cars blocking 91st Street. The front passenger door opened, and out stepped Detective Dan Gavin, a sight for sore eyes! He walked toward us at a normal pace, all the while taking in and assessing the scene, and when he reached us, he turned to the uniformed officers and held up his badge. "Thank you, officers," he addressed them. "Excellent police work."

The officers stared at him quizzically. Who was this man?

Dan knew the look. "I'm Detective Dan Gavin from the Suffolk County Sheriff's Office," he said without prompting to be asked.

"I'm the one who called for your assistance." The police all nodded in acknowledgment of the explanation, and Dan continued, "This man's name is Nikki Borisnikoff. He is a Russian industrialist who, we now know, has attempted to assassinate our president of the United States." Wide-eyed, the officers stared at him and then looked down at the man on the pavement with a sudden appreciation for what they had accomplished. I thought I caught a smirk on some of the officers' faces.

One of the policemen pulled Borisnikoff to his feet, treating him far more roughly than even Borisnikoff usually treated his subordinates. Borisnikoff glowered at the officer but didn't attempt to resist. He shrugged it off and stood up to his full height in a show of dignity among these lowlifes that surrounded him.

Dan stepped forward and started to inform him of his rights, "Mr. Borisnikoff, you are under arrest for attempted murder and conspiracy to commit murder. You have a right to remain silent—"

"You idiot!" Borisnikoff shouted. "Do you know who you are speaking to?"

"Of course I do. You have a right to be represented by an attorney—"

"You'll never prove anything. And when the US government is finished with you, you'll regret ever having heard of me, never mind speaking to me."

"Oh? Why is that?"

"I have friends in high places. Very high places, trust me. They will bring you down."

"Do you mean Vice-President Chernoff?"

Borisnikoff looked at him suspiciously but answered, "Yes, Rick Chernoff is a friend of mine."

"Well, as we speak, the vice president is being arrested on the same very charges for which we are charging you."

Borisnikoff suddenly blanched, his face losing all color.

"And we have a recording of you speaking with your man, Mikhail, in your car about what happened at West Point."

"That can't be! We turned off the recorder."

"Yes, you did, but the device was specially designed to remain on, even when the wearer attempts to switch it off, and to encrypt and transmit the recorded sounds. We received and heard your entire conversation."

Chapter 84

There is something about the realization that you have been caught at doing wrong that makes you finally want to tell the truth. It is a cathartic moment, and you need to talk to someone to explain yourself and justify your actions. It's the age-old adage: "If you were in my shoes, you would have done the same thing." The police have seen this time and time again.

What was unusual in this case was that Nikki Borisnikoff didn't need any prompting. He just stood there staring at us when he learned and understood that his life would change forever, and the words came tumbling out.

"You Americans! You are so self-righteous." He quite literally spat at Dan and the other officers with disdain and disgust and continued, "You have no right to lord over us. We in Russia are superior in culture, superior in technology, and superior in the way we do business, but you do not recognize it! We are *invisible* to you."

That was just the beginning of his tirade. We all stood there, transfixed, and listened to his stream of consciousness come pouring out. What follows is not word for word, mind you, but as best as I can remember, this is what he said:

"We in Russia were highly civilized when, in your country, you had nothing but a few colonial outposts with African slaves, living among your primitive Indians. Whatever knowledge and technology you had, what little there was, was imported from Europe and Russia.

"You set up a democratic government, I will grant you that. If there was ever a contribution you Americans gave to the world, it was the creation of your democratic government with your constitution and your bill of rights. But it takes more than a government to make a country.

"Since the time of the first czar in Russia, our people have excelled in the things that count. We live with our art, our literature, our music, and our ballet, all of which are unequalled by any other country. You Americans live through your bourgeois pop culture and have infected the world with this tasteless stuff while you ignore what we Russians have accomplished and contributed to civilization.

"Our science and technology has also led the world, but you Americans don't even know it. You think you invented everything. Alexander Bell invented the telephone. Thomas Edison invented the lightbulb, and the Wright brothers invented the airplane. Let me tell you something: We Russians were ahead of you every step of the way. Our Igor Sikorsky was far more advanced than the Wright brothers. While in Russia, he was the first to build and fly a multi-engine airplane. We would have had his helicopter too, if you had not lured him away from us with more money.

"We were the first to build a rocket and put a satellite in space, while you couldn't get a rocket off the ground even after getting Werner von Braun to design them. Eventually, you built a 'me too' rocket, and with your arrogance, you had to show us up by going to the moon.

"We were the first to build and test a hydrogen bomb, which was supposed to give us some measure of credibility in the world, but no. You Americans had to build and test one too. You were always the good guys. You did it for your 'self-defense,' while we Russians were the bad guys, and we did it to assert our power.

"You Americans have never given credit to Russia for anything that was good for the world, only things that were bad like world domination.

"Well, I was sick and tired of hearing the world was against us, with America leading the way, after all the good that we have contributed, so I said, 'What the heck? We'll just have to take over the world after all.'

"When I just happened to meet Rick Chernoff, who is now your vice president, I said to myself that this might be possible by creating an alliance with this man. Through the military business I did with my country and yours too by the way, I was able to support his campaign when he ran for congress and then for the senate. I made sure he always had enough money to win. When he finally ran for president, though, I couldn't control your primaries, and he ended up in second place behind Peter Bradley. But this got him on the ticket as the candidate for vice president.

"We didn't let that deter us. Once you are vice president, it is easy to become president because you are next in line. When the president dies, his becoming president was automatic. This is what we arranged to make happen."

By the time he was nearly finished, my mind was racing. This was all about his plot with Chernoff to assassinate the president and take over the world. No small matter, but what about Carl Collingwood? What about blowing up Carl and his aircraft? What about his taking over the military business from Mike Snead and Transport International? I had to press him, so while everyone just stood there dumbfounded in the face of the audacity and arrogance of this powerful yet powerless man, I stepped up and asked the simple question: "What about Andrei Gershuni?"

"Andrei who?" came the reply.

"Andrei Gershuni. You sent him here on a mission, too!"

"I do not know this Andrei . . . Gershuni. Who is he?"

"He planted a bomb that blew up a VTOL aircraft that was being developed for the military out on Long Island. This aircraft would have taken a lot of business away from InterMil."

"Nonsense! I know of no such man, and we would never have done such a thing. We Russians can compete with our superior technology. We do not have to resort to killing people to develop our business."

Hearing this, something suddenly clicked in my mind. I had the germ of an idea that just might work to acquit Mike Snead. I looked at Dan, and he looked back at me quizzically, obviously wondering what I was thinking.

"Dan, can take you me back to Suffolk with you? George needs to hurry home to write the story and get the breaking news on our website, and I need to be at that trial the first thing tomorrow morning!"

Chapter 85

The trial should have long been over, but Derek Taliz had been able to keep Mike Snead going on the stand for the past two days. Even Mike was tiring, Derek told me, in trying to stall by telling the jury his life story. Mike had been entertaining, but it was wearing very thin, especially on Judge Davis, who, Derek said, was becoming increasingly exasperated. Both he and Mike needed me to hurry back, and now I was on my way.

I had spoken with Derek that evening and had explained to him my plan. He said that in all the years of his experience as a criminal trial lawyer, he had never tried this tactic, but he felt that it just might work in this case.

When I walked into the courtroom the next morning, Derek and the DA, Helen Meisner, were both sitting at their respective counsel tables, getting ready for the day's testimony. I nodded hello to Ms. Meisner and sat down next to Derek.

"We're all set," I whispered "Everyone's agreed to come. George'll be here later too."

As before, the courtroom was overflowing with spectators and journalists. Once the court was in session, the chattering would stop, but at this point, the sound behind us was nearly deafening. I turned around in my seat to see who was there and noticed Aleksa in the front row. She must have been really miffed at having to stay with the trial these past couple of days, while other reporters were covering the big news stories of the day. If she was, she didn't show it though. She shot me a friendly smile, and I smiled back.

The door at the side of the room opened, and Mike Snead appeared, ushered in by two bailiffs. He stood there at the threshold for a moment, making his actor's entrance and looking very dapper in his striped, dark gray business suit, white shirt, and regimental tie. He scanned the courtroom, and when he saw me, he grinned from ear to ear like the Cheshire Cat. The only thing that revealed his status were the dangling chains connecting his wrists and ankles. He must have thought I had come to save him, that I held the key to his acquittal and release. Geez, no pressure!

The bailiffs brought him over to us and undid his chains. He sat down in a chair between Derek and me and came right to the point. "What have you got?"

Derek leaned over and spoke quietly into his ear while I watched his reaction. He cocked his head and looked back at me while he listened, his face in a quizzical expression.

"That's all? You still don't know who did it?" Derek nodded yes to both questions.

"Okay, then it looks like a plan."

"The court will rise. Justice Kathleen Davis presiding," came the call. Judge Davis entered with a flourish, sat on her perch, and called the court to order.

"Counselor," she began with a sharp tone, glaring at Derek Taliz, "I assume you are finished with your witness?"

"We are, your honor. But we still have two more witnesses for the defense."

"*What!*" Judge Davis practically fell of her chair. She had cut Derek a lot of slack in allowing Mike Snead to testify for two full days and had expected the trial to reach the summation phase today.

"Your honor, I apologize. But the witnesses will take no more than about fifteen minutes each."

"I don't see how that's possible. It will take longer than that even to introduce them to the jury."

"That won't be necessary. They have testified before."

"Really? You've piqued my interest. Just whom do you intend to call?"

"Shelley Bernstein and Bruce Collingwood."

"You have already cross-examined them. You had your chance."

"Some new evidence has come to light in the meantime, your honor."

"Within the past two days? I don't believe it."

"Yes, the last two days. I need to ask them both a few more questions."

"All right, I'll give you your precious fifteen minutes. But that's *all* I'll allow. Now, does the prosecution wish to cross-examine the witness we have heard at such length these past two days?" Judge Davis looked at Helen Meisner expectantly but with silent pleading that she show a little restraint.

"Just a couple of questions, your honor." Helen nodded to Mike Snead to take the stand again. Helen waited for him to sit and then addressed him. "You understand you are still under oath, Mr. Snead."

"Yes, I do."

"I have just a few simple questions for you. First, were you aware that Carl Collingwood was developing a new type of vertical takeoff aircraft?"

"Yes, of course."

"Were you aware that Carl Collingwood had been awarded a contract to sell the aircraft to the army if the test flight were successful?"

"Yes, I was."

"If his aircraft were sold to the army, would that have meant less sales of aircraft by your company, Transport International?"

"Objection!" Taliz shouted. "That's *speculation*."

"I'll allow it," the judge ruled. "Go on."

"Yes, it would."

"Did your company supply Collingwood the aircraft engine that exploded during the test flight."

"Yes, unfortunately."

"That is all I have," Helen said and walked back to her seat.

"Is there a redirect?" Judge Davis glowered at Taliz.

"No, your honor."

After Mike took his seat again at the counsel table, Derek stood and announced, "The defense calls Sheldon Bernstein," and turned toward the rear of the courtroom. The main door opened, and in walked Shelley. He looked at me as he came down the aisle and winked as he entered the gate. He knew what I wanted him to do, and this was a signal that he was going to do it.

Chapter 86

After Shelley took the stand, Taliz reminded him he was still under oath and continued, "I have just a few simple questions for you: First, were you aware that Carl Collingwood was developing a new type of vertical takeoff aircraft?"

"Yes, of course."

"Were you aware that Carl Collingwood had been awarded a contract to sell the aircraft to the army if the test flight were successful?"

"Yes, I was."

"If his aircraft were sold to the army, would that have meant less sales of aircraft by your company, Transport International?"

"Yes, it would."

"Did your company supply Collingwood the aircraft engine that exploded during the test flight."

"Yes, unfortunately."

"That is all I have," Derek said and walked back to his seat.

"Any redirect by the prosecution?" Judge Davis inquired.

"No, your honor."

"Then you may call your final witness, Mr. Taliz," the judge said.

"The defense calls Bruce Collingwood."

All eyes turned toward the door of the courtroom as Bruce Collingwood appeared and came forward. He took the stand, and Derek again reminded his witness that he was under oath.

"Mr. Collingwood," he began, "Were you aware that your father had been awarded a contract to sell the aircraft to the army if the test flight were successful?"

"Yes, I was."

"Did you have access to the aircraft engine that exploded during the test flight?"

"Yes, of course."

"That is all I have." Derek said and walked back to his seat.

"Is there a redirect?" Judge Davis glanced at Helen.

"No, your honor."

"Then after lunch, we will hear the summations." Judge Davis said and banged her gavel. "This court is adjourned until 1:30."

Chapter 87

"*Res ipsa loquitur*. The thing speaks for itself. That is the guiding legal principal of this case," Helen began in her summation.

"The legal principal is that where a certain instrument is in the exclusive control of one person or even a group of people, provided they are under the control of that one person, and where that instrument causes the death or injury of another person, that first person is automatically responsible for the death or injury and should be held accountable.

"In this case, we have shown that Mike Snead's company sold an aircraft engine to Carl Collingwood's company to be installed in a remarkable new prototype aircraft and that this engine blew up during the initial flight of the aircraft, killing its pilot, Carl.

"The thing speaks for itself. The aircraft engine blew up. Why? We don't exactly know, but we do know it shouldn't have. Where did the engine come from? A company called Transport International. Who was in control of Transport International? The president and CEO is sitting right there." Helen pointed accusingly at Mike and waited until everyone in the jury had taken a good look as he sat there dejectedly.

"The facts of this case speak loudly and clearly that the accused, Michael Snead, acted with malice to cause the death of an aircraft developer, Carl Collingwood, to squash his competition for military contracts.

"You have heard more testimony in this courtroom that you will ever need to be certain beyond a reasonable doubt that the accused, Mike Snead, is responsible for this crime and should be held accountable."

With these words, Helen launched into an hour's review of the evidence presented over the past two weeks and then finally concluded, "*Res ipsa loquitur.* The thing speaks for itself." The jury was spellbound.

When she sat down, Judge Davis called for a fifteen-minute break, and then it was Derek's turn. He didn't take nearly as long.

"Ladies and gentlemen of the jury," Derek said as stood up from his chair and addressed the jury. He wore a bow tie on a dark blue shirt with a white collar under a gray, pinstriped suit that was impeccably tailored to fit his large frame. "Beyond reasonable doubt. *Beyond* reasonable doubt. Beyond *reasonable* doubt. Beyond reasonable *doubt.* That is what this case is all about."

Derek walked slowly and reflectively from behind his counsel table to a spot directly in front of yet a respectful distance from the jury box. He was now in his element.

"You will soon be asked to retire to the jury room and deliberate whether my client, Mike Snead, is guilty or innocent of committing this dastardly crime. Before you do so, Judge Davis will instruct you that to find Mike guilty, you must conclude that the government proved *beyond a reasonable doubt* every element of the crime of murder.

"This standard of proof goes back to the beginnings of our system of jurisprudence, which we took over from England when our nation was founded. The US Supreme Court stated it this way in 1970, the case of *In re Winship.*"

Derek pulled a folded piece of paper out of his breast pocket and read to the jury:

> The requirement that guilt of a criminal charge be
> established by proof beyond a reasonable doubt dates
> at least from our early years as a nation. The demand
> for a higher degree of persuasion in criminal cases was
> recurrently expressed from ancient times, (though) its
> crystallization into the formula "beyond a reasonable
> doubt" seems to have occurred as late as 1798. It is
> now accepted . . . as the measure of persuasion by
> which the prosecution must convince the trier of all
> the essential elements of guilt.

"But how much doubt about the guilt of an accused is 'reasonable doubt,' requiring you to acquit?

"In order to find the accused guilty, must you be 100 percent certain that he committed the crime for which he is charged? Certainly not, for if that were the standard, then no one, and I mean *no one*, would ever be convicted of committing a crime. We can never be 100 percent certain of anything in this world.

"So how much doubt is permitted under the law for you to find the accused guilty as charged?

"Must you be 90 percent certain to find the accused guilty? Or to put it another way, can the amount of doubt in your mind be 10 percent?

"How about 20 percent doubt? Thirty percent? Fifty percent? Surely, that would be too much doubt, for in the reverse, it would mean that you were only 50 percent certain of the guilt of the accused. What is the percentage of doubt that is considered "reasonable" under the law?

"You may find this very odd, as I do, but even after more than two hundred years of history in our country, no court in the land has ever answered that question.

"The Supreme Court, in another case called *Victor v. Nebraska*, upheld a conviction where an instruction given the jury defined reasonable doubt as, among other things, *a doubt that will not permit an abiding conviction 'to a moral certainty' of the accused's guilt*, and an 'actual and substantial doubt' that is not excluded by the 'strong probabilities' of the case. That is as close as the courts have come in defining what is 'reasonable doubt.'

"If you are looking for a number, a percentage fixing the amount of doubt that is 'reasonable' under the law, you won't find a single case among the *millions* of criminal cases that have been decided and reported over the years since 1798 that provides a percentage.

"In other words, there is no standard or even a guideline for us to go on. But there is one thing we can agree on, I believe. An amount of *sixty-six and two thirds* percent is too much doubt to permit a conviction. If the percentage of doubt is that high or close to it, you *must* acquit.

"In this case, there are two witnesses, Shelley Bernstein and Bruce Collingwood, who share equally with Mike Snead in having a motive to commit the crime. All three had equal access to the engine that caused the explosion. So you might say there was no more than a 33 percent chance for each that he committed the crime.

"That leaves a 66 percent probability that each one *didn't* commit the crime. Clearly, the prosecution has not met its burden of proof that the accused, Mike Snead, was guilty *beyond a reasonable doubt.*

"Therefore, ladies and gentlemen of the jury, having heard all the evidence presented in this case, you can arrive at only *one* verdict. That is that Mike Snead is *not guilty.*

THE GABLES REPORT

WELCOME TO OUR WEBSITE

YOU ARE THE

023,456,789th

VISITOR

Breaking news story . . .

MIKE SNEAD AQUITTED OF MURDER CHARGE IN COLLINGWOOD CASE
The Collingwood Murderer Is Still at Large.

<u>New York, NY</u>. *After a two-week trial, Mike Snead, CEO of Transport International Inc., was completely exonerated in connection with the violent death of Carl Collingwood, aircraft pioneer and developer in Westhampton, New York.*

It took a jury in Suffolk County Court just one hour to reach a verdict of "not guilty" of all charges.

Carl Collingwood was piloting his new vertical takeoff and landing, winged aircraft on its maiden test flight when it exploded and burned, killing him instantly. The cause was traced to a bomb in the central engine compartment, and it appeared that an employee of Transport International, Andrei Gershuni, was responsible for placing the bomb in the engine. Gershuni subsequently died in his apartment under suspicious circumstances, but the cause of his death was never determined.

The prosecution, Suffolk County District Attorney Helen Meisner, charged Mike Snead, believing he had motive in removing a potential competitor to his company, Transport International. Defense attorney Derek Taliz proved to the jury that at least two other persons were just as likely to have committed the crime and argued that a 33.3 percent probability of guilt amounted to "reasonable doubt." The jury clearly agreed.

At a press conference following the trial, DA Meisner, said she was "devastated" by the jury verdict and condemned the "trickery" on the part of defense counsel Derek Taliz that led to what she called a "miscarriage of justice." Nevertheless, based on the trial record, she said she could not appeal.

Interviews with members of the jury revealed an odd fact. Most jurors thought that none of the three persons, each described by Taliz as equally likely to have committed the crime, were involved. The jury was left wondering who could have done it.

In the jury's view, no satisfactory evidence was ever presented to prove who was responsible for Carl's death.

The crime remains under investigation. Daniel Gavin, the Suffolk County detective in charge of the case, said they were "leaving no stone unturned" in their search for the truth about the murder but refused to disclose if they had any suspects or even "persons of interest" who might have relevant information.

With stories updated hourly, the **Gables Report** remains your best source of news.

Visit our Website *every hour, every day* to follow this breaking story. www.gablesreport.com/articles/collingwood

Breaking news story . . .

VICE-PRESIDENT CHERNOFF CHARGED
IN COLLINGWOOD CASE
Vice President Contends He Was Forced to Confess.

*An anonymous source revealed that Vice-President Chernoff has
confessed to the murder of Carl Collingwood.*

*Speaking "off the record," the source said Chernoff confessed after
investigators threatened to use the same tactics that he himself had
authorized for the "war against terror." These tactics were considered
torture under federal law, but initially, Chernoff invoked the Fifth
Amendment against self-incrimination and refused to cooperate in the
investigation into what authorities considered acts of treason.*

*Chernoff is under indictment for his involvement in an alleged plot
to explode a nuclear device at the US Military Academy at West Point.*

*Investigators denied threatening torture to extract a confession from
Chernoff. Immediately upon assuming his office some two years ago,
President Peter Bradley issued an executive order ending the use of any
type of torture by federal officials. If such methods were used, Chernoff's
confession as well as any evidence obtained as a result of the confession
would not be admissible during his forthcoming trial.*

*Chernoff now insists he is innocent of all charges and said, when
acquitted, he will sue the government for damages in the multimillions
of dollars. He will also leave his home in Washington, DC, and move
his family to Russia "to live in a civilized country."*

*Chernoff is said to have confessed that he ordered Maj. Gen. David
Bellamy to kill Collingwood to end the development of Collingwood's
aircraft, as a "gift" for his friend Nikki Borisnikoff, CEO of InterMil,
a Russian supplier of aircraft to the US military. It was Bellamy who
hired Andrei Gershuni to plant the bomb in the aircraft engine. Bellamy
subsequently killed Gershuni, and then Charles Brodsky, Chernoff's
former chief of staff, had Bellamy killed to eliminate any possible leaks.*

*Before he died, Collingwood had a premonition he might fall
victim to foul play. During discussions with Bellamy about the sale of
his aircraft, Bellamy told him that Borisnikoff had a "friend in high*

places" in the US government so that Collingwood should not count on getting an order from the US Army.

Borisnikoff is currently being held at an undisclosed location. His trial on charges of the attempted murder of thousands of Americans is scheduled for next month.

With stories updated hourly, the **Gables Report** remains your best source of news.

Visit our Website *every hour, every day* **to follow this breaking story.** www.gablesreport.com/articles/Chernoff

Epilogue 1

One Year Later

The legislative history of the "Save Humanity Act" will eventually be written by greater minds than mine, but I have to say something about it before I end this story and bring this chapter of my life to a close. It was a legislative battle that brought out the best and also the worst in our members of congress.

It all started—appropriately enough, I thought—with an innocuous bill sponsored by a congresswoman from California, whom I shall not name, who sought to regulate the use of the peace gas. There were times, it was thought, when the "PG" was considered to be too intrusive, like in the bedroom of a married couple, and possibly unsafe for use, like for women who were pregnant or who expected to become pregnant. But from the moment this bill was introduced and the news hit the media, it created a firestorm. Eventually, it pushed every other new story off front pages and even off the Internet. It was what everyone in the country and maybe even the whole world talked about. Everyone had an opinion, and they voiced it vociferously.

Poor Peter Bradley. Instead of leaving a legacy for mankind as he had naively hoped, the PG almost sank his presidency. By putting his name and reputation indelibly on the use of PG on that fateful day at West Point, he could not straddle the fence and allow the battle to rage and eventually burn itself out. He had to advocate and speak out for its unrestricted use, and to his credit, speak out he did. As a result, he became a lightning rod for the cause, and as the media coverage intensified, even those who supported him and were aligned with his liberal politics came to question his judgment.

The Republicans had a field day. It was a breakthrough political moment for them: another "liberal" cause that had to be stopped. This was an issue that even the most reticent conservative could get behind. Unlike gun control or eliminating tax loopholes for the rich, where they bucked wide public sentiment, they could ride this issue freely and at the same time bash the Democratic president, who was seemingly committing political suicide every day that the public debate raged on.

At best, the use of PG was called an "invasion of privacy." At worst, it was an intentional tort, inflicting permanent damage on the "victim" against whom PG was inflicted, and its use should be actionable just like the use of a poison.

Somewhere in between, the use of PG was considered to be a "manipulation" of another person's free will. Lost in the rhetoric was the president's point that it was the amygdala that caused the loss of free will and that the peace gas *maintained* one's free will in stressful circumstances where hate and anger took over and controlled one's personality.

Theologians and members of religious organizations were quick to take sides and voice their opinions, too, mostly advocating of a complete ban on the gas, believing that it interfered with God's eternal plan for mankind. This faith-based political action resulted in ramping up the rhetoric and increasing the heated exchanges of views between citizens, even among those who had never before cared to voice their opinions in public.

The Republicans, and even many Democrats, beat the drums to keep the issue alive as long as the public could stand to listen. They said the use of PG would turn us all into robots and zombies. They warned we would no longer experience joy and threatened untold dire consequences of the use of PG. God forbid, the gas would even cause an end to conjugal *sex* as we knew it!

A much more conservative bill was introduced in the senate and passed. The original bill in the US House of Representatives had long since been amended to add numerous clauses banning the use of the PG in family gatherings, governmental campaigns, parliamentary deliberations and debates, and vacation resorts. The whole city of Las Vegas was mentioned by name. This bill passed too and went into reconciliation with the senate bill, which was much more stringent.

What came out was a ban on the use of peace gas everywhere in the United States except in cases of business negotiations that might lead to blows and in negotiations between our government and foreign governments that might lead to war. This final bill passed both US Houses of Congress with a comfortable majority and was then sent to President Bradley to be signed into law. To a man and woman, the Republicans were all secretly gleeful that they could "stick it to the man." The Democrats feared the worst and held their breath, hoping the president would "bite the bullet" and go along with the signing.

Days passed, and the world waited for him to act. Congress was set to adjourn, but the Republicans insisted on keeping congress in session to avoid a pocket veto.

Article 1, Section 7 of the US Constitution states:

> If any Bill shall not be returned by the President within ten days (Sundays excepted) after it shall have been presented to him, the same shall be a Law, in like manner as if he had signed it, unless the Congress by their Adjournment prevent its return, in which case it shall not be a Law."

If congress were to adjourn, the president's inaction would result in a veto and the bill would not become law. If congress stayed in session, the president would have to take the affirmative step of vetoing the bill to prevent its becoming the law of the land.

The president, wishing to avoid the controversy, hoped that congress would be caused to adjourn; however, in the end, it continued in session, and he had no choice but to exercise his veto power. He did so, but only after he interrupted prime-time television with an address to the nation. His speech, which was announced just one day in advance, was watched by nearly sixty million Americans.

"My fellow Americans," President Bradley began, looking straight into the camera and the eyes of the millions of viewers. "Our nation and, in fact, the entire world community of nations have been handed an historic opportunity, the opportunity to end human violence as we know it and as we have known it since human beings first stood up and first walked erect upon this earth thousands of years ago.

"Our scientific research on the human brain has finally borne fruit. We now know how the mind works, and we can adjust and control its operation so as to avoid our naturally aggressive impulses. By restraining irrational thought and behavior, it is within our power to sharply reduce, and perhaps completely eliminate, all violence perpetrated by one person against another.

"There are some who do not trust humanity and, perhaps most importantly, the government to make proper use of this scientific breakthrough. They see it as a final fulfillment of George Orwell's *Brave New World*. But doesn't that same argument apply to all advances in science? Indeed, this reasoning was used in an attempt to halt stem cell research, to block atomic research, and even to naysay the invention of the aircraft. 'If God meant us to fly, He would have given us wings,' they said, but such talk did not stop or even slow the development of aircraft, which continues even to this day. As a matter of fact, our military procurement has just placed a large order for a new type of vertical takeoff and landing, winged aircraft that was developed on Long Island in the state of New York.

"In my judgment, the development of peace gas is one of the most beneficial breakthroughs in science since the beginning of human history, and I cannot, and I will not allow congress to ban its use. With this pen," President Bradley said and then held up a Mont Blanc fountain pen to show the television audience, "I will veto the bill that congress has euphemistically called the 'Save Humanity Act.' I am going to save humanity by signing my name on this document."

With that, the president lifted a sheet of paper off the podium in front of him and held it up. At the top, it read "veto" in letters large enough for all to see. He then returned the paper to the podium and, with a flourish, signed his name at the bottom.

The television audience was stunned. The very next day, both the US House of Representatives and the US Senate voted nearly unanimously to overrule the president's veto.

Both George and I were greatly saddened, for we knew that the president owed his life to my use of peace gas. After the law banning PG was enacted, regulations were quickly prepared, published for comment, and finally adopted, which designated PG as a "controlled substance" and established such strict rules that its use, even in the rare cases where it was permitted, became an administrative nightmare. Only the government's Secret Service, the CIA, and the FBI make use of it today.

Epilogue 2

Two Years Later

George and I drove east from New York City along the Southern State Parkway on Long Island and exited at Westhampton, where we drove north toward the Suffolk County Airport. Instead of turning right at the airport entrance, we turned left into an attractively gardened entranceway across the street and parked in one of the spots marked "visitor" facing an enormous, cement building. The building, which was about the size of an entire New York City block, was surrounded on three sides by a vast parking lot more than half filled with parked cars. In the back of the building, mostly hidden from view as I drove by on the road past the airport, was a huge, chain-link fenced-off area where dozens of new aircraft stood waiting for delivery. This was the home and the new manufacturing facility of Hummingbird Aircraft.

George and I entered the main door of the building and found ourselves in a small lobby, too small even for furniture, but we could see a receptionist sitting behind a glass window. George stepped up and announced our presence.

"We're here to see Bruce Collingwood. We have an appointment."

"You are?" The woman looked up from her computer screen. "Oh, please forgive me! I should have recognized you. Do come right in." She pressed a button under her desk, unlocking a door next to her station. I pushed open the door and let George go in first, his video equipment under his arm.

We stood there facing an open room filled with maybe a dozen clerical personnel at workstations. As we scanned the area, we finally noticed Bruce in the back, sitting at a desk no larger than the others in the room, waving at us to come over. "Over here, guys!" he shouted excitedly. "I've got something to show you!"

George panned the room with the video camera for a moment, and then he and I walked over to Bruce, who looked up at us, grinning from ear to ear.

"We just received an order from the US Navy. They want another ten thousand airplanes just like the ones we sold the army. That makes a total of about twenty-five thousand aircraft on order, and that's just the beginning. After the military uses are satisfied, we can start to fill orders from private industry and, who knows, maybe even the public will eventually want to buy them. This aircraft is going to be the next big thing!"

"That's wonderful!" I replied. "If anyone deserves to make it, and make it big, Bruce, you're the one. It's just too bad your father isn't here to see this happening."

"I know." Bruce's grin evaporated and he looked at me, reflective. "If he could only have seen this, it would have made it all worthwhile."

"How many employees do you have now?" I asked, trying to get us back on a positive track.

"We already have about a thousand, but we need more. We're hiring as fast as we can."

"That is so good for Long Island. You used to have a thriving aircraft industry. Grumman and Republic Aircraft together, and their suppliers accounted for over one hundred thousand jobs on Long Island during World War II. Thanks to you, Bruce, the industry is back again, and people have jobs."

"Let me show you!" Bruce stood up and led the way to a door in the back.

Bruce opened the door, and what we saw there practically took our breath away. The building walls housed one enormous, cavernous room that was two stories high, a room as far and as wide as the mind could take in at one time. Within this area on the factory floor below us were what appeared to be about one hundred aircraft being assembled from start to finish along an assembly line that snaked back and forth in the building and finally led out through a large open door on the far side. Oddly, there was hardly any sound, perhaps because whatever factory noise was being generated evaporated within the huge space, but the effect was like watching a movie with the volume turned way down.

"We can produce aircraft at the rate of about one every five minutes in two seven-and-a-half-hour shifts. If you do the math, you'll see we're set up to make one hundred and eighty aircraft a day."

As I watched, I could see the assembly line inch forward, and sure enough, it moved the aircraft from one station to the next in about five minutes, just long enough for the several workers at that station to add whatever parts they needed to add.

George worked his video magic from our elevated perch overlooking the room, capturing the scene for a report on our website.

"The finished aircraft go out through that door in the back, and we flight-test them before delivery. If they pass quality control, we take the wings off and ship them out by specially designed trailer trucks. At any one time, there's only about a day's worth of new aircraft out there, waiting to be shipped."

I didn't know what to say. I was so impressed and so proud of Bruce. I just stood there dumbly and took in the scene until I finally managed to remark, "You brought the aircraft industry back to Long Island."

"There used to be a good business here. It started at about 1910 with Curtiss. In the golden age of aviation in the twenties and thirties, there were more than twenty aircraft manufacturers on the island. Lindbergh took off from Roosevelt Field in Garden City, Long Island, on his flight to Paris in 1927," I recalled.

"What's even more remarkable, I think, was the very first flight across the Atlantic, from Long Island to England nearly ten years earlier in 1919, with a Curtiss Flying Boat made in Garden City. Nobody remembers it because they made two fueling stops along the way."

As we stood there and talked, I noticed George in the background out of the corner of my eye, training his camera on us. Just at that moment, we heard the door behind us open. George swerved and pointed the camera in that direction.

There in the doorway stood Aleksa, holding a tiny baby wrapped in a blanket. "Hello, everyone!" she said. "I heard you were coming and wanted to surprise you. Bruce and I would like you to meet the newest addition to the family, *Carl II*. Born two weeks ago at six pounds, ten ounces."

ABOUT THE AUTHOR

Karl F. Milde, Jr. is a practicing attorney, specializing in intellectual property law. He is registered to practice before the U.S. Patent and Trademark Office and is a member of the law firm of Eckert Seamans Cherin & Mellott LLC in White Plains, NY.

Karl is a graduate of Georgetown University Law Center and holds two Bachelor of Science degrees from M.I.T. (Physics and Electrical Engineering).

Karl has made numerous inventions, for which he received patents, principally in the fields of electronic music, automotive electronics as well as vertical take-off and landing (VTOL) aircraft.

Karl has also written a children's mystery series about a young inventor named "Jason" who joins with his friends to investigate suspicious criminal activity. Having written two novels, entitled "The Commuter Train" and "The Airplane," Karl is currently at work on his third novel to be called "The Tractor Trailer," thus completing a "transportation trilogy" about trains, planes and automobiles.

Karl is a member of the Rotary Club of White Plains (NY) and in 2009/2010 he served as the Rotary International "District Governor" for the Rotary District 7230, which includes New York City, The Bronx, Staten Island, Westchester County NY and the island country of Bermuda. Karl resides in Mahopac NY with his wife Cheryl and has three children and four grandchildren.